SAVING LOGAN (SPECIAL FORCES: OPERATION ALPHA)

SAVING SEALS, BOOK 4

JANE BLYTHE

Dear Readers,

Welcome to the Special Forces: Operation Alpha Fan-Fiction world!

If you are new to this amazing world, in a nutshell the author wrote a story using one or more of my characters in it. Sometimes that character has a major role in the story, and other times they are only mentioned briefly. This is perfectly legal and allowable because they are going through Aces Press to publish the story.

This book is entirely the work of the author who wrote it. While I might have assisted with brainstorming and other ideas about which of my characters to use, I didn't have any part in the process or writing or editing the story.

I'm proud and excited that so many authors loved my characters enough that they wanted to write them into their own story. Thank you for supporting them, and me!

READ ON!
Xoxo
Susan Stoker

I'd like to thank everyone who played a part in bringing this story to life. Particularly my mom who is always there to share her thoughts and opinions with me. The wonderful Cat Imb of TRC Designs who made the stunning cover. And my lovely editor Lisa Edwards for all her encouragement and for all the hard work she puts into polishing my work.

CHAPTER 1

September 6th

2:43 P.M.

Most people believed that Logan "Shark" Kirk didn't feel emotion.

They would be wrong.

It wasn't his training to become a Navy SEAL that had taught him to withstand torture or given him the ability to lock down his feelings. Those were skills he had learned long before he decided to join the military.

Long before he was old enough to do so.

His emotions were there, he just knew how to keep them locked safely away where they didn't have the ability to affect him. Shark found his life moved much smoother that way.

Didn't mean he was immune to feelings though.

His or other people's.

Right now, it wasn't his feelings about his mother's death that were forefront in his mind, it was the obvious tension rolling off the only woman on the helicopter.

The rest of his SEAL team were already in Afghanistan, having left a few days prior on what would be a two-month deployment, but he'd been delayed with his mother's death, making arrangements, and the funeral which he had attended yesterday before immediately boarding a plane to fly into Bagram. Since his team was currently at a different base, Shark had hopped on a helicopter to go and join them. Besides the two pilots, there were three other passengers not including himself, two men he had immediately dismissed, and a woman he couldn't seem to stop staring at.

It wasn't her looks that had captured his attention—although she was stunning with soulful brown eyes and long dark locks—it was her demeanor.

Shark might not have officially met the woman, he didn't know her name, hadn't exchanged anything more than a nod of greeting when they both climbed aboard the helo, but he knew as sure as he knew himself that she was afraid.

Of what he had no idea.

That he wanted to find out left him shocked and unsettled.

He didn't do relationships, he attended to his physical needs from time to time when he met a woman who wasn't intimidated by his large size and gruff attitude. He didn't do friendships either unless it was with his team—who were more brothers to him than his own brother was—and the women they loved.

This woman shouldn't be his concern.

She *wasn't* his concern.

She was merely a fellow passenger on a flight. When they got to base, he would join his team and go about their business, and she would go about whatever business had brought her out to Afghanistan. Although what that business was he had no idea. The woman didn't give off a military vibe, there were always various civilian contractors on base, but he couldn't seem to put his finger on what role this woman played.

Although she had been staring out the window, her hands calmly clasped together in her lap, he could see that her knuckles were white from the tightness of her grip, she turned her head, and for a second, their eyes met.

Fear bloomed in the chocolatey brown eyes that looked back at him, and a wall of regret hit Shark. Normally, he didn't care if people were afraid of him, so long as it wasn't his teammates' wives or children then he didn't much care if he scared people, in fact he often welcomed that reaction because it helped him keep some distance between himself and others.

But he didn't want *this* woman to be afraid of him.

It didn't make any sense, but for some reason he didn't like the idea of her thinking badly of him.

He must have been frowning at her because fear bloomed more prominently in her face and her gaze quickly skittered away as she resumed her stare out the window.

That made his frown deepen.

Although he had learned how to lock down his emotions, Shark had always been a protector, someone who had spent most of his life placing himself between those weaker and smaller than himself and whatever threat wanted to hurt them. That was how he'd gotten the nickname Shark. As a kid, he would roam the school halls or the park or anyplace kids congregated in search of bullies. With his empty black eyes and his reputation of beating up anyone who bullied another kid, he'd been compared to the supposedly soulless creatures that roved the oceans. The nickname hadn't bothered him. He'd been too busy searching for kids to rescue, and when he'd decided to join the military he'd kept the name. It was who he was, who he thought himself to be, but all this woman saw when she looked at him was a six-foot-four, two hundred pounds, angry man.

As a rule, Shark never initiated conversations with strangers unless it was a requirement of a mission he was working, he rarely initiated conversations with his friends either, but it sat wrong with him to let this woman think he was any sort of threat to her.

He was about to lean forward and tell her that there was no need for her to fear him when he heard something connect with the helicopter.

The woman startled, her gaze scanning the interior of the helo for whatever had caused the noise, but she wasn't going to find it in here.

"We're taking fire," the pilot's voice announced through their headsets.

Once again, fear filled the woman's expression only this time he was thankful that it had nothing to do with him. The man sitting beside him looked panicked, but the man sitting beside the woman maintained his composure.

Since they were in the air there wasn't really a lot he could do. If they survived the crash it wouldn't be because of anything he did or didn't do, it would all come down to the pilot, how badly they were hit, and pure dumb luck.

Shark had long since accepted the possibility of death. You didn't grow up in a home with an abusive father, and then join the military and become a SEAL and not become intimately acquainted with the notion, so he wasn't afraid, just calmly accepted his fate, whatever it might be. However, the idea of this woman dying upset him. He didn't need to know her to know that her death would come as a loss to the world.

Another bullet or missile hit the helicopter, and it tilted

sideways as the pilot struggled to remain in control of the craft.

"We're going down," the pilot announced.

The level of fear inside the small craft intensified, and Shark couldn't help but return his attention to the woman. She hadn't screamed or made a sound, but she was sitting ramrod straight, one hand pressed to her chest above her heart, the other covered her mouth. He could see fine tremors rippling through her small body, and while he wanted to say something that would reassure her, what was there to say?

They were going to crash, that was a given, and it wasn't likely they would survive, but if they did it wouldn't be without injuries, and they would be alone and unprotected in hostile territory.

There was nothing reassuring to say about their situation so he kept his mouth shut.

"Brace for impact," the pilot said as the helicopter swung wildly from side to side.

Shark checked to see if the woman knew the correct brace position, but she pressed her lower torso against the seatback and head against the headrest. Her hands slid under her thighs, and she sat there grimly awaiting her fate.

There was a resignation in her eyes that seemed incongruous with their situation, and he wondered again what had brought her to Afghanistan.

The helicopter quickly lost altitude and there was no time to wonder why the woman seemed oddly unsurprised to be facing almost certain death, or worse, capture. Nothing else struck the craft as the ground came up to meet them, but whoever had been shooting at them would be following their descent and would no doubt arrive on scene shortly after the crash to take care of any survivors.

Shark found himself praying that the woman didn't

survive impact, death would be better than whatever the terrorists would do to her if they found her alive. Capture—especially for a beautiful western woman—would have her praying for a death that would take far too long to come for her.

In the end the impact felt almost anti-climactic. It seemed to happen in slow motion. The ground was right there, they hit with a screech of metal and a bone-shattering force that tossed him about in his seat.

Then the world faded away.

There were hints of pain.

The sound of screams.

Footsteps.

Voices.

Fear.

He wasn't sure if he was dead or alive. He couldn't move, couldn't see, could barely hear, blanketed in a heavy burden of pain. His last thought before he died or passed out or whatever happened to carry him away was fear over what had happened to the woman.

* * *

3:30 P.M.

Pain.

It was all Claire Barrett could register.

She whimpered, her body squirming as though her pain were a physical thing that she could dislodge.

But she couldn't.

The pain was inside her, and it was getting worse not better the more she moved.

It took several moments for her to remember what had

happened, they were precious seconds wasted that she couldn't get back.

Claire knew she was in a world of trouble. She didn't know if anyone else had survived the crash, but even if they had, it didn't mean that she was any safer than if she was on her own. Someone on the helicopter might very well have been responsible for the crash, and if they were ...

Well, Claire wasn't ready to think about that yet.

For now, she had to get out of here, start moving, and pray that someone would come looking for her.

Someone who didn't want to kill her because of what she knew.

Blinking open her eyes, she squinted as the blinding light from the sun seemed to shoot right through her skull.

Headache; tick.

Sensitivity to light; tick.

Dizziness; tick.

Nausea; tick.

She could safely diagnose herself with a concussion. That would make hiking through the Afghani landscape more difficult, but she had just plummeted out of the sky so it wasn't like the injury was unexpected.

Doing her best to ignore the hammering in her skull, she slowly took stock of the rest of her body. She ached all over, her chest hurt every time it expanded as she took a breath but at least she could take a breath, she had survived the crash, and that meant she had a lot to be grateful for.

Maybe.

So long as she wasn't caught.

Scanning her surroundings, she saw that the man who had been sitting beside her no longer had a head.

Claire panted in terror, the sight enough to tip her out of her analytical daze and into the horror of her situation. That man had been sitting right beside her, that could have so easily been her. The man who had been sitting in the seat facing hers was nowhere to be seen, and she wondered what had become of him.

He'd scared her.

Those dark eyes had been so empty, so expressionless, even after the helicopter had been hit.

Was he the one?

She wished Raymond had told her everything before he'd killed himself. She hated only having half the story. How was she supposed to help if she didn't even know who she was looking for?

Knowing she'd already wasted too much time, Claire unsnapped the seatbelt that still kept her secured to her seat and staggered to her feet. Burning hot pain sliced through her shoulder as she stood, and when she glanced down she saw that the joint had popped out of place.

How was she going to put it back in on her own?

The other man who'd been in the back with her and the scary guy was clearly dead, and while she'd check the pilots before she left, she figured she was on her own. That wasn't anything new to her. Claire had left home when she was fifteen and had been on her own ever since, but being out here, knowing whoever shot down the helicopter would be coming, knowing she would be hiking through hostile territory with no one to watch her back was terrifying.

Beyond terrifying.

As carefully as she could, she stepped out of the mangled helo. She was going to have to search for anything she might need, all she had was a suitcase, she needed a survival kit of some sort, MREs, water, a first aid kit, something to make a fire with, and guns.

Clutching her arm to her chest so she didn't jostle her dislocated shoulder, she wobbled more than walked as she circled the helicopter. The man with the scary eyes was lying on his side, trapped under his seat which had also been ripped out of the broken vehicle.

Her feet headed toward him without thinking, intending to find out if he was dead or alive, but then she stopped. She should keep her distance from him in case he was the one. He'd been looking at her oddly, watching her as she'd been staring out the window worrying about what she'd be doing when she arrived at the base.

Why would he have been watching her unless he knew who she was?

Withdrawing, Claire was about to start her search when she heard voices.

Someone was coming.

It wasn't help, there was no way the military could have gotten anyone to them this quickly, which meant it was no doubt the people responsible for the crash.

She needed a weapon.

No way was she going down without a fight.

If there weren't too many of them, with the element of surprise on her side, there was a chance she could take them out before they could take her out. That the helicopter she was traveling in was shot down for any reason other than because she was in it never even occurred to her.

This was because of her. A desperate attempt to take her out before she could help to take them down.

Claire eased herself back inside the mangled craft, searching desperately for a weapon. She found a pack lying on the floor, partially open, and spied the black handgun inside. She wasn't a great shot, but she was proficient enough that she could hit a target at reasonably close range.

Thankfully, it was her left shoulder that had been dislocated so she still had full use of her dominant hand. She clutched the gun tightly enough that her knuckles turned white with the pressure. She wasn't a fidgeter. When she was anxious she folded in on herself, tensed up, locked herself down, locked everyone else out, but right now she didn't have time for anything other than intense concentration. One wrong move and she'd wind up dead.

Well, worse.

Before they killed her they would kidnap, torture, and rape her, and then they would give her a long, slow, painful death.

Four men dressed in traditional Afghani clothes approached the wreckage cautiously. They were each carrying an assault rifle and were muttering amongst one another. They were speaking to one another, but she didn't know either Pashto or Dari so she had no idea what they were saying.

One of them approached the scary man, and he moaned.

He was alive.

The insurgent lifted his weapon, and Claire aimed her own weapon, there was a chance the scary guy wasn't the man she was looking for, and even if he was, she couldn't let him be gunned down in cold blood.

Once she fired, she would have to take out the other three men quickly because she'd give away her position.

Focusing just on her next action and not all the fear, and pain, and worries that crowded in her mind, jostling for her attention, Claire aimed and fired.

The first man dropped.

The other three whirled around in her direction, and she aimed at the second and fired off a shot before they could start firing on her.

Crouching down so she was mostly hidden by the seat and what was left of the helicopter, she suppressed the scream that wanted to erupt and waited until the men finished firing before darting up and shooting the third man.

The fourth raised his weapon, but she took him out too.

Silence.

It seemed deafening and the world no longer felt solid beneath her. At any second she was going to sink through it and disappear.

Claire blinked against the light, which felt more like a sword slicing through her aching skull, and crept out of her hiding place. No one was moving, but she knew she would have to check to see if the four insurgents were dead.

The scary man moaned again. "Hello? Who's there?" he called out.

"H-hello?" she said hesitantly as she took a step closer to him. She didn't want to go near him, wanted just to curl up and hide from the world, but she couldn't do that.

"You're the woman from the helicopter," he said when she entered his line of sight.

"Uh ... yeah," she said, caught off guard by how good-looking he was. She was a psychologist who worked as a civilian contractor for the military. Sexy, built military men weren't new to her, but this one ... well, if she wasn't so afraid of him and who he might be then she would have felt very attracted to him. However, right now her fear was like a bucket of cold water on her libido.

"What's your name?" he asked, his gaze raking over her, and she shivered even though she sensed nothing untoward in his expression.

Self-preservation made her want to keep her mouth closed, but she was stuck out here with him, they could be the only two survivors of the crash, and she was going to have to rely on him to remain alive and get to safety. "Claire. Claire Barrett."

"Nice to meet you, Claire, although I wish it were under better circumstances. I'm Logan Kirk, but my nickname is Shark."

Shark.

She could see that.

It was his eyes. There was an emptiness to them, a predatory gleam that reminded her of sharks.

Logan shifted, tried to shove off the seat that pinned him down, but winced and sunk back against the ground. "Can you help?" he asked, looking up at her.

Claire hesitated. If she helped him get free and he was the man she was here to identify, she could kiss her life goodbye. He would simply lead her into the lion's den, then allow her to be tortured for information, or maybe he would be the one to interrogate her. Either way, trusting him could be the equivalent of signing her own death warrant.

"Claire?" Logan was looking at her with those inky black eyes, and she couldn't suppress her shudder.

Trust him or not?

She was so afraid to make the wrong decision.

"You okay?" He sounded genuinely concerned about her, and she sighed. It wasn't like she had a choice, she couldn't just leave him here to await certain death.

"Yeah, I can help." Moving closer, she leaned down to grip the back of the seat with her good arm and managed to curl her fingers around it as she fought off a wave of dizziness. Logan planted his own hands on the seat and pushed while she pulled, then he dragged himself backward and sunk down again.

Blood drenched one side of his light blue shirt as well as one side of his head, he was injured, but he was still a good foot taller than her five-foot-three frame and had over a hundred pounds on her. If she had made a mistake helping him get free then she was about to come face to face with the agent of her death.

* * *

4:08 P.M.

"You're bleeding," Claire said, pointing at his stomach.

It didn't go unnoticed that as soon as she'd helped him get free she shuffled backward a few paces, putting a little distance between them. It was obvious she was terrified, and while the logical assumption was because they'd just been in a helicopter crash and were now stranded in enemy territory, he couldn't forget her nervous tension during the flight.

A nervous flyer? Or had she suspected something bad was going to happen?

Ignoring the pain in his side for the moment, Shark pushed to his feet. He swayed slightly, fought back a sickening wave of dizziness, and then drew himself up to his full height. If this woman was a threat to him, everyone on base, including his team, and the country he served, he had to know now.

And if she was then he would eliminate her.

He wouldn't enjoy it, she was a small, slight, almost fragile-looking thing. However, despite her obvious injuries, she'd helped him when she could have left him, and he recalled gunshots and voices and could see bodies strewn about. Since Claire was the only other one standing, she had to have been the one to kill them. Again, if she was up to something she could have stood by and let the insurgents kill him, but she hadn't.

Allowing the coldness inside him to seep into his eyes, he took a menacing step toward her.

Claire sucked in a scared breath and backtracked further until her back pressed up against the wreckage. It was obvious she was terrified witless of him, and while he internally flinched at the idea, he kept his emotions hidden. If she was a traitor then he had to know.

Her huge dark eyes stared up at him. She was shaking all over, one arm clutched tightly against her stomach, and yet she made no move to run, no move to go for one of the weapons he could see lying about. She just stood there and shook and stared at him like she expected him to … hurt her? Kill her?

Because she knew she'd done something bad or because she feared *he* was the bad one?

Shark froze at the thought. That was exactly the vibe he got from her. She was afraid of him, just like she had been on the helicopter.

"Why are you in Afghanistan?" he growled.

Claire flinched at his tone and seemed to shrink in on herself. "I'm a psychologist, a civilian contractor who works with the military." Despite her fear, her voice was clear and strong. She might be afraid of him, but he doubted she would back down from a fight even if the odds were stacked against her.

Shark allowed himself to relax a fraction, he didn't sense anything evil from her. Maybe her nerves on the flight had just been about her job and the horrors she knew she'd be hearing from her patients. Letting it go for now if he felt anything change, or if he learned anything about Claire Barrett that caused him to become suspicious, he could easily restrain her and take care of the problem.

When he took a step back, Claire let out a relieved breath, and he realized she *had* believed he was about to hurt her, the notion made him frown. He didn't do gentle or sweet unless he absolutely had to, but for some reason Claire made him want to try.

"Your shoulder is dislocated, and you have a head wound. Are you hurt anywhere else?" he asked.

She shook her head but couldn't hide her wince at the

movement. "Just bruises," she said softly, "but you're bleeding badly."

He nodded, the pain in his side was bad but certainly not the worst pain he'd ever endured. His first priority was checking to make sure the men who had come for them were really dead and seeing if anyone else had survived the crash. Since Claire had been up on her feet longer than he had, and they were about to take a dangerous hike through the Afghani desert, he gestured at the ground. "Why don't you rest for a moment?"

Claire hesitated but then relented, her knees buckled, and she dropped hard onto her backside. Again she winced, but she didn't say anything as she curled her legs up to her chest and rested her head on her knees.

As a rule, Shark never voluntarily touched anyone, and certainly not to offer comfort, but the psychologist made him want to gather her into his arms, hold her and rock her, and tell her that everything was going to be okay.

Instead, he walked over to the men dressed in traditional Afghani clothes. Each one had an AK-47 beside his fallen body, and Shark found himself impressed that an injured Claire had been able to eliminate all four targets without getting shot herself. She was much stronger than he had given her credit for and that eased some of his concerns about their upcoming hike. He had a feeling that Claire Barrett was more than capable of holding her own.

Quickly, he bent beside each to press his fingers to their necks. The first three were dead, but the fourth moaned when Shark touched him. Scooping up the man's own weapon, Shark shot him once in the head to finish him off.

"Oh ... oh my ..."

He turned to see that Claire was watching him with wide eyes, her skin had paled, she was breathing hard, and she pressed a hand to her mouth then scooted onto her knees, leaned over, and threw up.

Shark crossed over to her, crouched beside her, and placed a tentative hand on her arm. Instead of shrinking away from him like he expected, she grabbed onto his hand with her own much smaller one, holding onto him with a vicelike grip.

"Th-they were g-going to k-k-kill you," she stammered. Her breath was now sawing in and out of her chest, and he was worried she was about to hyperventilate.

"You saved my life," he said simply. While it had been the approaching of the four Afghani men that had woken him from unconsciousness he had been unarmed, trapped, and too out of it to defend himself. If Claire hadn't regained consciousness first and been alert and on her feet, then he'd be dead right now. As would she.

The idea of Claire dead affected him in a way it shouldn't, but he shoved aside the unwanted feelings. He had an injured woman to tend to and then somehow get to safety, he had to remain focused.

"Breathe with me," he ordered maybe a little harsher than he should have, but this woman unsettled him, and he didn't like or appreciate it. "In and out," he coached. When he'd helped her get her breathing under control, he gently pried his hand from her white-knuckled grip and stood. "Rest for a moment, I'll check to see if anyone else survived, then gather everything I can. Then we'll put your shoulder back in and get out of here."

"And your side," she said, pointing to the blood soaking his shirt.

He merely nodded and went in search of supplies. Both pilots were dead, as were both of the men who had been traveling in the back with him and Claire, one had been decapitated, and he hated that Claire had seen something so horrific. There was nothing he could do about it though, so he found his pack, which was thankfully stocked with MREs, water, a fire starting kit, a well-stocked first aid kit, some extra clothes, and weapons. His job had taught him to be prepared, and he never went anywhere without a well-stocked pack. You never knew when you would be shot down out of the sky and forced to go on a hike through enemy territory with a sexy psychologist who set alight parts of his soul he'd thought didn't exist.

Shark also gathered the assault rifles from the insurgents, he had no idea how long it would take for him and Claire to be found or how many hostiles they would encounter. The more weapons they had, the better.

"Hey," he said when he walked back over to Claire and found her staring at the bodies of the men she had killed. Her gaze swung slowly to his, and when he knew he had her attention, he said, "You had to do it. It was you or them."

"I know," she whispered. "I've just never … I've never killed anyone before." Her bottom lip wobbled, but she clamped her teeth down on it hard enough to draw blood.

Reaching out, before he could even process what he was doing, Shark had brushed his thumb across her lip. She sucked in a surprised breath, but for once, she didn't pull away from him, just stared at him as though he confused her.

Welcome to the club.

No one in his life had ever confused Shark as much as this beautiful, battered woman huddled on the ground before him.

"You did the right thing, tell yourself that as many times as you need until it sinks in. This is going to hurt, but I have to put your shoulder back in."

Claire didn't protest, knowing it had to be done, and since worrying about how much it was going to hurt was only going to make her tense up more, he grabbed her wrist and guided her arm forward. The joint popped loudly as it went back into place and Claire screamed, her eyes rolling back as she passed out.

Shark caught her head in one of his hands, then gently eased Claire down until she lay flat on her back. Despite her claim that she was fine besides the shoulder and her head, he suspected that declaration had more to do with trying to stop him from touching her since she was clearly afraid of him. While he didn't want to invade her privacy or make her feel uncomfortable, he had to know if there were any other injuries he had to be concerned about, so as clinically as he could he ran his hands over her arms and legs. There were no broken bones as far as he could tell, and although it made him feel like a pervert he lifted her t-shirt to check her torso. Bruises were already forming on her chest beneath the white lacy bra he tried very hard not to notice, they were bad enough that he was sure she'd cracked ribs. At least they'd have to hope the ribs were cracked and not broken.

Smoothing her t-shirt down since there was nothing he could do for that other than offer her some painkillers when she woke up, he turned his attention to his own injuries. His ribs hadn't fared much better than hers, but it was the deep gash in his side that had him the most concerned.

Using the supplies in the first aid kit, Shark cleaned and stitched the gash, applied antibiotic cream and a bandage, then gave himself a shot of antibiotics in the hopes that he could stave off any infection because out here an infection spelled his and Claire's deaths.

It had been a long time since anyone other than his team had depended on him for anything, but Shark vowed here and now not to let Claire down.

* * *

4:26 P.M.

"Wake up."

Someone was patting her cheek, and Claire moaned and tried to roll away, but she was held in place. "No," she muttered, trying to swat at whatever was touching her.

"Yes," a voice tinged with humor contradicted. "I need you to wake up now, Claire."

That voice, she recognized it but she couldn't remember from where.

It was a nice voice, deep and sexy, smooth, although somehow she got the impression it was a voice that wasn't used to being used a lot.

She understood that.

Despite her job, which was basically encouraging people to talk about their problems so she could suggest possible solutions, she actually wasn't one for talking much herself.

It had been her experience that oftentimes people weren't really interested in what you had to say. That was why she always made sure that every single one of her patients knew that she cared, that she wanted to help them, that they weren't just a paycheck, that helping them to heal was important to her.

It must have worked because Raymond had opened up to her, trusted her, and no one else with what he had done.

Raymond.

Afghanistan.

The helicopter.

The crash.

Logan.

Pain.

"Come on, Claire, wake up for me."

That was Logan's voice, the scary, intimidating, but

somehow also gentle man who had survived the crash along with her.

Claire blinked open heavy eyes and saw relief wash over Logan's face. "I couldn't get you to wake up, you scared me."

She'd scared him?

His easy admission went a way toward easing her lingering fear that he was the man she had been sent here to identify. If he wanted her dead, he wouldn't care about whether she was okay or not. Right? Unless he needed her to tell him and whoever he worked with what she knew, what Raymond had told her.

"You need to drink some water," Logan announced, sliding a hand behind her head to lift it and holding a canteen to her lips.

His hand was warm, big, strong, it comforted her even as she continued to have doubts about him.

"Come on, Claire, drink some water for me," he urged.

Obediently, she swallowed the water he poured into her mouth. She hadn't even realized she was thirsty until the cool liquid slid down her throat. Too soon he moved the canteen away, she would have asked for more water, but she knew they might not have much and that what they did have they would have to ration carefully.

The gravity of their situation settled over her heavily. They were both alive and considering that the other four people in the helicopter weren't, they had both walked away relatively unscathed.

"Do you need me to tend to your wound?" she asked, tilting her head to indicate his stomach. For now they were stuck together, their survival—their lives—intertwined. If she wanted to live, she would have to work with Logan not against him, which meant making sure he was okay.

"It's okay, I took care of it while you were out."

"Oh, sorry," she said as he helped her sit up. She hadn't

meant to pass out but the pain in her shoulder when Logan put it back in combined with the head injury and fear must have taken a toll on her.

"It's fine. You saved my life, it was my turn to take care of you." Logan smiled at her and it transformed his entire face. He was shockingly handsome when he wasn't looking all deadly and cold. His dark eyes sparkled like black diamonds, his dark hair was just long enough to have a soft wave to it, and his body was the kind that melted women's panties.

His smile did things to her insides that she'd never experienced before and she squirmed uncomfortably to relieve the sudden tingling between her legs.

Logan obviously mistook that for pain because the smile vanished and creases lined his forehead. "Do you want to take something for the pain?"

"No, I need to keep a clear head and painkillers make me go loopy, even the mild ones." They were in a fight for survival, she should not be getting distracted by a sexy stranger who very well might want her dead. "We should get out of here."

"We should," he agreed. "Let's put this on you."

While she'd been out, he'd made her a sling from a bandage he must have gotten from his first aid kit, and he helped her position her injured arm in it. Immediately some of the pain and pressure in her shoulder eased. "What's the plan?" she asked as she accepted his hand and allowed him to help her to her feet.

"We get up into the mountains," he said, pointing to their left where there was a steep mountain range. "We both need rest, and there should be caves up there where we can spend the night, but for now, we need to put as much distance between ourselves and the wreckage before more men come looking for us."

Claire highly approved of that plan.

"Are you okay to walk?" Logan asked, eyeing her sling and her head. "If you're not I can carry you."

Heat flushed through her body at the idea of being cradled in those strong arms of his, and she felt her cheeks redden. "I'm fine," she mumbled as she wracked her brain for a question to distract herself. "What kind of temperatures should I be expecting?"

"First time in Afghanistan?" he asked as he hefted a pack onto his back, then slung all four assault rifles that had belonged to their would-be killers across his chest.

"Yes. I can carry something," she offered.

"You have cracked ribs and a dislocated shoulder."

She frowned. "How do you know about my ribs?"

"Saw the bruises. Sorry, Claire, I had to check you for injuries, I had to know whether you were going to be ambulatory or if I would be carrying you out of here."

Logan didn't look particularly apologetic, nor did he sound it, but since she supposed she couldn't argue with his logic she let it go even though the knowledge that he had seen her bra and her breasts left her oddly … jealous? He'd seen her, or at least some of her, and yet his long-sleeved black t-shirt hid his sculpted body.

"Mid-eighties during the day, low sixties or high fifties overnight."

"What?" she asked as he started walking and she hurried to trail along behind him.

"Temperatures."

"Oh." She'd forgotten she'd even asked him that. Those temperatures didn't seem too bad, not so hot that dehydration would be a major factor, although they would still need to be careful to remain hydrated, and not so cold that they would freeze at night.

Despite the injury to his side and the weight he was carrying, Logan set a grueling pace, and it wasn't long before she was struggling to keep up. She was wearing comfortable cargo pants and boots that offered a fair amount of tread for traipsing across the rocky terrain, but she wasn't much of an outdoorsy kind of girl, she'd never been hiking, and certainly not in conditions like these.

Still, she didn't want to be the weak link that got them both killed, so she kept walking, urging her bruised body not to fail her when she needed it the most.

A bead of sweat formed at the base of her neck, she felt it trail down the curve of her spine, settling at the waistband of her pants.

Her muscles began to burn with fatigue. Claire considered herself reasonably fit, she went to the gym a couple of times a week and watched what she ate, but none of that prepared her for this. After a while, her burning muscles turned numb and heavy, lifting her foot to take each step became more difficult and she started to stumble, tripping over rock or shrubs, or sometimes just her own feet.

The minutes blurred together and eventually her vision blurred along with it and when she swayed and dropped to her knees, she knew she wasn't getting up again. At least not without a short break and some water.

"Logan," she called out. He spun around to look at her, a glare on his face, and she wondered what she'd done wrong to make him angry. Was he mad she needed a break? No, he knew she was injured and didn't have the same training he did. Was it his name? Was she supposed to call him Shark? "Oh … um … sorry. Shark? What am I supposed to call you?"

His features smoothed out and he backtracked to close the small distance between them, offering her his canteen. "No, Logan is fine, I'm just not used to it anymore."

She knew military guys loved their callsigns and nicknames, but it felt weird to her to call someone Shark, even if the name did suit him. "You're special forces, right?"

Logan nodded. "SEAL."

She could see that. What else could a man who went by the name Shark be other than the biggest predator in the ocean?

The cool water went a long way to restoring some of her strength, and she handed it back to Logan and went to stand. "Sorry for slowing us down, I can keep walking now."

"Take a moment," he said.

"We have to put more distance between us and the helicopter, and it's getting dark, we won't be able to walk much longer."

"Rest."

Logan was a man who didn't waste words, and he definitely had a bit of a bossy side, although she should expect that since he was a SEAL. However, she was still dizzy and she did need another couple of moments before she was ready to get back to hiking.

Claire closed her eyes and focused on locking her pain away in a box to be dealt with later, it was a trick she had mastered as a kid, and now it just might save her life. She took deep breaths, let her aching muscles relax as much as they could, and let her body take these few precious moments to recharge.

"I'm good," she announced a few minutes later.

When Logan gave her a scrutinizing once over and then nodded, she went to stand up again and put her good hand down to help her get her feet beneath her, but she overbalanced.

The next thing Claire knew, she was sliding down the side of the mountain.

* * *

6:16 P.M.

. . .

One second Claire was behind him, and the next, she wasn't.

She must have lost her balance, and it had sent her sliding down the twenty-foot sloped side of the mountain they'd been walking up.

Why hadn't he helped her to her feet?

Shark knew the answer to that because he hadn't wanted to touch her again. He was a little too attracted to her for his liking. If he'd seen her in a bar that would be one thing, he might have approached her, seen if she was interested, and if she was they would end up in bed.

But he hadn't met her in a bar.

And they certainly wouldn't be ending up in bed together.

This was about survival, and he had already made the vow to himself that he would get Claire out of here and to safety, it was a promise he intended to keep. Thinking of anything but their survival wasn't the way to make that happen.

Claire had screamed when she first started falling but now she'd gone silent.

She lay still.

Too still.

There weren't any trees on the mountain or any large rocks that she would have hit on the way down, but she still could have snapped her neck in her tumble.

Not wanting to draw any more attention to them if someone was nearby, Shark reined in the need to call out to her, and instead he hurried down to join her in a controlled slide. When he got to her, he dropped to his knees, and this time he ached to touch her, confirm that life still flowed through her veins.

Shark pressed his fingers to her neck and was reassured by the steady thumping of her pulse.

"Claire?" he called, lightly tapping her cheek. "Come on, Claire, open your eyes for me."

"Logan?" she murmured. Like he'd told her earlier, he wasn't used to hearing anyone call him by his given name, he'd been Shark for so long and it was a shock to hear the name fall from her lips. But he'd liked it. Definitely a whole lot more than he should.

"Are you hurt?" he asked, then realized that was a stupid question. She'd been in a helicopter crash and she'd just taken a tumble twenty feet down the side of the mountain, of course she was hurting. "Let me rephrase, any new injuries?"

"I don't think so," Claire replied as she slowly moved each part of her body. "Sorry, I just lost my balance."

"Don't apologize," he said so fiercely she flinched. "You're hurt, you haven't complained once, and you kept up with the pace I set. You need to rest."

"We need to keep going, we're not far enough away yet," she protested.

Again he reminded her that pushing too hard was going to be counterproductive. "You push too hard and you crash. This is a marathon, not a sprint."

"But we're behind now because of me, we have to redo all that distance I made us lose." Tears shimmered in her big, brown eyes and he wanted to wipe them away, wanted to make her smile even though there was nothing to smile about with their situation.

"Claire, relax." He wished he had some idea of what to say to ease her fear, even if just for a moment. He'd never been a man of words. When his father had beat his mother, he hadn't tried to talk him out of it, he'd just stepped in between them and used his own fists. When his father had tried to beat up his younger brother he'd done the same thing, he'd fought back, given as good as his father gave. When he'd seen kids who were being bullied he hadn't tried to convince the bully with words that it was wrong, he'd simply given them a taste of their own medicine. Now he was a SEAL, and again he didn't solve problems with words, but now he would give anything to know the right thing to say.

"I'm trying." She sniffed.

Shark sighed, he had to find a way to do what didn't come naturally to him. He reached out and slipped an arm behind her shoulders and helped her sit up. "I know you are, and you're doing just fine. Better than fine."

"Really?" she asked hesitantly, needing a little reassurance.

"I know we don't know each other, but there is one thing you need to learn about me right now. I don't say things that aren't true. Usually, I don't say much at all, I leave the talking that needs to be done to my team, but they're not here right now, and I don't know what you need me to say to reassure you, so just know that I don't see you as a liability."

Much to his surprise Claire relaxed and actually smiled at him. "What you just said was perfect, it was what I needed to hear. Can you help me up?"

He stood, then reached out a hand for her to grab and gently pulled her to her feet. Shark rearranged the sling, making sure it was offering her shoulder the support it needed. Then he gave her a once over to make sure she wasn't trying to hide any injuries from him under the guise of not worrying him or wanting to slow them down.

When she looked relatively steady on her feet, he started walking, taking them back up the mountain. This time he made sure that he kept a closer eye on her and when he noticed her starting to flag again, after another thirty minutes or so of walking, he changed their hike from covering the distance to searching for a place to spend the night.

Ten minutes later, he found a small cave in a position that would allow him to keep watch on anyone approaching and be able to take them out before they even knew he and Claire were there.

"Here we go," he said, guiding her inside.

"Home sweet home," Claire said with a lopsided smile as she sunk down and leaned against the rough stone wall of the cave.

"You might want to go do your business before it's completely dark out."

Claire groaned but used her good arm to lever herself back up and disappeared. Wanting to give her some privacy, Shark resisted the urge to keep watch, trusting that she would call out if she needed him and that it was too dark now for anyone to be out hunting them. Instead, he busied himself getting out the emergency blankets and MREs for them to eat. They'd also have to ration their water until he could find more, but they had enough for them both to hydrate before they lay down to sleep.

"That wasn't fun," Claire grumbled when she joined him, sinking once again down to rest against the wall.

"Not a fan of camping?" he asked as he handed her an MRE.

"What is this?" she asked, scrunching her nose up as she looked it over.

"Dinner. Meals ready to eat."

"Are they ... good?"

Shark shrugged. "They're all right. They're fuel, and your body needs fuel."

Claire nodded her agreement and then opened the meal sniffing it suspiciously before tasting it. "It's actually better than I thought. And no, not a fan of camping, I've only been once, with my dad before he ..."

His chest constricted at the mention of fathers. His was not a man he chose to think about. "You lost him?"

"Yeah, he ... uh ... committed suicide. He was in the military, he was special forces too, a Ranger. He couldn't live with the things he saw and did so he ended his life. That's why I decided to become a psychologist and why I wanted to work with men and women who served. My way of trying to do my part in making sure no one else went through what my mom and I did." Claire shrugged sadly and returned her attention to her dinner.

"I'm sorry," he said softly.

"Thanks." She offered him another lopsided smile. "What about your family? Are your parents still alive? Together? Do you have any siblings?"

His airway seemed to close, no way was he talking about his family with Claire. He didn't even talk about his family with his team let alone some stranger fate had tossed into this nightmare with him.

Yet almost against his will, the words came out. "Father died in prison when I was twelve. I have a brother who's two years younger than me, he's a cop, married with three kids. My mom just recently passed away, she had a heart attack. That's why I was flying out alone, my team is already on base."

"I'm so sorry." Claire reached out, hesitated for a moment, then rested her hand on top of his. "Losing a parent sucks even if they aren't a great parent."

She said it like she had firsthand knowledge of deadbeat parents, the sense of loss he'd felt from her when she talked about losing her dad told him it wasn't her father. He bet there was a story there about her relationship with her mother, one that didn't have a happy ending. He'd ask if she wanted to talk about it, but he didn't know what to say, and to be honest, he was a little afraid of what she'd tell him if she did talk. What if she told him something really awful and he made it worse by saying the wrong thing?

Claire seemed to be content to drift into silence as they

finished their meals. When they were done he put away the packaging in his pack and gestured to the blankets.

"You should get some sleep. I want to get an early start in the morning."

"Are you going to lie down with me?" Claire looked torn between not wanting to get close to him and also not wanting to be alone.

This was an easy out.

Tell her no, he was going to be sitting by the entrance to the cave keeping watch. He wasn't any more comfortable lying down and spending the night under the same blanket than she was only he suspected for entirely different reasons. She still didn't completely trust him, why he didn't know, but he could see it written all over her face. His reason for not wanting to sleep beside her was the way she made him feel. Or more accurately, that she made him feel at all.

Better to be safe, keep things professional, get her out of here then bid her farewell.

Instead, he nodded. "I'm just going to go and do a perimeter check and then I'll be back."

Frustrated with himself and his inability to make good decisions and saying things he didn't mean to say, Shark stalked outside to do his perimeter check.

What had he been thinking?

Why had he agreed to sleep with Claire?

Nothing good could come from it, and yet it was done now, and he wasn't going to backtrack.

Even worse he wasn't sure he wanted to.

Shark groaned, it was going to be a long night.

CHAPTER 2

September 7th

5:22 A.M.

Claire was deliciously warm and toasty.

Comfortable too.

Wait a minute.

Wasn't she in the middle of Afghanistan sleeping on the floor of a cave? Why would she be comfortable?

Blinking open sleepy eyes, she immediately saw the reason she was so comfortable. During sleep, she had draped herself all over Logan. Her left leg was hooked over his, her head was pillowed against his broad chest, and her left arm—still tucked into her sling—was tucked comfortably against his stomach.

When they'd both lied down to go to sleep, they had been careful to make sure there was a sliver of space between them. Even so, they had been close enough that she could feel the heat pouring off him. It had been like sleeping with a hot water bottle. Despite how he'd made the cold, hard floor of the cave somehow less cold and less hard, she wanted to put more distance between them because he made her uncomfortable.

She wasn't really scared of him anymore, not much anyway, but he made her feel things that no man ever had. Claire avoided men like the plague, well romantically anyway, she had guys who were just friends. She was quite happy with that arrangement, she didn't like men touching her, even those who were her friends, and yet when Logan touched her she got this weird fluttery feeling in her stomach.

It was odd and she didn't like it.

But sleeping on opposite sides of the cave wasn't an option, there was only one blanket, and even though it wasn't cold enough for them to freeze, it was cold enough that they needed the blanket. Apparently, her sleeping mind didn't care one iota about how unsettled Logan made her feel because it had sought him out and well and truly taken advantage of the comfort his body offered.

It didn't seem like he minded, he had one arm curled around her, anchoring her against him, his large hand settled on her hip. It was very intimate sleeping like this. *Too* intimate.

Claire carefully slipped out from under Logan's arm, then tucked the blanket back around him so he didn't get cold. She needed to put some distance between them, getting attached in any way to Logan Kirk was a bad idea. When—because she couldn't allow herself to believe it was in question—they got to base she had a job to do. A job she still didn't know for sure didn't involve Logan. Once she'd done what she'd been brought here to do then she would go back home, Logan would join up with his team, complete whatever mission they were here to do, and then he'd go back to his life.

Which for all she knew included a wife or girlfriend.

Somehow the thought of that bothered her.

But it shouldn't.

And it wouldn't.

She wouldn't let it.

Stepping out of the cave, she stood for a moment to watch as the sky lightened. The sun would be up soon, and Logan would want to get going, but she was happy for this couple of quiet moments before she had to face him again. Her gut told her that he was a good guy, not the man she was here to find, but Claire wasn't sure if her gut was being influenced by the fact that she depended on Logan for her survival.

Without him she doubted she would make it back alive, her life was literally in Logan's hands, and she prayed he wasn't going to take advantage of that.

Sighing, Claire headed off to the place where she'd relieved herself last night, and once she was done she'd go back to the cave. Logan would no doubt have woken up when he realized she was no longer draped all over him, and then the grueling walking would begin. She had no idea where they were heading, but it seemed like Logan had a plan, maybe she should ask him about it, just in case the worst happened and she wound up on her own.

She was so distracted with her thoughts and trying to figure out if Logan was the traitor or not that she didn't see the men until it was too late.

She'd just pulled up her pants, wishing she had never taken toilet paper for granted, when she saw them. There were two of them, and they were both heavily armed. It was obvious they weren't expecting to find her because their eyes widened when they spotted her.

What should she do?

Claire had zero training when it came to this, she had never even taken a self-defense course before. The only reason she knew how to shoot a gun was because her friend Dahlia Black, who was studying to be a physical therapist and worked at a VA rehab facility back home, had come from a military family and had insisted on taking her to the range and teaching her the basics.

If Dahlia hadn't done that, then she and Logan would have been killed back at the site of the wreckage.

Now terror zinged inside her. Should she try to run? It was obvious she couldn't attack them, they were armed, and she wasn't, which she was really going to have to talk to Logan about. She needed to have a gun on her at all times in case they were separated.

Instead of doing anything even vaguely useful she stood there, frozen to the spot, for several long moments, wasting the precious seconds that might have made the difference between her living or dying.

One of them kept a weapon pointed at her while the other one approached. Since she didn't speak their language, she had no idea what they were saying, but their intent was clear. They weren't leaving here without her.

She was grabbed roughly, a hand around her right bicep, dragging her closer until her body was touching the man's. He reached out with his other hand to grab her breast, squeezing painfully hard, and she could feel his growing erection against her stomach. Whether he knew who she was and what she was doing in Afghanistan or not, this man knew she was a Westerner and that she was out of place so far out here in the middle of nowhere, and he intended to use that to his advantage.

When he tried to kiss her, Claire finally snapped out of her shock-induced stupor and stopped standing there like an idiot doing nothing to protect herself.

Without conscious thought, she slammed her left fist into his nose, satisfied when she heard a crunch, and he released her with a howl, his hand flying to his nose as blood streamed from it.

The strike might have got the man to let go of her, but it hardly saved her, and it also cost her as pain throbbed in her injured shoulder. The two men exchanged heated words, and she could see that the one who hadn't touched her was laughing at his friend whose face was turning as bright red as the blood that poured from his broken nose.

No doubt irked by his friend's laughter, adding insult to the injury of being hit by a woman, he lifted his assault rifle and aimed it at her.

Claire dove behind a nearby rock as the rat-tat-tat-tat sounded exorbitantly loud in the otherwise quiet dawn.

She screamed without thinking and wondered why she hadn't screamed earlier. She was only about a hundred yards from the cave where she and Logan had spent the night, now she wished she was closer, but at the time she'd been embarrassed to pee too close to Logan, which seemed silly now. If she'd screamed as soon as she'd seen the two men she could have immediately brought Logan running. He was armed and a SEAL, he was more skilled than both these men put together and she knew that he wouldn't hesitate to throw himself between her and any threats.

Unless he was working with these men.

Had he contacted them somehow?

Told them where she was?

The thought was enough to snap her lips closed, not wanting to do anything to draw Logan's attention although it was probably already too late for that.

The two men appeared around the rock and her fingers curled around a smaller rock in the ground, it wasn't really a match to an AK-47 as far as weapons went, but it was better than nothing.

The one she'd hit came up to her, backhanding her immediately and screaming something at her that she didn't understand. When he shoved her back against the rock, pinning her in place with his larger body, and shoved a hand up her shirt, mind-numbing fear took hold.

This wasn't the first time she'd been pinned down like this.

It wasn't the first time a man had used her body for his own pleasure, stealing something from her she could never get back.

But the fear numbed only the conscious part of her mind allowing instinct to take over.

Claire rammed the rock into the side of the man's head, then grabbed a handful of soil and threw it in his face.

He screeched as the dirt got in his eyes, and she threw the rock in her hand at the other man as he swung the gun in her direction, no doubt thinking he'd had enough of her and was ready to eliminate her and be done with it. He dodged to miss the rock but lost his footing and slammed down hard on his backside.

Unfortunately, the man who had assaulted her recovered quicker than she had anticipated and before she could make a run for it he grabbed her, his fingers digging painfully into her injured shoulder, and slammed her head against the rock hard enough that she saw stars.

* * *

5:39 A.M.

. . .

He had woken the second his sleeping mind sensed that Claire was awake, but apparently, he was a coward because he faked sleep until he heard her sneak out of the cave.

What was it about this woman that got to him?

Nobody got to him.

Any person, any situation, it didn't matter he responded the same way.

Until Claire Barrett anyway.

Frustrated with himself, he sat up and began to fold up the blanket, shoving it back into his pack with a little more force than strictly necessary. Shark knew one thing for sure, when he got out of this mess he was adding a second blanket to his pack so if he was ever stranded with a sexy woman again they could each have their own blanket and space to sleep.

Claire had woken him during the night when she'd plastered herself all over him, snuggling against him like they were lovers instead of two strangers sleeping side by side out of necessity. It wasn't her sleeping on him that had bothered him, she'd been asleep, she hadn't made the conscious decision to use him as her pillow, it was his reaction to the physical closeness.

He liked it much more than he should have.

Instead of gently easing her off him and rolling over onto his side with his back to her to discourage that closeness, he'd thrown an arm around her, settled his hand on her hip, and actually enjoyed having her slight weight against him.

What was she doing to him?

The worst part about it was that he was pretty sure she had no idea how much she affected him. There was a naiveté about her that hinted that she perhaps wasn't very experienced when it came to men and relationships. She didn't seem to know how beautiful she was, she didn't seem to understand how alluring those dark eyes were or how kissable her lips looked, and that only made her that much sexier.

Shaking away all thoughts of the stunning psychologist, they were a waste of time, not only would they never see each other again once this was over but even if they did what would a woman like Claire see in a man like him?

Annoyed that Claire had managed to rattle him when he'd thought he had long since perfected the art of not allowing anyone or anything to rattle him, Shark pulled out two energy bars, one for each of them. They were going to have to ration their food, he had no idea how long it would take them to be found, but he was more worried about their water situation. They were going to have to find a well or something soon so he could restock.

Claire still hadn't returned, and he started to worry about her.

Actually worry.

The only people he was used to worrying over were his team and their families, and yet he was as concerned over Claire as he would be if he had been thrown into this situation with Ryder "Spider" Flynn's wife Abigail, Eric "Night" McNamara's wife Lavender, or Owen "Fox" LeGrand's wife Evie. He loved each one of those women like sisters, and he would do anything it took to make sure they survived.

Same as he would do for Claire.

Who really should be back by now. How long did it take to do your business? He had assumed she had slipped away to go to the bathroom, but even if she's had a stomach upset she should still be back by now.

Shark was just debating whether or not it was too big of an invasion of privacy to go looking for her when he heard the sound of gunfire, closely followed by a scream.

Claire's scream.

She was in trouble.

Fear cut through him as he snatched up one of the stolen weapons and hurried out of the cave. The sun was just rising, and he headed in the direction of the gunshots. It didn't take him long to spot Claire. She wasn't alone, two men were crowding around her. One had a weapon trained on her, the other had her by the shoulders and slammed her head into a rock.

He saw red.

No one put their hands on Claire and got to live.

The man touching Claire put his hands under her shirt and Shark didn't hesitate. He fired one shot at the other man who was still armed to eliminate the biggest threat. At the sound of the shot, the man assaulting Claire spun around, searching for his weapon. With the man a step away from Claire, he could now take the shot without worrying about her getting caught up in the crosshairs and getting hit her.

With both men down, Shark scanned the area but didn't see any other threats, either these two had no knowledge of the crash and weren't looking for him and Claire, or they were scouts, and there were men all over the mountains searching for them.

For the moment his priority was Claire and making sure she was all right, then they were going to have to get moving, he wanted to put more distance between them and the wreckage. Shark had been hoping that today after they'd both gotten some much-needed rest they'd be able to make good progress, but now Claire had new injuries he needed to worry about, and that plan seemed to have flown right out the window.

"Claire," he said as he reached her side, kneeling beside her.

She was curled up against the rock, her back pressed against it, knees to her chest, head resting on them, her arms wrapped around herself as though in an attempt to hold herself together.

"Claire," Shark said again, his concerns growing when she didn't react to his voice. It was obvious she was in shock, and while he couldn't blame her and didn't hold it against her, he needed her to snap out of it so they could get out of here. "Come on, Claire, come back to me."

When he reached out and touched her shoulder, hoping that it might help to bring Claire out of her shock-induced haze, she screamed, her head snapping back, eyes wild as she looked right through him. She tried to scramble backward, but there was nowhere to go. Like a cornered animal, her gaze searched for an escape. Her breath sawed in and out of her chest so fast she was on the brink of hyperventilating.

Feeling way out of his depth here, he drew on what he knew about psychology from what he'd learned from his mother, who ironically had been much better at helping others while always being unable to help herself.

Keeping his voice low and soothing, but also speaking calmly and straightforwardly, Shark said, "Claire, it's Logan. The men who hurt you are dead, you're safe now. I need you to try to focus on me, I need to check out your injuries, and then we need to get out of here. Come on, Claire Bear, I need you to look at me."

She blinked in slow motion and then her gaze cleared and she looked right at him. "Logan," she said on an exhale.

"Right here," he assured her.

Her gaze shifted to the bodies behind him. "Are they d-dead?"

"Yes," he said firmly. "They won't hurt you again." He wanted to ask what they'd done to her, if she had been raped, but he didn't know how to ask. He could see there was a red mark on one of her cheeks, and he had seen the man slam her head into the rock, but he had to know if there were other injuries he needed to be concerned about.

Claire had tilted her head to the side and was studying him now with open curiosity and a bit of confusion.

"What?"

"You called me Claire Bear, why?"

To be honest, Shark hadn't even realized he'd done it, he'd just been trying to calm her down, and the name must have slipped out. Now that she'd drawn his attention to it, he felt self-conscious. Pet names like that implied an intimacy that he and Claire most definitely did not share. "I'm sorry, I didn't realize I said it."

"Don't be sorry, it's just ..."

"Just what?" he prompted when she didn't continue.

"Claire Bear is what my dad used to call me. I hadn't thought about the name in a long time, not until you just said it." She gave him a sad smile. "I remember the first time he called me that. I was four, and we had spent the whole day at a carnival, me, my dad, and my mom. We'd had so much fun, we'd ridden on the Ferris wheel and the carousel, I'd eaten way too much cotton candy and popcorn, then my dad won a teddy bear for me in one of those silly little games, I can't remember which one. Then he got down on one knee and held it out to me, it was pink and fluffy and had a big gold bow around its neck. When he gave it to me, he said, 'Here's the most beautiful bear in the world for my Claire Bear'. After that, he used to call me Claire Bear all the time. That day is one of my favorite memories of my dad. I still have the bear at home, but the name, I hadn't realized I'd missed it until you just said it."

Without warning, Claire moved forward, he caught her as she wrapped her arms around his neck and held her, assuming she wanted comfort, but then she shocked him when she pressed her lips to his and kissed him.

* * *

6:00 A.M.

He tasted so good.

Kissing Logan hadn't been a conscious decision. He'd come running to her rescue, killed two men to protect her, he'd been so nice, then he'd called her Claire Bear, and the name sounded so sweet falling from his lips, and before she even knew what she was doing she'd thrown herself at him.

Although it didn't seem like Logan minded.

He had one arm wrapped around her waist, holding her close against his body, and his tongue was nudging at her lips. She'd never done this before. She'd been scared off men before she'd reached an age where she found them attractive, and so she'd always kept her distance, but somehow she couldn't seem to do that with this man.

Tentatively, Claire parted her lips, and Logan's tongue swept into her mouth. A multitude of things she'd never felt before flew through her body. It was like only having ever seen the world in black and white only to discover that there were in fact thousands of colors, each one adding a unique beauty to the universe.

Pleasure surged through her body, like small ripples at first but growing stronger until they felt like tidal waves.

How had she never known that this existed?

All her life, Claire had maintained distance between herself and everyone else, it was better to be alone and lonely than it was to be hurt and betrayed. But she felt something pulling her toward Logan. She'd never believed in that kind of thing, she'd always thought soul mates and happily ever afters were for fairytales, and books, and movies, not for real life.

And yet, she couldn't deny the almost otherworldly forces pushing her toward this too sexy SEAL.

When Logan suddenly pulled back, Claire couldn't help but moan her disappointment, but when he reached up to brush across her cheek with the pad of his calloused thumb she realized that her cheeks were wet with tears.

"What's wrong?" Logan demanded, something close to panic morphing his usual calmly stoic expression. No guy liked women's tears, and especially not tears from a woman who had just been kissing him.

Embarrassed both by her impulsive kiss and the fact that she had ruined it by crying, even if they weren't tears of pain or regret, she ducked her head. "Sorry," she mumbled, scrambling out of Logan's arms and pressing herself back against the rock.

"I shouldn't have kissed you."

Logan said it so pragmatically like what they'd just shared meant absolutely nothing to him. Of course, why would it? That had been her first real kiss, but he was a SEAL and built like most women's fantasy. He was obviously much more experienced than her, so why would he want to settle?

Fighting back tears, she shuffled a little further away, maybe if she put enough distance between them she wouldn't die of mortification. "R-right," she said, hoping she sounded like she agreed.

Cocking his head, Logan studied her in silence, and she fought the urge to squirm. "I said I shouldn't have done it, not that I didn't like it."

Claire's eyes went wide, and she allowed herself a glimmer of hope. It shouldn't matter what he thought, it shouldn't matter if they would ever share another kiss, it shouldn't matter if there would ever be anything more between them. But it did. It mattered more than it should considering she'd known Logan for a whole fifteen hours or so, all of that time they'd spent fighting to survive.

Was that what this was?

These feelings she thought she had, the attraction she couldn't deny, the pull she couldn't ignore. Were they all just as a result of their situation?

Her brain said yes, but her gut said no.

"The kiss made you cry," Logan said, remorse clear on his face. "You've just been attacked, I shouldn't have taken advantage of you like that. I apologize."

Tentatively she shuffled closer. "I wasn't crying because I felt taken advantage of. I … I *liked* the kiss."

Logan's brows knit together. "You have a funny way of showing it."

His confusion over women and what made them tick had her smiling. "It doesn't make sense, but I … like you," she said shyly, already preparing herself for him to brush her off. When he didn't say anything, she started to babble. "I know, it's silly, we just met, we don't even know each other, but I'm not saying I want to marry you tomorrow, well not that we even know if we'll still be alive tomorrow. I don't even know if you have a wife or a girlfriend, and I don't know where you live when you and your team aren't deployed, or if you even want a girlfriend, not that I'm saying I want to be your girlfriend. I don't know how long I'm going to be here, but I was wondering, well, I was thinking that if you felt the same way, that I don't know, maybe we could hang out together a bit, get to know each other, because …"

"You like me," Logan finished for her. His expression was a mixture of amusement at her rambled monologue and disbelief.

Claire shrugged, she didn't know what else to say. This wasn't her at all, she never *ever* threw herself at men, had never even met one who she'd wanted to, and now she felt like an idiot offering a stranger a soliloquy practically begging him to spend time with her.

Talk about a turnoff.

Yet, Logan didn't look turned off, he looked ... turned on.

"I don't play games, Claire, don't have time for it, nor any interest in it, and I only do things one of two ways, all in or all out. You sure that's what you want?"

The seriousness in his eyes scared her. Not on a physical level, she wasn't afraid of Logan anymore. She didn't believe he was the traitor she had been sent to weed out, to believe he was would mean she would have to discount that he'd saved her life yet again, something he wouldn't do if those men had been sent to find her. Yet still his warning rang in her ears. Was she really ready to commit to something and go all in?

She liked Logan, and she was the one who had kissed him and said she'd like the opportunity to get to know him better with the understanding they would become a couple if they got along and liked each other. But all in was a terrifying possibility. How could she go from never being in a relationship to jumping all into one?

Still, as much as the idea scared her, it also excited her. She'd spent her entire life playing it safe, never putting herself into a position where she might be hurt again, but here, in the middle of Afghanistan, knowing there was a good chance she might not live through this, she felt like she'd been missing out. Maybe the scales had finally tipped, and it was no longer enough just to play it safe, now she wanted to actually live.

"I ... I ... I'd be okay with that," she said, fighting through her nerves. She'd fought so hard to rebuild her life after it had been torn to shreds, surely she could fight just as hard to take this next step.

A small smile curled his lips up, he leaned forward,

grasped her hips, physically lifting her and setting her in his lap, then he covered her lips with his in a soft, gentle kiss. While it might not have been as passionate as the last one, this one had a proprietary feel to it, almost like he was claiming her.

And that didn't twist her insides up like she'd thought it would.

In fact, Claire thought that she could definitely get used to this.

Being held in such strong arms gave her a sense of security that had been lacking from her life since her dad's death. She'd had to learn to take care of herself and look after herself because no one else was going to, but Claire knew without a shadow of a doubt that things wouldn't be like that with Logan. He was a protector, a hero, a man who had chosen to risk his life for what he believed in.

He was a man she could fall in love with.

"We should get back to the cave," Logan announced, standing with her in his arms and carrying her back to their cave. "I'll check out your head, then we'll get your arm back in its sling. You can eat something, drink some water, and I'll deal with the bodies."

She liked how he took control of the situation and seemed to know everything that needed to be done and how to get it done, which was good considering she was so far out of her depth out here. Claire was so grateful that of all the people who could have been on that helicopter with her, it had been Logan Kirk.

* * *

1:21 P.M.

. . .

He tapped his foot as he waited for the man on the other end of the phone to pick up.

He was anxious, but not in a worried way, more an annoyed kind of anxious. Every time he made a call he was risking exposure. He was playing a dangerous game, teetering between two worlds where one wrong move could wind up with him dead in either one of those worlds.

When the phone was finally answered, he didn't bother with pleasantries. "What were you thinking?" he demanded. "You got impatient, I told you I would take care of the Barrett woman once she got to the base, but no, that wasn't good enough for you. You had to go and shoot her helicopter out of the sky."

These idiots could have ruined everything.

Now, if Claire Barrett survived, she was going to know that she was in danger, as would everyone else, which meant if she ever made it back to the base she was no doubt going to have a security detail, making it that much harder to get to her.

Idiots.

They were making an already difficult job so much harder than it had to be. This was why he preferred to work alone. Every time he let someone else in it just ended up in disaster.

Case in point; Raymond.

If the man hadn't grown a conscience at the wrong time then he wouldn't be in the position of having to clean up a mess.

Raymond had been right by his side in the beginning. They'd agreed together to do this, they'd split the money, they'd both get what they wanted, and then suddenly Raymond couldn't go through with it. Which would be one thing if he'd just backed out, but he hadn't. Instead, he'd gone running to the pretty psychologist and spilled his guts before taking his own life.

Raymond was a coward, he'd turned on him, thrown him under the bus, ruined what they had spent months planning, and now it was all falling apart. Unfortunately, he didn't know how much Raymond had told Ms. Barrett, but he knew it was enough that the military was sending her in to help identify someone he could only assume they believed was Raymond's partner.

But what else did they know?

If his friends hadn't been so hasty and shot the helicopter down, then he could have an answer to that question by now.

His plan had been to seek out the psychologist when she arrived on base, get her alone somewhere where he could scare her into leaving. If that hadn't worked, then he would have interrogated her to find out what she knew. Then depending on how helpful she was he would decide her fate.

She was very attractive, with long dark locks, large brown doe eyes, she had a nice slim figure, and while her breasts were a little too small for his liking they were round and perky and suited her frame perfectly. He wouldn't have minded the chance for a little time alone with her, maybe give her the opportunity to keep herself alive by providing certain services that were sorely lacking over here.

Now all of that was ruined.

Thanks to these idiots.

Again, he'd be so much better off if he was handling this himself, but there were certain things he couldn't achieve without their assistance, so for the time being, he was stuck with them.

"We didn't think she would survive."

He rolled his eyes. "Didn't think she would survive, well so much for that plan. And now she's out there somewhere with a SEAL as her guide, and there's a chance she'll make it back here. If she does now she knows she's in danger. That's going to make it so much harder for me to get access to her."

"It is not our fault that Raymond betrayed us."

"Well, it's not my fault either," he snapped. He had been so sure that Raymond was on his side, after all, they both would have gotten what they wanted, and they had talked in great detail about it. While their reasons for choosing this path were vastly different, when it boiled down to it they both wanted the same thing, and this had been the perfect way to get it.

Raymond's betrayal cut deeper than it should. He had truly liked the other man, and there weren't many people he liked. Most annoyed him, making it near impossible to control his emotions and not let what he really felt come bursting out. Then there were those he hated, those who had forever changed the course of his life, those who claimed they cared about others, about freedom, love, and hope. Those who were nothing but liars. Those he wanted to destroy.

Those he *would* destroy.

"Don't interfere again," he muttered into the phone.

Stony silence met him.

He knew what that silence meant. It meant that if they got their hands on Claire Barrett first, they would kill the SEAL, take her, and do their own interrogation. Despite his plans for the beautiful woman, he couldn't help but feel a smidgen of compassion for her. If she found herself in the hands of those men she would pray for a death that wouldn't come. They wouldn't end her life until her body gave out and they could no longer enjoy her, there was no telling how long that would take, but he knew they had women they'd kept captive for years in their possession.

"I mean it," he said, infusing every ounce of his position of power that he had into his tone. "The Barrett woman is mine.

I will deal with her if she makes it here." The group he was associated with weren't the only ones out in the mountains of Afghanistan that were a threat to the psychologist and the SEAL, the only two survivors of the crash.

"We shall see."

Frustration beat a steady drum inside him. He hated being out of control like this, he was used to people following his orders, but the men he was working with weren't afraid to let him know that he needed them every bit as much as they needed him. Their relationship was symbiotic, and there was no way around that. There was no way he could do what he had planned without them, so he had to tread carefully.

"Fine." He sighed dramatically. "But if you get your hands on the woman I want to know about it. I need to know how to mitigate the damages here." Everyone on base knew about the helicopter crash, the higher-ups were in a panic over the woman, needing her to find the traitor they knew was in their midst, while the SEAL's team was out there searching for their missing teammate.

"Fine," the other man snapped back.

Unimpressed with the attitude he was being given, he was ready to end this call. "I'll speak to you later. In the meantime keep me updated." Before there could be any disputing the fact that he was to be kept in the loop at all costs, he hung up, tossing the burner phone onto his desk in disgust.

He'd waited a long time for this, and he wasn't letting anyone ruin it for him.

This was personal for him. He wasn't on some religious quest like the men he had aligned himself with, he wasn't out to prove that his God was the better God, and he didn't want to change the world.

No, he wanted to punish the world.

Well, at least the world that had destroyed him.

Ever since, he had been consumed with the need for revenge, the need to punish, the need to lash out at the world because it was the only way the pain inside him wouldn't consume him.

Raymond might have been in this for the money, which was probably why he had backed out at the last moment and tried to stop the inevitable from happening, but he was in this to find the only measure of peace he was ever going to find.

Because this was so important to him, he wasn't letting anyone ruin it. It would happen, no one was going to stop it. Not Raymond, not a pretty psychologist trying to fulfill a dead patient's final wish that she stop a tragedy from occurring, and certainly not a Navy SEAL who might be the only thing standing between the one person who could destroy him and her death.

* * *

5:44 P.M.

It was about time to call it a day.

Shark watched as Claire weaved on her feet again, her eyes had a glassy look to them, and he knew she was moving only because of fear of what would happen if they didn't keep going.

Knowing she was hurting, he had made her take regular breaks. She'd complained about it at first, insisting that she was fine and didn't need to take a break, but those insistences dwindled as the hours ticked by. Over the last hour or so she'd been barely able to put one foot in front of the other and had lost her balance several times, falling to her knees more than once.

Each time she did, Shark knew that it jostled her injured shoulder, but she didn't cry out in pain or rant and rave about their situation, she would just wince, clutch at her arm, and then accept his help and get back on her feet and keep walking. Her inner strength and determination were even more appealing than those lips he couldn't stop remembering the feel of.

Claire had startled him when she'd thrown her arms around him and kissed him, then terrified him when he'd felt her tears dripping onto his skin. But it was her declaration that she was interested in him that had knocked the air from his lungs.

This beautiful, smart, strong woman was interested in him.

His natural inclination to disbelieve anything positive urged him to deny it, to come up with a reason why she'd said what she said. And yet, all he'd seen in her eyes when she was babbling was a mixture of sincerity and apprehension.

She was nervous about telling him how she felt, but she'd done it anyway, and then the next thing he'd known he was vowing that he was all in.

All in with what?

They'd known each other a little more than a day and shared one kiss—albeit an amazing one. Why was he claiming that he was all in to her?

Claire staggered, bumping into him then sagging to the ground at his feet. That was it, she was done in. They were back up in the mountains again, there should be another cave nearby where they could make camp for the night, and tomorrow—barring anything unforeseen—he hoped to make it to the spot where he prayed his team would come looking for him. The first mission they'd gone on after his teammate Spider had first reunited with his now-wife Abigail, they had spent days hiding out in a small ravine when they'd been outnumbered and outgunned by a terrorist cell. He hoped that knowing the approximate vicinity the helo had gone down, his team would expect him to head there as the caves went underground, and if you weren't aware of them, you would pass over it and never even know of its existence. It was the perfect place to hide out, especially with an injured and untrained woman relying on him to get her home.

"Here, I got you," he said as he bent and scooped Claire up into his arms. She made a small sound of protest before sinking down against him, her eyes fluttering closed as her head came to rest against his shoulder.

As he stared down at her, his heart hitched in his chest. The longer he spent with this woman, the more she embedded herself inside him. She was under his skin for sure, quickly burrowing deeper, and he wasn't sure that he wanted to try to cut her out. Shark had a feeling that if he did, he would quickly start hemorrhaging.

With the sun setting and the dark crawling in, he started walking again, finding them a small cave to hide out in. It was smaller than the one they'd slept in the night before, but it offered him the same ability to see danger coming before it saw them. A lot of good that did though if Claire went traipsing off on her own again, he'd have to talk to her about that because the last thing he wanted was to ever see her in danger again.

Setting Claire down, Shark debated making a fire but decided it wasn't too cold and the risk of being seen would outweigh any possible benefits. Water, food, then sleep, that was what Claire needed, him too, although he could certainly go a lot longer before his body truly needed to rest.

"I'm just going to check your head," he told her as he knelt before her, gently running his fingers through her hair. Thankfully the skin on the back of her head hadn't been split when the man attacking her had slammed her head into the rock, but she had a large lump back there. He was concerned about the effects of two head injuries within twenty-four hours, but she had been alert all day, so he assumed she was all right.

Claire didn't say anything, but she blinked open tired eyes to watch him, or more accurately stare at his lips, but he ignored the desire thrumming through his body. Claire depended on him, and he couldn't let his libido distract him. If she was serious about being interested in him there was plenty of time to discuss it when he got her out of here.

He handed her a bottle of water and a pizza MRE, but after watching her drink no more than a single mouthful of water and nibble at her pizza he realized something was wrong. Was she feeling sick? Hurting worse than she was letting on? Or was she thinking about them? Having second thoughts maybe? Now that he thought about it other than his comment that he only did things all in or all out, he hadn't actually answered her when she'd asked if he was involved with someone, nor had he outright said that he was interested in her too.

"Logan?" It was dark in here despite the small light from one of the glow sticks he'd activated, but there was enough light for him to see the anxiety written into every line of her face.

"Yes?"

"I'm scared."

"I know you are, but I'll get you out of here." Shark didn't make vows. There was no possible way anyone could make a promise about the future because human beings had zero control over it. Yet at the same time, he knew without a shadow of a doubt that there wasn't anything he wouldn't do to make sure Claire lived.

She edged closer toward him until she was right against

his side. "I know you will, but that's not the only thing I'm scared about."

Remembering the fear he'd seen on her face on the helicopter, he asked, "You weren't surprised we got shot down."

"I was, and yet … you're right, I wasn't."

"What are you doing over here?"

"I'm not supposed to discuss it with anyone." Although she said the words, he sensed she intended to tell him exactly what was scaring her, so he sat quietly and waited. "You know I'm a psychologist and that I work exclusively with the military, well, about a month ago one of my patients committed suicide."

She'd told him about her father and how he had also taken his own life so he knew how hard that must have been for her. Tentatively, he reached out an arm and wrapped it around her shoulders, he wasn't used to having to offer comfort and support like this, but once he'd taken that small step he found he was pleased when she immediately snuggled closer and reached out to curl her small fingers around his.

"I'm sorry, that must have been hard for you."

Her head nodded against his shoulder where she'd rested it. "He killed himself in the parking lot right after he left my room, but before he did he told me something. Something that someone would be willing to kill me over."

Something akin to panic sliced through him at the thought of someone wanting Claire dead. "What did he tell you?"

"That he was working with a terrorist cell called The Atash—it means the fire—in Afghanistan. That they were planning on blowing up several sites on American soil. He said that they'd paid him a lot of money to give them information to make it happen."

"He was a traitor," he seethed.

"Yes. Although guilt ate away at him to the point where he couldn't live with what he had done. It's why he ended his life. But he wasn't working alone, Logan, he had a partner, but he wouldn't give me the man's name. Raymond was here before he came home. That's why I was sent here, to try to find the man he was working with, the second traitor."

"You're the only one Raymond told."

"Yes."

"The only one who might be able to identify the traitor."

"Yes."

"That's knowledge this man and the terrorist cell would be worth killing over."

"Y-yes."

"If they get their hands on you they'll torture you for information before they kill you."

"Yes." A shudder rippled through her, and she pressed closer against his side.

An echoing shudder rippled through him. He couldn't stomach the idea of sweet Claire being tortured and murdered. This situation had suddenly got a whole lot more dangerous because now, even if he did get Claire to the base, she wouldn't be safe. The only thing that would protect her was identifying the traitor.

With a growl of frustration that Claire had been thrown into such a situation, he grabbed her arms and hauled her over and into his lap, then crashed his mouth against hers and kissed her with a hunger and desperate need he'd never felt before.

* * *

6:03 P.M.

. . .

Claire moaned in delight and sunk down against Logan, the kiss making her feel weightless.

It wasn't a gentle kiss, it was hot and hungry and made her feel like she was being devoured. It also made her wonder what his mouth would feel like touching other parts of her body. Since she was completely inexperienced she had no idea what she was doing, but Logan didn't seem to care, he took control of the kiss just like he took control of everything else.

One of his hands cradled the back of her head, his fingers tangled in her hair, his other hand had been on her hip, but he moved it across to her stomach, his bare fingers tracing her skin. Immediately her body felt like it had been set on fire. These feelings were so new to her, so foreign, that she couldn't help tensing.

Of course Logan noticed and immediately removed his hand but that wasn't what she wanted.

She wanted this.

Wanted him.

She trusted him, felt comfortable around him in a way she never had with a man. What had happened to her when she was young had changed everything about her including how she viewed herself. Even her male friends weren't allowed to touch her in a friendly hug, or pat on the shoulder, or anything else. But when Logan touched her, she didn't get that panicky feeling she was accustomed to, she just felt wonderful.

As well as moving his hands back to rest on her hips—although lightly this time, his fingers no longer digging into her, holding her like he never wanted to let her go—he also lightened the kiss until his lips were barely touching hers. Realizing that he thought she wasn't comfortable with what he'd done, Claire knew that if she didn't reassure him quickly he would pull away from her, emotionally as well as physically, and she would lose all the progress they'd made today.

That wasn't what she wanted.

"Logan, you misunderstood," she told him. Her hands on his shoulders gently kneaded because she wasn't ready to let go of him yet. She found she liked touching him every bit as much as she enjoyed him touching her.

Dark eyes just stared back at her. He'd blanked his expression so she couldn't tell what he was thinking. At least he'd tried to, but Claire found that even when he tried to use his empty shark face on her, she could still tell what was going on inside his head. It was weird, but weird in a good way.

"You thought I was tensing because I didn't like what you were doing, but it was the opposite. I'm glad you kissed me, and I liked what you were doing, it's just that I'm ... not very experienced." No way was she admitting to him that she was basically a virgin because she knew without being told that that would put an end to any making-out. Despite him trying to appear as though he didn't have feelings, Claire knew that Logan was smart and intuitive and thoughtful, and since they'd just met if he knew just how little experience she had he wouldn't want to touch her again until they knew each other much better. But Claire wasn't sure she could wait that long.

The seconds seemed to tick by with excruciating slowness, and with each one that passed, Claire felt herself deflate.

It had been stupid to kiss this strong, sexy SEAL.

Even stupider to tell him that she was interested in him.

And stupider still to actually admit that she wasn't experienced with men.

This was exactly why she kept to herself. It was so much better to be lonely than it was to hurt, and while this man shouldn't hold the power to hurt her, it turned out that he did.

Because she was hurt by his rejection.

It was what she had expected, what man like Logan would be interested in a woman like her? She had just turned thirty last month, and she had never had a boyfriend, not even in high school or college. She'd been perfectly happy with that until Logan had to come along with his muscles, smoldering eyes, and thick dark hair, he was the very epitome of tall, dark, and handsome and he had thrown her world off its axis.

As much as she would like to blame it on the helicopter crash, their trek through dangerous enemy territory, and the stress she'd been under lately, Claire didn't think that she could.

She'd wanted him.

Really wanted him, and she'd thought that maybe he might want her too.

Embarrassed, Claire tried to slide off Logan's lap, but he tightened his hold on her, refusing to let her go. If it was anyone but Logan she would think he was playing some kind of sick game to add to her mortification, but she knew that wasn't him, he wouldn't do something like that.

One of his large hands covered the side of her head, and he tucked it under his chin before wrapping his arms around her and holding her snuggly against him.

"Someone hurt you," he said, not a question but a statement.

She could deny it, but she wasn't sure he'd buy that. "Yes."

"Not your father. The light in your eyes when you talked about him says you loved and adored him and miss him now he's gone."

"My dad was the perfect father," she said, pressing her cheek more firmly against the hard planes of his chest. "He was gone a lot, but when he was home he was *home*, you know? He was there one hundred percent. He'd drive me to school, read me bedtime stories and tuck me in, go to my ballet recitals and soccer games, help me with my homework, and he'd play dress-ups and princesses and fairies with me."

"You were lucky to have him." The tone of Logan's voice conveyed a sense of longing, and she remembered he'd told her his own father had been in prison.

"I was."

"I'm sorry you lost him."

"Me too," Claire whispered. When she'd lost her father, she hadn't just lost him but the family, the home, the life she had been used to. Her whole world had been upended when her dad took his own life, and she wasn't sure it had righted in the twenty-four years that had followed.

"You were young when you were hurt."

Despite the connection she felt to Logan and the longing he stirred up inside her, she wasn't ready to tell him everything. The only time she had ever talked to someone about what had happened to her it hadn't gone at all the way she had expected. In fact the opposite. It had been such a horrifically scarring experience that it had ended up hurting her worse than what he'd done to her.

"Most women and children are assaulted by someone they know," Logan continued. He wasn't pushing her, yet she sensed he wanted to know. If she knew him it was out of a desire to know how to fix the problem and protect her from further pain, but this wasn't something that could be fixed. It had happened, and the wounds inflicted on her were too deep to ever completely heal.

A heavy weight of exhaustion covered her, not just physical exhaustion from the grueling hike today, but a mental one of spending two decades carrying around a burden with no one to help. She'd never had anyone in her life that she could trust to hold her up while she shouldered those burdens, even if just for a little while. She'd always had to depend on herself, but now, here, curled up on Logan's lap, his arms steady and strong around her, she felt the need to rest. Really and truly rest, she might not be ready for him to know everything, but he knew enough for now.

Lips touched her forehead, hovered there for a moment before she felt a warm puff of air against her skin. "Close your eyes, Claire, and go to sleep, we have another long day ahead of us tomorrow, but tonight you can rest and know you're safe. I won't let anyone hurt you."

That sounded like a promise that hung in the air between them. A promise that went beyond tonight, beyond this ordeal they found themselves in, and the thought of this big, tough man wanting to be there for her brought more tears to her eyes.

She snuggled closer, needing to feel more of him, and she curled her fingers into his shirt, holding onto him like he was the only solid thing in her world, because in a way he was. He was the first solid thing she'd had in so long she almost didn't know what to do with it.

"Logan?"

"Yeah?"

"Thank you." Closing her eyes and letting her entire body go lax, Claire allowed the calm presence of the man who held her so gently to soothe away some of her pain and drifted off into a deep sleep.

CHAPTER 3

September 8th

11:26 A.M.

"What?" Shark asked as he looked over to see Claire staring at him.

"Nothing," she said with a smile and a shrug, "you're just kinda nice to look at."

Since he didn't know what to say to that, he just grunted and rifled through his pack to find protein bars for both of them. They were going on forty-eight hours now since the crash, and he was basically out of food. There was one final protein bar left which they would have to share, and he had enough MREs for them to have dinner tonight, but that was it.

He hated not knowing what was going on, what his team knew about what had happened, what had been organized to find him and Claire. Had the helicopter wreckage been found? Did they know he and Claire were out here somewhere? Did they know which direction they'd headed? Had they mounted a rescue?

While he wouldn't allow his concerns to show, he found that the idea of adding to Claire's worries was so unappealing that he had forgone what would be his usual procedure which was to not sugarcoat anything and give the facts as they were, he *was* concerned about their situation. He'd been able to find a well yesterday so they'd restocked their water supply, but the lack of food was going to become a problem quickly. Thankfully he knew from experience that the cave he was heading for had a water source nearby, but he was loathed to leave Claire alone and unprotected to go and try to find them something to eat.

She was already getting weaker. Her injuries from the crash and being assaulted by those men yesterday morning were taking a toll, as was the lack of food. She hadn't slept well last night either, pain and fear kept startling her out of sleep. He knew this for a fact because he had held her on his lap for a lot longer than he should have.

After she'd tensed while they were making out, he'd been sure he'd ruined things by pushing too hard too fast, but then she'd admitted she wasn't experienced. That hadn't come as much of a surprise, he'd gathered as much from their first kiss, but the realization that her lack of experience came from trauma had hit him hard.

He'd been filled with a deep, vicious protective rage he'd never experienced before.

Shark may have spent most of his life fighting for the underdog, protecting those who couldn't defend themselves, but he'd never felt anything like the rage that speared him when Claire all but admitted that she had been assaulted by someone she knew when she was young.

Even now, thinking about it, his fingers curled into the bar, squeezing it as rage pulsed a steady beat inside him.

"You know," Claire said, drawing his attention back to her before he said or did something that would scare her off. For some reason, this woman didn't seem fazed by his aloof attitude, but he was afraid one slip up, and she'd see the dark ball of anger inside him and go running for the hills. "It's customary when someone gives you a compliment that you return the favor."

She was smiling teasingly at him, but he caught the undercurrent of doubt in her eyes. This was all new to her, and she wasn't confident in her beauty, inside and out, and clearly had no idea just how attractive she was.

Instead of answering her with words, which he had long since learned achieved absolutely nothing, Shark grabbed her, dragged her to her feet, and crushed his mouth to hers, kissing her thoroughly so there could be zero doubt about how she made him feel.

"So, I guess I can assume going forward to expect compliments to come in the form of kisses," Claire said, teasing smile still in place but the doubt wiped away.

Looking at her standing there, lips full and plump from just being kissed, hair tousled from his fingers just running through it, he knew that once they got to know each other it wouldn't be kisses he'd be giving her. He'd be throwing her down on the nearest piece of furniture, ripping off her clothes, and ravishing every inch of her body.

Apparently, what he was thinking was written all over his face because heat flared in her eyes and the tip of her tongue peeked out to run across her bottom lip.

Shark groaned and reached out to brush his thumb across said lip. "Don't."

"Oh?"

"Clinging to control here, Claire Bear." This was the most

inappropriate time and place to be thinking about sex, yet it was pretty hard not to think about it when he looked at Claire. But they weren't safe out here, he had vowed to get her home safely, and besides both of those things he was pretty sure that Claire was a virgin. Therefore their first time had to be special and perfect, not things he was used to thinking about when it came to women, and he had no idea how to do it, but he would figure it out. For Claire.

"I really make you want to ...?" The self-doubt was back in her eyes, and he hated to see such a strong, beautiful woman unsure of herself.

Not wanting to scare her but also needing her to know the truth, he reached out to circle her tiny wrist with his hand and guided her to his crotch. He brushed her fingertips against his hard length and then looked her straight in the eye. "Still got doubts?"

Her cheeks had gone bright red, but she shook her head and chewed on her bottom lip. When he groaned, she quickly released it and giggled. "Okay, you made your point."

"Did I?" he asked, not sure that he had. If she had been abused as a kid by someone she knew, she would have major trust issues. Helping her deal with that wasn't something he was equipped to do, his own trust issues could fill the ocean.

Claire opened her mouth to answer but whatever she'd been about to say was swallowed up by the sound of gunfire.

Damn.

He'd allowed himself to get distracted, allowed his attraction for Claire to get in the way of doing his job, a mistake that might get them both killed.

They were in a pretty good position. He'd made sure that he didn't stop until they had somewhere that provided cover and a good view of their surroundings. Although a lot of good that did if he wasn't focused on those surroundings.

Yanking on Claire's wrist, which he still held, Shark

threw her sideways. As they fell, he did his best to roll so his body took the brunt of the fall, but still he heard her pained breath as her injured shoulder was jostled.

Shoving her so that her body was wedged between his and the large rock that they'd been standing beside, he hoped it should be enough to protect her from the flying bullets, at least he prayed it was.

For now, it didn't look like they were surrounded, he could see six men approaching from directly in front of them, making things much easier for him.

Lifting his weapon, he grunted as pain shot through his side, the opposite side to where he'd been injured in the crash. One of the bullets must have got him. Better him than Claire, at least so long as the wound wasn't bad enough to incapacitate him.

Aiming at the closest of the terrorists, he picked them off one by one, satisfied to see each body drop, eliminating the threats against Claire.

When the last one fell, he started scanning the surrounding mountains for any caves where he could stash Claire. The sound of gunfire would have been enough to alert anyone in the vicinity, and if these men were part of the terrorist cell hunting Claire, then there could be others nearby.

He would not allow Claire to fall into their hands.

What would happen to her if she did was enough to have him break out into a cold sweat. He had seen what men like these were capable of doing, and being a woman Claire would be subjected to pain and humiliation unlike anything she could imagine, even in her darkest nightmares.

That would never happen to her on his watch.

He needed to take out any other men searching the area, then once he got her to the base, he would help her find the traitor, and once they did he would get the intel he needed to dismantle The Atash and make sure they never got to carry out their plans to bomb American targets, and could never again be a threat to Claire. Shark knew his team would help him, but this was personal for him, Claire was personal to him, and he took care of what was his.

* * *

11:58 A.M.

The shooting had stopped, but now things were quiet.

Too quiet.

That kind of eerie silence that said things were only going to get worse.

The only sounds Claire could hear were of her ragged breath and the harsh gasp of Logan's breathing.

Something wet and warm was soaking into her clothing, but she didn't feel any pain. Well, that wasn't entirely true, her injured shoulder burned from Logan throwing her to the ground, and her bruised ribs had also protested the sudden movement, but other than that she felt okay, whole.

The wet feeling was against her legs. She'd curled her knees up to her chest when Logan had shoved her against the rock, curling his body protectively around hers to try to protect her from getting shot.

The blood was his.

Logan had been shot.

Terror clawed inside her. How badly was he hurt? Was he going to bleed out in front of her? Had she lost him just as she'd found him?

Claire knew first aid, but there was a difference between knowing in theory what to do and having to use that same knowledge to try to save someone's life. Even if she could stop the bleeding they were still lost out here, alone, so far no one had found them, and she had no idea where this cave Logan had been heading for was or how far from it they were.

Her breathing accelerated as fear and shock took over.

This was impossible.

They were going to die out here.

And if The Atash found her first, her death wasn't going to be a pretty one.

They didn't care about Logan. His body would be left out here, his team might never find it, and there would be no closure for them or for Logan's brother. They would be left to wonder what had become of him, and the thought made her eyes well with tears. As awful as her father's death had been at least she'd known what happened, she hadn't been left wondering if he was dead or alive and being held captive, suffering unimaginable torture.

"Claire, you're bleeding."

The accusatory voice and the hands that dragged her to her feet tore her out of her shock-induced terror, and she wildly shook her head.

"You are, there's blood all over you," Logan growled. He looked so angry, so intimidating and fierce, but instead of wanting to run from him what she wanted to do was throw herself into his arms and cling to him, making him promise to never leave her.

But she couldn't do that.

Because Logan was hurt.

"It's your blood," she said. Her voice was hoarse with fear, but not for herself, for Logan. She shoved away his hands and pushed the sling out of her way, then ran her hands over his body. He hissed in a breath when she touched his side, and she knew she'd found the source of the bleeding.

"We need to get you somewhere safe, could be more men

coming," Logan said, but his voice sounded off, and he swayed on his feet.

"No, we need to check your wound and stop the bleeding," she countered.

"I'm fine."

"You're not."

"I am." He tried to growl that at her, but he sounded more like a kitten than a lion right now.

Placing her hands on his shoulders, she pushed and was surprised and afraid when she was able to get him down on his backside. He was hurt worse than he wanted her to know and that only made her fear grow.

She ripped open Logan's pack—he made no move to stop her, just sunk down to rest heavily against the same rock he'd used to save her life—and rifled through it, searching for the first aid kit she knew he had in there. When she found it, she looked through it, finding some QuickClot which she tore open, shoved up his blood-drenched shirt, and used to bandage his wound.

There was so much blood, it was clear Logan had lost enough to leave him impaired, which meant now it was on her to somehow keep them both safe, only she was woefully unprepared for the job.

Stop it, she ordered herself.

She could do this.

She had to, Logan had taken that bullet saving her, she owed it to him to do whatever was necessary to get them both somewhere safe. Since she had no idea where the cave he'd been heading for was, she was just going to have to find the nearest shelter she could, then she'd position herself at the entrance and shoot anyone who came toward them.

It wasn't much of a plan, nor did it solve the problem of them being lost and alone out here, but it was the best she had, and it gave her something to focus on.

Repacking Logan's pack, she put it on her back then took one of the assault rifles and slung it over her shoulders, then she hooked an arm around Logan's waist and tried to pull him to his feet. Of course that was easier said than done when he outweighed her by a hundred pounds.

"Logan, please," she begged. She didn't like this Logan, so quiet, his eyes closed, skin way too pale, she wanted her big, strong, tough protector back. Knowing that his protector side was what she needed to appeal to right now, Logan cared way more about her life than he did his own, she tried a different track. "Logan, please, I need you to get up and help me move you. I'm not safe here, I need you to help me get somewhere where we can be safe."

That seemed to do the trick because he started to move, and somehow between the two of them, they were able to get him on his feet. Her injured shoulder protested with a vicious stab of pain when she took a large percentage of his weight, but she ignored it, Logan needed her, and she wasn't going to let him down.

Her body had already been teetering on the edge of exhaustion. Her sleep last night had been plagued with nightmares even with Logan cradling her in his arms, and two solid days of doing nothing but walking had depleted her reserves of energy. But Claire was determined not to give up, not to fail the man who had become very important to her, and somehow she found strength she hadn't known she had to keep walking.

She had no idea how far they'd gone or how much distance they'd covered, when she saw two men appear before her.

Claire didn't think, she just reacted.

Letting Logan slide to the ground she swung the weapon in their direction and fired off a volley of shots, all of which appeared to miss the two men.

"Ma'am, United States Navy, put the weapon down," one of them ordered.

Yeah, she wasn't going to do that.

Knowing they were from the USA didn't reassure her in the slightest, for all she knew the traitor had sent them here after her with orders to kill her or capture and interrogate her, she wasn't going down without a fight, especially not when she had Logan to protect.

"S'okay, Claire, my team," Logan murmured behind her.

His team?

Logan said he trusted them, but she didn't know them, she knew Logan though, and he seemed to have a good ability to read people. If he said they could be trusted, then they probably could, but still, she didn't seem able to move her arms.

The two men approached cautiously, and then suddenly she was grabbed from behind. A strong arm circled her waist, while a hand grabbed the weapon and shoved it up so it was pointing uselessly at the sky. The arm holding her was firm, meant to restrain and incapacitate her, but at the same time, she could tell whoever had grabbed her was being careful not to hurt her.

"It's okay, ma'am, we are Shark's team, we're not going to hurt you."

Beside her Logan growled, leveling a look that could kill at whoever was holding her. "Let her go."

Immediately she was released, and when she turned to see who had grabbed her, she saw a man with bright blue eyes looking at Logan with surprise. The two men who had been in front of her had reached them, and there were two other men she hadn't even noticed who quickly joined their little group.

"That's Spider," Logan said, nodding at the man who had grabbed her. "Fox and Night," he said, indicating to the two men who she had almost shot. "And Chaos and King. This is Claire Barrett."

"Nice to meet you, Ms. Barrett," Spider said while Night dropped down beside Logan.

"Seen you look better, man," Night said.

Logan just grunted in response, he seemed happy to see his team, but Claire found herself shaking in fear. She should be happy, they'd been found, Logan's team would get them out of here, but these men terrified her. They were so big, so intimidating, and if they had orders to take her they could and there would be nothing she could do to stop it from happening.

She'd worked with special forces men before but that was different. Then she'd been in her cozy little office, sitting in one of the comfortable leather armchairs that faced the electric fireplace. She'd been confident and in control but out here, surrounded by these men, she felt anything but.

Spider turned his attention to her, taking the weapon from her, sliding the backpack off her shoulders, and then sitting her down. He crouched in front of her, running his hands over her body to check for injuries, and she wondered why he didn't just ask her where she was hurt.

It wasn't until he wrapped something warm around her that she realized it was because she was shaking violently, her teeth chattering loudly. Seemed like her body had chosen now to shut down and send her into shock.

"Exfil location is two klicks from here. Can you make it?" Fox was asking Logan, who nodded.

No one asked her if she could make it. Spider's assessing blue eyes gave her a onceover, apparently decided she was more of a liability walking on her own than if she was carried because he picked her up and draped her over his shoulders.

His shoulder dug painfully into her bruised ribs, her own

shoulder throbbed, her head ached, she was shaking, and tired, and cold, and she wanted Logan more than she wanted anything else. But Logan was propped up against Night, and then they were all moving.

They reached the helicopter, where she was set in a seat on the far end of the craft from where Logan was placed on a gurney and buckled in. No one paid her much attention, Logan's team was preoccupied with him, and sitting here alone, unable to reach out to Logan, she felt a sense of loss and loneliness second only to what she'd felt when her father committed suicide.

* * *

4:32 P.M.

To say Shark was in a bad mood would be the understatement of the century.

They'd arrived on base over two hours ago, he'd been whisked straight to the hospital where the wound in his side had been stitched, and he'd been given a transfusion, antibiotics, and painkillers. He'd been lucky the bullet hadn't hit anything important and hadn't needed surgery to close the wound. He'd also been lucky that the wound on his other side from the crash hadn't become infected.

Now he was sitting here, in his hospital bed, alone, waiting to be given his discharge papers, cranky but mostly pain-free, wondering where Claire was and why she hadn't come to see him. He didn't think she'd been shot because somehow she'd managed to get the gunshot wound treated, then get him on his feet and moving, before his team had arrived and found him. Was she hurt more badly than he had realized?

It was really the only explanation he could think of why she wouldn't have come to see him.

She'd been amazing out there, held her own despite her fears, and the fact that she had actually shot at his team when she hadn't realized they were there to help her and not hurt her had him uncharacteristically grinning. She was something else, and it still hadn't quite sunk in that she was actually interested in getting to know him.

Maybe that was because at the back of his mind he had been preparing himself for the possibility that they didn't make it back. But now they were here, they were both alive and mostly in one piece, and the need to see her was growing with each passing second.

Shark was just about to disconnect his IV and go searching for Claire when the door to his room opened, and three men walked in. One was the Colonel, the other two were dressed in suits and were no doubt associated with one of the alphabet agencies—CIA if he had to guess.

Immediately he knew something was off.

"Chief Petty Officer Kirk," Colonel Gaulding greeted him with a nod of the head.

One of the men lounged disinterestedly by the door, the other stood to the side of the bed and waited to get down to business. Well Shark was on board with that, he wanted to know what these men were doing here, and then he wanted to get out of here and go find Claire, reassure himself that she was all right.

Other than a nod in Gaulding's direction, Shark simply sat there and waited for them to say whatever it was they were here to say. As much as he wanted to know he wasn't going to be the one to crack and speak first.

"This is Michael Sims, he's with the CIA," Gaulding said, gesturing to the blond suit, "and Jeffrey Tanaka, who is with NSA," he said, gesturing to the brunette by the door.

"I understand you didn't arrive with the rest of your team because you were attending your mother's funeral," Sims said. Apparently he liked to just jump on into things.

"Yes," Shark replied, wondering where this was heading. His team had gone straight to debriefing once they'd arrived, and he'd known that both he and Claire would also be debriefed, he just hadn't expected it to be done by the Colonel and a CIA spook here in his hospital room.

"Sorry for your loss," Sims said, sounding anything but. "Your mother had been ill for quite some time?"

"Yes." If they knew that, then that meant they'd actually investigated him before coming to speak with him. And just like that the pieces fell into place.

They had made the same assumptions he and Claire had that the helicopter being shot down was no accident and that she was the target.

They suspected him as the traitor Claire had been sent here to find.

They'd already started looking for a motive.

Hadn't Claire told them that he'd saved her from the two men who'd been going to assault and then no doubt abduct her? Hadn't she told them that he'd taken a bullet for her when they'd been attacked just before his team arrived? Hadn't she told them that after having spent two days with him as they fought for their lives that she knew he couldn't be the man she'd been sent to find?

No.

Of course she hadn't.

Because obviously, she still thought there was a chance that he was the traitor. What he'd thought was interest and attraction on her part had been a calculated ploy to make sure he had a reason to get her safely here. She wasn't military, she had no training to fall back on to help her survive, she'd needed him, and she'd done whatever it took to make sure he had a vested interest in keeping her alive.

He could have told her it wouldn't have mattered. No matter who she was or what she had done he would have done everything in his power to make sure she survived. It was simply who he was.

Anger at Claire battled with fury with himself for falling for the oldest trick in the book. Men—even him apparently—often thought more with the little head than they did with the big one, and Claire had used that to her advantage.

Forcing himself to do what he had always done, Shark ruthlessly shoved the emotions down, burying them under an ocean of well-practiced calm. So Claire had played him, big deal, so he'd actually been interested in her, oh well, lesson learned. Better to keep things strictly physical when it came to women. Claire had been the first to crack through his shell, make him want more, and she would also be the last.

"A long illness, lots of medical bills, that can be rough," Sims continued.

"Not really." Shark shrugged indifferently. "My mother had good insurance, and I invest most of what I earn. Between the insurance and my brother and I splitting costs, we were able to cover everything." If they thought he had turned on his country for cash they were idiots, money was the last thing in the world he cared about.

Sims nodded as though he was already aware there was no medical debt, but clearly continued with his next theory. "Your father died in prison when you were a kid? What was he in for?"

"Yes he did. Domestic violence and assault charges."

"I see." Sims nodded thoughtfully. "Did you know Claire Barrett before you both got on that helicopter?"

"Never met her or heard of her before."

"Ah." The man nodded again in what was obviously a habit. "And no one had approached you and spoken with you about her. Perhaps mentioned that she was a problem that needed eliminating?"

"If they had, do you think I would have risked getting on that helicopter knowing I might not get off it?" he asked through clenched teeth. This was ridiculous. He had an exemplary record, had dedicated over a decade to serving his country, and now he was being accused of being a traitor.

"No, no, of course not." Sims smiled agreeably. "We don't really think you had anything to do with the crash, but of course we must dot all our i's and cross all our t's, after all, Ms. Barrett is here on a matter of national security."

From the look on Sims' face it was clear he wanted to know if Shark knew just why it was Claire had been sent over here, and he was happy to oblige, too bad if it got Claire in hot water for telling him, she should have thought of that before she used him. She must have said something to Gaulding after they were brought here that implicated him in the plot to bomb American targets and kill her to make sure it happened.

"Ms. Barrett mentioned being here to look for a traitor that a former patient of hers informed her about," he said. "I can assure you that man is not me." Shark let every ounce of darkness that lived inside him, every bit of the cold, empty lack of emotion that he'd always been accused of housing shine through his eyes as he held the CIA agent's gaze unwaveringly.

The man actually shivered under the stare, and Shark felt a surge of satisfaction. This was what he was, who he was, he didn't do relationships, and he certainly didn't do falling for a woman that he'd known all of two days. What he'd thought was a connection with Claire was obviously nothing more than the situation they had been thrown into. She had doubts about him, wondered if he was a traitor to his country, and he had to wonder if everything she'd told him was a lie.

Regardless, it didn't matter, Claire didn't matter.

"We had to ask these questions, Chief Petty Officer. I hope you understand that given the seriousness of this situation, we have to cover every base, however unlikely. But what you did, getting Ms. Barrett back here safely, I understand the Navy will be giving you a commendation medal. Rest, recover, and I hope you'll feel at home during your stay here despite the rocky start." With that, Gaulding turned and left the room, Sims following along behind, as did Tanaka—who had done nothing but lean against the wall with his arms crossed over his chest—leaving Shark alone with his feelings.

Or lack thereof.

Because he didn't do feelings, and a certain sexy psychologist wasn't going to change that no matter how beautiful she was.

* * *

10:52 P.M.

Claire was exhausted.

It had been a grueling several hours. She'd barely finished being treated when Colonel Gaulding, CIA agent Sims, and NSA agent Tanaka had descended on her. Then came the questions, the millions of questions, going over again everything Raymond had told her, everything she knew about the traitor, everything she knew about the plots to plant bombs across the US. After that, they moved on to her and her life over the few weeks between Raymond's death and getting on that helicopter. Had anyone harassed her? Followed her? Had she received any threatening letters, emails, phone calls? Had anyone gone through her house or her office? Had she had contact with any military personnel who had taken an inordinate amount of interest in her?

She'd wanted to scream at them yes to that question and that it was the three of them peppering her with questions until her head spun and pounded so badly that she'd felt like she might pass out.

"Is that enough for tonight?" she asked tiredly, realizing that if she didn't assert herself then the others weren't going to take the hint and leave so she could rest.

"Of course, we can meet again in the morning," Gaulding said, finally pushing his chair away from her hospital bed.

"You staying the night here, Ms. Barrett?" Sims asked.

"No, I want to go to my room where I can get some real rest," she said. If she stayed in the hospital the lights and sounds would keep her awake, and what she needed most was a good night's sleep.

"I'll have someone come by to show you to your quarters," Gaulding said, and she gave him a grateful smile.

The three men said their goodnights, well two of them did, Tanaka just stood there and watched like he had during the entire interview, and then finally she was alone. A glance at the clock on the wall showed it was almost eleven, she hadn't realized just how much time had passed. Now that she wasn't being peppered with questions, she could focus on what she really wanted to think about.

Logan.

It had been hard to keep him out of her thoughts while she'd been answering questions. Was he okay? She hadn't seen him since they'd both been whisked off to separate rooms to be examined and she hadn't had a chance to ask about him.

He must be worse off than she'd thought because he

hadn't come by to check on her. Worry was bubbling inside her when a nurse entered her room, and Claire immediately pounced on the woman. "Would you please organize my discharge papers? And there was a man I was brought in with, his name is Logan Kirk. I was wondering if I could get an update on him."

"Are you family?" the woman asked.

"No, it's just we were out there together, he's the reason I'm still alive, and I just wanted to make sure he was okay," Claire explained.

The woman gave her a sympathetic smile. "I'll see what I can do."

"Thank you so much. Umm, I'll also need something to wear," she said, indicating the hospital gown. She could hardly leave dressed like this, but all her clothes were in her suitcase back at the helicopter crash site.

"I'll bring you some scrubs," the nurse promised.

Once she was alone, for the first time since Logan had saved her from those two men the morning after the crash, the reality of what had happened sunk in. There was no sexy SEAL to distract her, no walking to stay alive to occupy her thoughts, no one shooting at them, there was nothing but her fear.

Someone wanted her dead.

Had been willing to shoot down a helicopter, killing others who had nothing to do with her situation, to make it happen.

Just because she was here now didn't mean the danger was gone.

Whoever had tried to kill her would still want her dead, and even though she was on a military base, it didn't mean they couldn't make it happen.

Chewing on her lip to try to hold back the sobs that wanted to break free, the last thing she wanted to do was break down and show weakness in front of her would-be killer. She trusted Logan, and he trusted his team, maybe they could keep her safe until they identified the traitor because that was all that would keep her safe.

That only worked if Logan was okay.

If he wasn't then she wasn't sure she trusted a single person on this base. Any single one of them could be who she was looking for.

"Here you go, ma'am, discharge papers and scrubs," the nurse announced when she came breezing into the room. "And the gentleman you were enquiring about has already been discharged."

"Oh," Claire said, confused at hearing that. Logan had left without coming to check on her. Without saying goodbye. He hadn't even left a note or anything.

Oh.

Reality sunk in.

Logan hadn't bothered to check on her because he didn't care. She had just been a responsibility, someone in need of saving, and when she'd expressed an interest in him, he'd probably thought pretending to reciprocate was a good way to keep her calm so she didn't hinder his efforts to get them back in one piece.

Quickly she signed the papers and threw on the scrubs, desperate now to get to her room so she could be alone because the second she was, she was pretty sure she was going to fall apart.

Outside her room was a young man who directed her to where she'd be staying. She didn't ask for his name, didn't care what it was, she didn't even really wonder if he was the traitor, her dark haired SEAL with the purposefully empty eyes that hid a warm heart he didn't want anyone to know about occupied her thoughts.

Only he wasn't hers.

He never had been.

She'd seen only what he wanted her to see.

Finally they reached her room, it had only a bed, and a desk with a chair, but thankfully it had its own tiny bathroom, and she quickly stripped off her clothes, rummaged through her suitcase—which according to the man who walked her here had been found at the wreckage and brought back—for her toiletries. The second she stepped under the shower's hot spray she broke. Claire sunk to the floor, curled into a ball, and sobbed into her hands.

She was here alone.

Really and truly alone.

She had no one to turn to for help, no one to have her back, every person she looked at she would wonder if they wanted her dead, and worst of all, she didn't have Logan.

It shouldn't matter so much, she'd only known him for a couple of days, but in that time he'd managed to crack through barriers she had thought were impenetrable. He was special, and she'd been silly enough to think he thought she was something special too.

Although the tears kept coming, Claire wasn't sure how much hot water there would be, so she stood and shampooed her hair and scrubbed every inch of her body three times.

Tears were still streaming down her cheeks as she turned the water off, dried herself, and threw on her pajamas.

They hadn't stopped as she climbed into bed and pulled up the covers. When she and Logan had slept on the ground the last two nights she'd wished for a bed, but now that she was in one, she would gladly trade it to have Logan's comforting presence by her side.

She missed him so much her heart ached.

Actually ached.

At some point, Claire must have cried herself to sleep because the next thing she knew she was bolting upright as the door to her room shook as though someone was trying to open it. Thankfully, she must have automatically locked it when she got here, but now she jumped out of bed and approached it cautiously.

"Hello?" she called out. It was still dark out, she couldn't see any light coming through the room's only window, and the person at the door hadn't announced themselves. Could it be the traitor?

There was no answer but something brushed against her barefoot.

Claire jumped a mile and was opening her mouth to scream when she realized it was a piece of paper. Snatching it up, she flipped on the lights and debated opening the door but decided if it was the traitor she would be just handing herself over to him. Instead she read the note that had been left for her.

A warning.

And a threat.

An order to leave now and drop this or suffer the consequences.

An order she couldn't fulfill.

There was no way she could live with herself if she went slinking home with her tail between her legs and didn't do everything within her power to stop the attacks Raymond had told her were coming. She couldn't let her fear send her running because if she did, innocent people would pay the price. She had to see this through even if the idea of being here and the danger she was putting herself in terrified her. Nothing was going to make her stop.

But, oh, how she wished she had Logan here to watch her back.

CHAPTER 4

September 9th

6:44 A.M.

"How're you doing?"

Shark grunted at the voice and didn't stop the set of bicep curls he was in the middle of.

"Is that an affirmative grunt?" Grayson "Chaos" Simpson continued cheerfully as he breezed into the gym, his light green eyes twinkling merrily.

He just glowered at his teammate. Despite the horrors they saw and dealt with in their job, Chaos was in a near-perpetual good mood. The man loved practical jokes and was like a tornado of energy, hence the nickname.

"How's the lady?" Charlie "King" Voss asked as he and the rest of the team joined him in the gym.

In an effort to remain aloof, he asked nonchalantly, "Which lady?"

As soon as he saw the surprised looks on his friends' faces, Shark realized he had made a tactical mistake. In trying to make it sound like Claire meant nothing to him, he'd actually given away that he did in fact care about her.

"Umm, the one who you spent forty-eight hours with trying to stay alive in the Afghanistan desert while you were being hunted and shot at," Night said, looking amused.

"So the big man has fallen," Chaos sing-songed, his smile growing wider.

"It's amazing people don't punch you in the face more often," he growled.

Chaos just tossed his head back and laughed like that was the funniest thing he'd ever heard. "You're totally right, dude."

Shark rolled his eyes at Chaos and started on a set with his other arm. Maybe if he just didn't talk about Claire, his team would get the hint and let the topic drop. Unfortunately, one look at their eager and expectant faces and he realized that wasn't going to happen.

"So?" Fox prompted.

"So, what?" he asked defensively. He didn't do this, he didn't sit around like he was in junior high and discuss his feelings, he didn't even *have* feelings.

"So, you and Ms. Barrett," Fox prompted again. "You're a ..."

"A what?" he asked stubbornly, refusing to cave and have this conversation.

"A couple," Spider said with exaggerated patience.

"No," he said shortly.

"The way she was standing there all mama bear shooting at me and Fox to protect you says otherwise," Night said.

"She was trying to protect us, we'd just been shot at," Shark said, gesturing at his injured side.

"So you didn't kiss her?" King asked.

He just grunted.

"You did kiss her," Chaos said delightedly. "Shark and Claire sitting in a tree, k-i-s-s-i ..."

Shark swung a fist at his friend who easily dodged it. "What are you? Twelve?"

"Did you two have sex?" King asked.

"No, of course not. You really think I was thinking about sex in the midst of being injured, and hungry, and thirsty, and dirty, and trying to keep on the move so we didn't get hunted down and shot?" He glowered at King, mostly because he *had* been thinking about sex in the midst of all the things he'd just mentioned.

"So you kissed her, but you're not a couple?" Spider asked, looking confused.

Obviously, they didn't intend to let it go, but he wasn't about to go blurting out that he'd actually liked the woman, felt a connection to her, and then found out when he got back here that she'd been using him and still wondered if he might be a traitor.

A *traitor*.

The idea was so ridiculous, and he felt another rush of fury flood through him.

How dare Claire believe he was capable of that. She didn't even know him, she had no right judging him.

"Can we assume the stony silence is because you do like her and don't want us to know?" Night asked.

He sighed long and deep, they weren't dropping it, and he realized they were really going to do this.

Discuss a woman.

His woman.

Well, Claire wasn't his, but he'd ... wanted her to be.

And that was the crux of his problem. He'd cut himself off from feeling anything but anger as a kid. Watching his father beat up on his mother over and over again, it was too hard to care about someone who kept themselves in a position where they continued to be hurt. Even admitting that he was interested in Claire opened him up to a world of possibilities to be hurt.

Something he wasn't sure he could do.

"Don't forget who you're talking to here," Fox said, indicating himself, Spider, and Night. "I think we could write a book on how to mess up a relationship. Did you forget how badly I messed up with Evie? I'm lucky she even talks to me let alone married me and gave me a son." Fox beamed as he talked about his wife and two-month-old baby son Sullivan. Shark knew how hard it had been for him to leave his wife and infant son, especially given that he'd lost his first wife and almost lost Evie almost eighteen months ago when the two had reconnected.

"And I took three tries to get it right with Abby," Spider added. "I let other people come between us." He shot an apologetic look at Night who was Abby's older brother and one of the people who had come between them. While it was water under the bridge, Shark knew Night still—and probably always would—felt guilty about it. "It took her being missing for fourteen months to wake me up and realize if I didn't fight for her, I'd lose her. Now we've been married for almost two years, and we have a seventeen-month-old son." Ryder Junior, RJ, had been the first baby to join their SEAL family and was ridiculously spoiled by all his SEAL uncles, including him.

"If Lavender hadn't been abducted doing aid work over here then we would never have become more than friends. I wasn't even thinking about falling in love, then all of a sudden everything changed, and then she was pregnant, and

I realized I was falling for her, and now I have two wonderful women in my life, Lavender and Anastasia." It was hard to believe that Anastasia was going to be one at the end of the month.

"But I'm not in love with Claire," he reminded his friends. Their stories had all worked out because they'd been in love with the women in their lives.

"No, 'course not," King agreed, "you only just met. But you do like her."

Reluctantly, he nodded. Yeah, he liked her, but what good did that do him when she thought he was capable of betraying the country he had vowed to protect.

"So, what's the problem? She's here, you're here, you can get to know her, see where things go, doesn't have to be any pressure," Fox said.

Setting the weights down, Shark raked his fingers through his hair. He could brush his friends off, but part of him was too angry to do that, he needed to vent. Over the years, he'd learned not to direct his anger to his fists, but that urge to beat something up was still there. "Claire is a civilian contractor, a psychologist, one of her patients admitted to her that he had sold information to a terrorist cell planning to set off several bombs across the US. Then he committed suicide. Before he did, he told her he was working with someone but wouldn't give up the person's name. Claire is here to find that person. She thinks it could be me."

Spider's brow furrowed. "You?"

"You mean like right after the crash? Because I could see that. She's afraid, she knows she's in danger, and you can be kind of intimidating. It's perfectly reasonable she might have wondered if you were the man she'd been sent to find," Fox said.

Shark nodded in acknowledgment. "I agree. But we spent two days together, and the first thing she did when we got back was send the Colonel to my hospital room to interrogate me." That shouldn't sting, it was a smart move, and one that he could agree was logical if he hadn't liked Claire, if that move hadn't made him feel betrayed.

"Not cool at all, dude," Chaos said, shaking his head. The rest of the team quickly and vigorously nodded their agreement.

"Yeah, man, that sucks," Fox agreed. "I'm sorry."

He shrugged like it wasn't a big deal, desperate to downplay the whole situation, desperate not to let them know how badly it had hurt. He was Shark, the man without emotions, the one who was always calm and collected, who nothing touched, nothing ruffled his unflappable composure. Nothing ever had, not until a small brunette who had proven herself tougher than he'd originally given her credit for had managed to slip beneath his defenses.

"It is what it is," he said, feigning calm as he stood and grabbed a bottle of water. "Can't get that upset over someone you only met."

Not wanting to discuss it any further, he'd done more talking already today than he usually did in an entire twenty-four hours, he was ready to just forget about Claire and move on. They might be stuck on the same base for however long it took her to complete her mission, but that didn't mean they had to see each other. Besides, what possible reason would she have to seek him out when she didn't trust him?

* * *

8:09 A.M.

.   .   .

She was no more rested than she'd been when she climbed into bed last night.

After being startled awake by the knock on the door and receiving the threatening message, Claire hadn't been able to calm herself enough to go back to sleep. Part of her had wanted to go looking for Logan's room, but since he hadn't made any attempt to contact her, not even to check to see about her injuries, she wasn't sure where they stood with each other so she'd stayed put.

The shock of having it confirmed that the helicopter was targeted because of her and that she was in danger had left her with an icy ball of dread sitting heavily in her stomach. Cold and unable to stop shaking, she'd spent the last couple of hours sitting in bed, her back pressed against the wall, the blankets wrapped tightly around her as though they were a shield that could protect her from whatever was coming next.

But of course they couldn't.

As much as she wanted to hide out in here, away from everyone and everything, Claire knew she couldn't do that forever. She was here to do a job, a job that had become vitally important to her survival, and to do that job she had to leave this room.

With a sigh, Claire slowly uncurled her stiff fingers from around the covers and forced herself to get up. As she rifled through her bags in search of clothes, she made a plan for the remainder of the day. Although she was nauseous, Claire knew she had to eat, so she'd go to the mess hall, have some breakfast, then she'd go looking for Logan. Whether he had viewed her as just a responsibility to get to safety or there was another explanation for him keeping his distance, he was the only person on the base that she trusted, and she wanted to tell him about the note she'd received. Claire was positive that whatever he felt for her, whether the things he'd said to her had been real or not, that he was a good guy and would help her.

Once she felt like she had an ally, someone she trusted to have her back, then she would find Gaulding and the CIA and NSA guys, and they would get to work making a list of suspects to investigate.

The plan helped her feel a little more in control of her situation, and she pulled on the jeans and sweater she'd chosen. The sweater would probably be too warm if she ever actually warmed up, but right now, she was cold and needed the comfort of the soft, fluffy wool.

She was still bothered by her shoulder. Sitting most of the night gripping the blankets probably wasn't the best of ideas. The joint felt as stiff and painful as it had when she'd left the hospital. Slipping her feet into a pair of sneakers, she awkwardly managed to tie the laces without moving her shoulder too much and then slipped her arm into a sling. In the bathroom, she ran a brush through her hair, brushed her teeth, and then debated putting on makeup. It would help to cover the dark circles under her eyes, but she decided she couldn't be bothered, so with a one-sided shrug, she dismissed her reflection and tentatively crept out of her room.

Claire half expected to find whoever had left her the note still lingering around, but when she did open her door, she didn't see a single person.

Relieved that for the moment she was safe, she hurried off in the direction of the dining hall. She'd been left a map of the layout of the base so she knew where she was going, well, she hoped she did, but map reading had never really been a skill of hers.

A few minutes later, she was stepping inside the dining hall, which was busier than she'd been expecting. Busier than she'd been hoping too. It was hard to be around these people when she knew that one of them wanted her dead. Not just wanted, was no doubt more than ready and willing to follow through and actually kill her too.

Keeping her head down so she didn't attract anyone's attention, Claire joined the line, and a couple of minutes later, she was sitting down at an empty table, way over in the corner of the large room, with a bowl of cereal.

As expected, her stomach was not interested in food even though she'd barely eaten in days. She picked at the food, swirling the cereal around in her bowl more than actually eating it. Even though she knew her body needed the fuel that it was severely lacking, every mouthful she managed to swallow only added to the nausea.

Claire was about to give up and just abandon the idea of eating when she saw Logan and his team enter the room. She hadn't gotten a good look at his team yesterday when they'd come to rescue them, she'd been in shock, and they'd been dressed in their fatigues with their faces painted, but now that she could see them properly she noted they were a good looking group of men.

Her gaze focused on Logan. He looked good, moved smoothly like he didn't have wounds on both sides of his torso. He wasn't smiling, but then she knew he wasn't a big smiler, but it was clear that he loved and respected his team.

For the first time since he'd been taken away from her and they'd been put in separate hospital rooms, she felt an inkling of safety. Logan was here, and he wouldn't let anyone hurt her no matter what was—or wasn't—between them.

Quickly disposing of her bowl of mostly uneaten cereal, Claire headed straight for Logan and his team. She had closed maybe half the distance between them when he noticed her.

The look Logan gave her was cold, and her steps faltered.

Why was he looking at her like that?

Okay, she'd wondered if maybe he hadn't really been interested in her and simply used it as a ploy to keep her calm and get her to safety, but she hadn't considered the possibility that he apparently hated her guts.

It made zero sense, and sure she had misinterpreted the look and had put her own insecurities on him, she kept walking until she reached him.

Nervous, she couldn't not shuffle from foot to foot. "Hi."

Logan merely gave a curt nod.

Okay, so he *was* angry with her for some reason.

The rest of his team was no more welcoming. They all stood there and stared at her with stony expressions. She had no idea what had happened between yesterday and this morning, but it was obvious from the tension she didn't understand that something had.

Her heart dropped.

Logan really wasn't into her.

Maybe he was annoyed that he'd had to put up with her for two days straight, been forced to kiss her, and listen to her talk about her father, and tell him that she liked him.

Mortification mixed with a sense of betrayal that he could so callously manipulate her emotions, and with both emotions came a heavy dose of loneliness. She couldn't count on Logan to support her or keep her safe, she was in this on her own, just as she had been for most of her life.

Tears threatened to erupt, and Claire quickly spun around and hurried from the room, praying she could make it back to hers before she fell apart.

How stupid could she have been to allow herself to open up to Logan? She didn't let people in, ever. She was always so careful to keep some distance between herself and the people in her life, it was safer that way. But Logan had made her feel things no one else had, and for once, she had trusted those feelings and allowed herself to be vulnerable to him.

A mistake.

One she wouldn't be repeating.

Ever.

Claire was so distracted that she didn't realize that someone had been following her until she was almost to her room and the man made his move.

She was grabbed from behind and shoved roughly up against the wall face first. Her already bruised head protested as her forehead bounced off the wall, making her see stars. The man pulled her injured arm from its sling and shoved it up behind her, making her cry out in pain.

"I told you to leave, to drop your investigation, and get out of here," a voice snarled in her ear.

She did her best to remember exactly what it sounded like in case she made it out of this alive so she could use it to identify him, but her pulse was thundering in her ears, and he was purposefully keeping his voice quiet. And why did she think she was making it out of this alive anyway? She knew she wasn't.

"You're going to walk with me, you're not going to turn around, you're not going to make eye contact with anyone we see," the man instructed, and she knew he intended to kidnap her and take her somewhere he could torture her for information before killing her.

* * *

8:20 A.M.

Shark breathed a sigh of relief when Claire spun around and all but ran from the room.

Seeing her again was more difficult than he'd thought it would be. It didn't help that she was clearly nervous, or that he could see the tight lines of pain around her mouth, or that it was obvious she hadn't gotten any rest, the dark circles under her eyes looked worse than when he'd seen her the day before.

But none of those things were his problem.

She'd used him to make sure she got back here, and now here she was. His vow to save her had been fulfilled, and now he could wash his hands of the entire situation and move on.

So why had she come over here?

That seemed incongruous with someone who had just used another person.

If she had come just to thank him then she would have just said it and left, she wouldn't have run out of here on the verge of tears.

And she *had* been on the verge of tears. In fact, she'd been looking at him like she didn't understand why he was being so cold and distant.

Again that was incongruous with someone who had just used another person.

Something didn't feel right, and he was starting to wonder if he had misread the situation. What if there was another explanation for him being grilled as though he were the traitor.

"I have to go," he muttered to his team, already heading out of the dining hall and heading in the direction of Claire's room, assuming that was where she would retreat so she could have the privacy she needed to let her tears fall. He knew where Claire's room was because he'd asked, not because he cared, just so he could make sure he stayed away so that they didn't accidentally run into one another.

Definitely not because he cared.

That lie flew from his mind when he turned the corner and saw a man holding Claire up against a wall, her injured arm pulled behind her back.

Shark saw red.

He heard an angry growl but had no idea it came from him until the man assaulting Claire turned and looked at him, then released her and ran.

Shark had every intention of going after the man and ripping him to shreds with his bare hands, but instead, he found himself stopping beside Claire and hauling her into his arms.

She was shaking and crying, and she clung to him, burrowing closer as though there was no way she could get close enough, and in that moment he knew. Claire didn't believe he was the traitor and she hadn't sent those men to interrogate him.

He held her until she gently pushed at him, then reluctantly released her. He watched as she straightened her spine, wiped her face clean, and visibly pulled herself together.

"Thank you," she murmured.

Shark nodded, though he wasn't interested in her thanks. "Do you know who that was? What he wanted?"

Her gaze dropped to her feet, and she clutched her injured arm to her chest but didn't answer him.

That got his hackles up.

"Claire? Who was he?"

"I don't know," she said softly.

"But you know what he wanted."

Reluctantly, she nodded.

"Claire, tell me," he demanded, and her wide, scared eyes snapped to his, making him regret the harsh tone. Actually it made him regret a lot more than that. He regretted not checking on her last night before he left the hospital, he regretted believing that she was the kind of woman who would use him and then dump him. He regretted not looking for her this morning and being cold to her in the dining hall. Dragging in a breath, he shoved his fingers through his hair, then exhaled slowly. "I'm sorry, I didn't mean to yell. What's going on, Claire?"

Hesitantly, she reached into her pocket and pulled out a single sheet of paper. It was folded into quarters, and she silently handed it to him.

Shark unfolded it and swore when he read what it said. "When did you get this?"

"It was pushed under my door last night."

"Why didn't you tell me?" It hurt to know that she had been in trouble and hadn't come to him for help, and yet how could he expect her to when she was no doubt confused about why he'd left the hospital without checking on her.

"I was going to, I was going to look for you this morning, and in the dining hall I would have but ..." she trailed off, but he didn't need her to finish the sentence. She'd been going to tell him, but his cold demeanor had instead had her running away in tears.

He growled, at himself not her, but Claire took a fearful step back, and he realized they were back to her being afraid of him.

"I'm s-sorry," she stammered. "I know I should have told someone, but I didn't know who to trust. And I was going to tell you but then you were ... and it's okay, I mean, I understand. You felt responsible for me, and you played along with my delusions so it would be easier to get me back here. I'm not mad ... I'm just ... well, anyway."

Claire gave him a tight smile and then turned to leave, and Shark wanted to beat himself up. He knew better than to let a misunderstanding get in the way of anything. He should have gone to Claire last night, confronted her with what he thought, instead he'd allowed her to doubt him. Yet despite her doubts about his motives, she'd still planned on going to him with her problem because she trusted that he would keep her safe.

While he'd been ready to forget all about her, banish from his mind those kisses and those moments holding her in his arms while she slept, she'd been ready to trust him despite her doubts about him.

He was an idiot.

"Claire, wait."

Of course she didn't, and he quickly closed the gap between them. Clasping her good shoulder, he gently spun her around to face him.

"You got it wrong."

Her brow crinkled. "About us? I know, and it's okay, I really do understand."

She said it so sadly that he couldn't help himself from reaching out and brushing the backs of his knuckles across her damp cheek. "No, sweetheart, actually you don't understand."

They both startled at the endearment that had fallen from his lips. Shark rarely used them, even with the people he loved and considered a part of his family.

Since he knew it was better to be honest than keep secrets, he explained. "Last night the Colonel, and a man called Sims from the CIA, and Tanaka from NSA came to my hospital room to interrogate me. I thought you had sent them."

"Me?" She stared up at him clearly confused, and then her eyes widened as she obviously put the pieces together. "You thought I used you to get me back here and that the kisses and everything I told you were manipulations, and I really did still wonder if you were the traitor." Hurt and sadness flickered through her dark eyes. "I wasn't lying when I said I'm not experienced, Logan. And by not very experienced I mean not experienced at all. I've never dated anyone, never kissed anyone before you either. I would never pretend something like that. Admitting to you—and myself—that I liked you was one of the hardest things I've ever done, and I'm still bracing myself for you to realize how out of your league I am and dump me. I mean, look at you." Her gaze roamed him from head to toe and back up again before dropping to the ground. "And look at me."

Sad that she didn't see herself as others saw her, and furious at whoever had led her to believe she wasn't worth anything, Shark circled her waist and drew her close, careful not to jostle her injured arm. "You're right, look at you. A smart, tough, determined woman who won't back down from her job even though she knows she's in danger. A woman with sweet lips, perfect curves, and soulful eyes. And then there's me. The man people call Shark because they think I don't have any emotions. A man whose whole life has been spent fighting and killing. Tell me again, who's out of whose league here?"

Claire opened her mouth to protest, but he silenced her by kissing those sweet lips. She immediately melted into him, the fingers of her good hand lifting to curl into his shoulder, and the rest of the world faded away.

Was this how it would always be with Claire?

Would the anger at his father's abuse, and his mother's refusal to leave, the clawing need to protect anyone weaker than himself, would it all fade away when Claire was in his arms?

She was a sweet balm to his battered soul, and he never wanted to let her go.

* * *

8:34 A.M.

How did he do that?

99

How did Logan manage to make all her fear, sadness, and loneliness fade away with one kiss?

Much too soon as far as Claire was concerned, Logan pulled back. Framing her face with his large hands, his thumbs stroking softly across her cheekbones, he leaned in to kiss her forehead. "I'm sorry."

Just like that, the last of her hurt faded away. "It's okay. I can see why you would have thought that, but I swear I didn't send them. I told them that it wasn't you, that if it had been, you would have let those two men assault me and then kidnap me that first morning after the crash. I suppose given that you saved my life they thought there was a chance that was blinding me, making me trust you when I shouldn't, and they wanted to clear you themselves."

She could tell by his expression that he agreed with her assessment. "I should have thought of that instead of doubting you and your motives."

"Maybe you doubted me because it matters to you what I think." She said it in a teasing tone, but it was obvious Logan took her words seriously.

"You're right. It matters to me what you think, and it matters to me that I keep you safe. It's clear you aren't safe here. We need to bring my team in on this as well. I told them a little of what you told me, but I'd like it if you came and explained it all. Maybe we can help narrow down your suspect list."

Claire hesitated. She was intimidated by Logan's team, even more so after they had all given her the cold shoulder this morning. The idea of being with all of them, at the same time, scared her.

"They'll apologize for earlier," Logan said, noticing her hesitation and deducting what it was about. "We're a close team, we have to be to do what we do, when someone hurts one of us they hurt all of us, and they think that you used me.

Plus, they're not thrilled with the idea that you think I'm a traitor."

She felt her cheeks burn because at first she *had* wondered if Logan was the traitor. "You know at first ..."

"At first you didn't know me," Logan interrupted. "Now, let's get you to our building, then once we go through everything you know you can get some rest. Did you sleep at all last night?" he asked as he took her hand and started leading her across the base.

"Not after that note got slid under my door, I was too scared."

"Then you definitely need sleep. You're going on seventy-two hours without proper rest."

"More probably, I didn't really sleep well the night before we left to come here. Actually, I haven't really slept since Raymond dropped that bomb on me then killed himself, and that's going on a month ago now." Claire rubbed at her eyes, they were gritty from lack of sleep, and there was a heavy layer of exhaustion she couldn't shake. Maybe if Logan was close by she'd be able to let go and get the rest her body so badly needed.

They made the rest of the walk in silence, and too soon Logan was opening the door to one of the buildings, and she was face to face with his team. Their cool expressions moved from her to Logan and then to their joint hands, and Claire had to fight the urge to fidget.

"It was a misunderstanding," Logan said without preamble. And although she waited for him to explain exactly what the misunderstanding was, he didn't, just ushered her inside and over to the table in the middle of the room where he pulled out a chair for her and eased her into it.

Apparently, his team didn't need an explanation because they all stopped what they were doing and came to join her at the table, all except the blond one who went and retrieved a first aid kit. Gone were the cold and guarded expressions, and in their place were warm and reassuring ones, and she felt herself relax. These guys were protective of their team-mate. There was nothing wrong with that, she just wished that *she* had a team like this guarding her back.

"Claire was attacked on her way back to her room, and someone left her this last night." Logan held out the note, and the blue-eyed one—Spider she thought—took it and read it, whistling and shaking his head when he did, before passing it on to the others.

"He hurt her?" Chaos asked Logan as he knelt in front of her chair.

"Twisted her arm behind her back, the one she dislocated in the crash," Logan replied.

Chaos frowned as he looked at her, but she knew he wasn't angry with her but the man who had attacked her.

"Chaos is our team medic," Logan explained, sitting down in the chair beside her.

"May I?" Chaos asked, nodding at her arm.

Claire nodded, and the man very gently took hold of her wrist, taking her pulse before carefully probing her shoulder joint and moving her arm. When he was done, he put her arm back into the sling and opened his first aid kit. "What do you want for pain? I have morphine, codeine, aspirin, and ibuprofen."

"Umm, just the ibuprofen, I need to be able to keep a clear head to figure this out, and I need to be on guard at all times since someone is after me."

Chaos scowled at her as he returned to her side. "Don't you get it?"

"Get what?" she asked, feeling as confused as Logan's team looked.

"That you're one of us now and we won't allow anyone to hurt you," Chaos replied.

Shocked by the declaration, she'd exchanged only a handful of words with these men, and just minutes ago they believed she had betrayed one of their own, and now they were vowing to step up and keep her safe.

"That's the way this team works, Claire," Fox told her, smiling as he unscrewed a bottle of water and handed it to her.

"Shark likes you, I think it's pretty clear you like him back, that means you're part of our family now," Spider added as he took a seat at the table.

"But Logan and I hardly know each other," she protested. Just because she liked him didn't mean things would necessarily work out between them.

"Do you remember what I told you when we were still out there? That I only do things two ways?" Logan asked.

"I remember."

"Then this shouldn't be a shock to you."

Okay, so they expected her to just accept that she had all of a sudden acquired five over-the-top protective older brothers, and Claire found that she wanted to. She'd never had any siblings, and the idea of having surrogate big brothers was nice. "Okay," she agreed.

"Good, now that's settled, take your pills and tell us what you know," Chaos said, tipping two white pills into her hand.

Claire swallowed the painkillers, washed them down with a few mouthfuls of water, and then looked at the six SEALs who were waiting at the table to hear what she had to say. Her nerves gone now, their acceptance of her had earned her trust, and she started talking. "Logan said he told you about Raymond, so I'm guessing you know that part already." At their nods, she continued, "The idea was that I come here as a psychologist, let people come to me if they need to talk, and while I'm here try to figure out who the man working with Raymond is."

"Do you have any ideas?" Fox asked.

"Well, I have a few suspects. I was given files on everyone who was based here after I reported what Raymond had told me, and I was able to eliminate some, but there is a bigger pile of ones I'm not sure about. Raymond had a money problem, he had five kids to five different women, and child support pretty much tapped him dry. What didn't go to his kids he spent on gambling. He was so deep in debt he'd gone to a loan shark."

"Is that what convinced him to turn traitor?" Night asked.

Claire nodded. "Yes, he was in it for the money, but the guilt ate at him, it's why he confessed and ended his life."

"Why not tell you the other man's name?" Spider asked. "If he felt guilty enough to spill his guts you'd think he'd be guilty enough to want to stop the bombings they're planning."

Again Claire nodded, she agreed. "I'm assuming that whoever else is involved is someone who Raymond was close to, which is why I was able to eliminate anyone who had never served with or been stationed with him. Between military personnel and various agencies who have men and women based here that's still a lot of people."

"Off the top of your head, who are the top suspects?" King asked.

"Well, I don't like the NSA guy Tanaka, but that's just because he creeps me out," she said with a shiver.

"Trusting your gut is important," Logan reminded her, taking her hand in his and squeezing reassuringly.

"There was the guy the CIA assigned me as a bodyguard, I did wonder if it was him, but he died on the helicopter," she explained, banishing a picture of the beheaded man from her mind.

"What made you suspect him?" Night asked.

"He always seemed a little too interested in if I was making progress, he was always asking about the case."

"So if it wasn't him maybe it was that guy Sims from the CIA. He assigns you someone to watch over you and tells his man to follow your progress. Sims would also know exactly when you were on the helicopter and be able to organize the extremists when and where to shoot you down," Logan suggested.

That was a definite possibility. "There were also a few others who Raymond had served with for years, friends of his, a couple who also gambled with him, that are on the top of my list, but there's also ..." Claire trailed off, not wanting to verbalize her suspicion in case the others thought she was crazy.

"Also, who?" Logan prompted, his steady presence beside her and the gentle but firm grip he had on her hand reassured her.

"Well, Colonel Gaulding said something last night when he was interviewing me in the hospital that made me wonder. It wasn't an admission or anything, it was just a small thing. Maybe it's silly, it's not really proof or anything, and he could have gotten the information easily enough. It just surprised me that he knew and that he mentioned it." She was rambling and she knew it, still worried about what the others would say, but when she looked at them she saw they were all waiting attentively for what she had to say. "He knew the exact amount of money that Raymond was in debt, I mean down to the cent. As I said, he could easily get that information, I was just surprised that he knew it off the top of his head."

"Was it Gaulding who attacked you earlier?" Spider asked.

"I don't think so," she replied.

"No, it wasn't," Logan said more confidently. "But that

doesn't mean anything. If it is the Colonel then he could have built his own army here. He could have men that are loyal to him and his causes, not to the country."

If it was the top man on the base who was a traitor to his country, then every second she spent here she was in danger, there could be any number of men waiting for an opportunity to abduct or kill her, and not just the one man she'd thought when she'd agreed to come here. The only ones she trusted were the six men in the room with her, who were the only thing standing between her and death.

* * *

3:40 P.M.

He was in a foul mood today.

Nothing appeared to be going right.

First, Claire Barrett and the SEAL had been found yesterday afternoon and brought back to the base. Unfortunately, neither of them had been badly injured, the SEAL had a gunshot wound to his side, but nothing bad enough to require surgery, and other than bumps and bruises the only real injury Claire had was a dislocated shoulder.

Second, he'd had a note delivered to her room last night, a note that was designed to send her running for the hills. Well, more accurately, go running straight back to the US to leave this whole thing alone.

But she hadn't done that.

Nope, she'd gotten up this morning, not contacted anyone about flying back home, and instead sauntered over to the dining hall for breakfast like she didn't have a care in the world.

What was wrong with the woman?

Why was she hanging around?

Didn't she value her own life?

If the stupid woman would just leave then he would be prepared to wipe the slate clean and let her live. But hanging around here was only going to mean things ended one way.

With Claire's death.

Was that really what she wanted?

He shrugged, stupid was as stupid did. If the woman wanted to wind up tortured, raped, and dead, then she certainly could continue to do what she was doing. In the end, it was no skin off his nose. He didn't care one way or the other if the woman lived or died, all he cared about was making sure she never got a chance to figure out who it was she was looking for.

To that end, he'd had someone go after her, it was meant to be a quick and easy abduction. Walk the woman to a quiet place on the base, knock her out, stash her someplace where no one would find her, and then get her out of here when the opportunity presented itself.

Only that hadn't happened.

The SEAL had interrupted.

The SEAL was starting to become a problem. He'd saved Claire out in the desert, interrupted the first abduction attempt, and then he'd killed the second lot of men sent to find the woman and take care of her. Not only that, but according to his sources the SEAL had taken the woman to meet with his team so now he didn't have just one highly trained special forcers man to contend with, but a team of them.

Hence the bad mood.

He didn't have time for this mess. He was so furious that Raymond had thrown him into this situation, but unfortunately there was no opportunity for him to rail at the man, unleash his anger. Which worked to Claire's disadvantage because when he did finally get the woman—and he *would*—she would be the convenient target for all of that anger.

What he needed was to know just how close Claire was to figuring out he was who she was looking for. Although he'd participated in meetings with her today, she was playing things tightlipped, she wasn't giving a lot away. She knew that she was in danger, she knew that she was on borrowed time, that sooner or later he would get her, so she was being cautious, hiding behind the SEALs as her protection, and today it had worked.

Tomorrow was another day though.

Pulling out the burner phone he only used when he had to call the men he was working with, he placed a call. It annoyed him that he wasn't completely in control when he was dealing with them. He certainly wasn't anyone's lackey, but there was a power struggle between him and Anvar, the head of the group. Anvar provided the cash and the manpower, but there was no way they could achieve what they wanted without him, and he made sure he never let them forget it.

No way was he going to be pushed aside.

"What?" Anvar snapped when he answered.

"Do you know the mess you've left me to clean up?" he demanded.

"What mess?"

"What mess?" he echoed. "The mess you and your idiots caused by being overzealous and shooting down the helicopter. The psychologist made it back to the base, now she knows that someone is trying to kill her and she'd aligned herself with a team of SEALs. Do you know how hard it's going to be to get to her now?"

"That's your problem," Anvar said, sounding bored.

"If she figures out it's me then it'll be your problem too. She can ruin everything, and if you hadn't interfered, then I would have been able to snatch her when she got here without her ever even knowing she was in danger. Now I've got to figure out a way to get her alone."

"Use your men," Anvar said.

"Like I never thought of that," he snapped. "But I only have a few, and one of them already made an attempt to get her. An attempt the SEAL foiled. I can't use him again in case they were able to recognize him. Next time don't do anything to mess this up because despite you thinking this is my problem, the reality is that if I go down, we all go down."

"Then fix the mess," Anvar said it like it was easy, but they both knew it wasn't going to be.

"I will, but you keep your men under control, I know they like to blow things up, but they're going to have to wait until the time is right. Don't cause me any more problems. Just remember that I can get you shut down, send you straight to prison."

"And never forget I can do the same to you."

The phone went dead, and it took every ounce of his restraint not to send it flying into the wall. As satisfying as it would be to shatter the phone, he wouldn't be able to get another and he needed to be able to keep the lines of communication open with Anvar.

What he was doing was serious, he had to keep in control, letting his emotions get the best of him would see him serving the rest of his life in prison.

Well, in theory anyway.

There was no way he was going to allow himself to be captured.

His tongue touched the small capsule that was his backup plan. The cyanide pill could be cracked if he found himself in a situation where he was about to be captured. It wouldn't be a pretty death, but it would get the job done, and then maybe he'd find the peace he sought.

This plan was supposed to give him that peace, he'd been so angry and this had seemed like the perfect antidote to that fury, and while it had been, it had kept him occupied, given him a way to lash out at those who had hurt him, but so far he hadn't found any peace.

It would come.

When the bombs started going off, and he could see the destruction they caused, he was sure he would feel it.

He had to.

If he didn't then all of this would have been for nothing.

That wasn't going to happen, he wouldn't allow it. He pulled his game face on, he would figure this out, all he had to do was take it one step at a time. The SEALs couldn't watch Claire all the time, sooner or later they'd be sent out on the mission they were here for, leaving her alone and vulnerable, so he could either wait for that opportunity or he could make one of his own.

He'd never been one to sit back and wait, he'd always been proactive, he'd always gone after what he wanted. It was why he had gotten to this position in his professional life. He wasn't about to change a lifetime of thinking, especially not when the stakes were so high, he would find a way to force the SEALs' hand and get them out of the way so he could get to Claire Barrett.

Once she was out of the way, there was nothing standing between him and his revenge.

CHAPTER 5

September 10th

3:56 P.M.

Shark ducked a punch Fox threw, then kicked out his leg and took his team leader down.

"Woah, man, you're going all out today," Fox said with a grin as he picked himself up off the floor.

After spending the morning in meetings with Claire, they managed to cut the list of suspects down, which was good, but there were still far too many people left for his liking. Having Claire in danger was unlike anything he'd ever experienced before. As a kid, violence and abuse had always been a part of his life. He couldn't remember a time when his father didn't beat up his mother, and while his mother was a psychologist she could never seem to apply her advice to her own life.

Because of his home life, because he knew what it was like to be too small to stand up to and stop a much larger opponent, as he'd gotten bigger, learned to fight back against his father, he'd started developing a need to save anyone in need of a protector. But that hadn't involved any emotion, he'd simply stepped in because he could, and he didn't want to see anyone else get hurt.

He knew what that felt like, and he felt compelled to stop it if he could.

Of course he'd cared when Night's sister Abby had gone missing, and been relieved when they found her alive. He'd felt similar concern when a pregnant Lavender had disappeared, and when a cartel had taken Abby and Evie, but nothing had prepared him for this.

There was a ball of tension sitting in his gut that wouldn't go away. Even in sleep he'd remained on alert, aware of the fact that all wasn't right with his world. In a lot of ways, it unsettled him that Claire had been able to swoop into his life and make such an impact in just a few short days.

Still, unsettled or not, he wasn't walking away, and he wasn't backing down from his feelings. Instead, he and his team had decided to do some sparring, it was a great way to work out his anxious energy. While he may have gotten his anger under control back when he was a teen, he had always enjoyed using his fists, there was a cathartic side to it, almost like he could undo the damage his father had caused with his, but using his own fists to save others.

"He should be saving a little something in the tank for when the lovely Claire comes by," King said with a grin. "Too bad you saw her first, man, because I can tell you if I'd been the one to find her we would have been well acquainted with each other's bodies by the time ..."

Shark launched himself at his friend, taking him to the ground and pinning King beneath him.

The irritating man just laughed and shoved good-naturedly at his shoulders. "I never thought I would see the day where the big man fell for a girl."

As satisfying as it would be to shut King—their resident ladies' man—up with a fist to the mouth, Shark resisted and climbed off, confident that he had made his point, any talk about Claire was to be respectful. Yes, she was a gorgeous woman, but she was shy when it came to her body and lacked confidence when it came to men. The last thing she needed was King and his flirting. While he knew King didn't mean any harm, and there was no way he would ever consider touching a teammate's woman, he also knew it would make Claire uncomfortable, and that was the last thing she needed right now.

"Just so you know, dude, we have an audience." Chaos flicked his head behind him toward the door of the gym where Claire was standing, her eyes wide as she took in his half-naked body.

He wasn't shy about his body, he worked out hours every day and knew he was in perfect shape. Women were always attracted to him, something about loving the silent and broody type, but there was something different about knowing a woman he cared about found him attractive.

Claire had crashed yesterday after they'd talked through all her suspects, sleeping for a solid eight hours before she'd woken. She'd had to go and see the Colonel, and after she'd informed him of the note and the attack, he had agreed to have Shark's team watch over her since they knew for sure none of them was the traitor. Overnight he and his team had taken turns watching over her room, as much as he would have loved to stay there he knew he needed to remain rested if he wanted to keep her alive.

"Hey," he said, walking toward her. The smile she gave

him was bright, and she kissed him back when he dropped a quick kiss to her lips.

"Should you be doing that with your wounds?" she asked, gently touching the bandages on his sides.

"I'm fine," he assured her. Today she'd had more meetings but had also been set up with an office so she could start seeing people to keep her cover. "Did you have anyone stop by your new office?"

"Just one woman, nothing related to this situation. She's just been struggling with being away from her young daughter." Something in the way Claire said that had alarm bells sounding in his head. She hadn't told him yet what had happened to her, who had hurt her, and he wondered if her mother had been involved.

"Do you want to go lie down? You still look tired."

She gave him a one-sided smile. "We're going to have to work on your compliment skills, but no I'm okay, I didn't mean to interrupt whatever you guys were doing though."

"You didn't interrupt," Spider assured her.

"You can go back to your fighting if you want," she said.

"I have a better idea," Night said, "why don't you do some training with us."

"Me?"

"You know any self-defense?" Shark asked her.

"No, not really. I mean, I've never taken a course, just what I've seen on TV," Claire replied.

Fox chuckled. "Real self-defense is nothing like that. Shark here could run you through a few scenarios."

Shark rolled his eyes at his team's blatant attempts at matchmaking, but since he wasn't going to say no to more time with Claire, he handballed the decision to her. "If you want to we can do a few moves, we'll just have to be mindful of your shoulder."

"I guess that is a good idea. I mean, someone is trying to

kill me, and I'd like to know I have a chance at defending myself if it came down to it. It would have been nice to be able to fight back yesterday when that man grabbed me," Claire said.

While he hated her motives were based on fear, he was pleased she wanted to learn how to protect herself. Maybe if his mom had taken a self-defense class, she wouldn't have let her husband beat her up. "All right then, let's try something like yesterday, only I'll put my arm around your neck, which is more likely to happen. He went at your arm because he knew it was already injured.

A flicker of uneasiness sparked in her eyes, but she acquiesced and allowed him to guide her over to the wall. He'd helped train his teammate's women in self-defense, but it felt different putting his hands on Claire in a way that was meant to scare her. He would be gentle, careful, and it was for her own good, and yet he still didn't quite like it.

"Okay, when I put my arm around your neck your initial reaction is going to be to focus on that, but if I'm bigger than you and stronger than you then it's unlikely you'll be able to dislodge it. Instead, what you need to do is aim at other body parts, knees, feet, groin, try going for that," Shark explained.

"I don't want to hurt you," Claire said.

"You won't, you don't have to go all out, but also don't pull back too much."

When Claire nodded, he put his body right behind hers, then, mindful of her shoulder, he wrapped one arm around her neck.

Claire didn't move.

Didn't do anything but tremble in his hold.

"Stomp on my foot, Claire, or kick at my knee, or you can put a fist to my groin," he coached, wondering if she was having a flashback to yesterday's assault.

She didn't try any of the things he'd suggested.

His concerns amped up.

"Claire?"

"L-let me g-go, p-please," she stammered.

Instantly he released her. The second he did she turned and flew from the room.

"You know what that was about?" Fox asked.

"She just had a panic attack," Chaos noted.

"You have to go after her, and not in a make sure she isn't killed way," King added. "In a she's your girlfriend and she just freaked out about something and you need to talk about it way."

"I know that," he muttered. Although Shark couldn't deny as he headed out after Claire that he'd much rather protect her from an outside threat, someone who wanted to cause her harm than he would from an inside threat. Because pain inside from old hurts was something he couldn't fix, and talking about feelings and emotions was something he was woefully unprepared for. But this was Claire, and he'd suck it up and find a way to give her what she needed because what other choice did he have?

All in meant all in.

* * *

4:17 P.M.

This was one of the most embarrassing moments of her life.

It had been so long since she'd had a flashback that Claire had been caught completely off guard by it.

She'd known that particular self-defense move wasn't a good one to try, not after being attacked yesterday, not when her life was in danger, not when the past was trying to shove its way into the present.

Only she wasn't going to let it.

The past was long since over and done with. She'd got out, built a life for herself, and for the first time, that life actually included someone other than herself.

There was no way she was letting anything blow it for her, not even herself.

Reaching her room, she burst inside, slamming the door behind her and snipping the lock into place. If only it was that easy to keep out her thoughts, her memories, the disconcerting feeling of being stuck between the past and present, helpless to break the link that kept her tethered to things she wished didn't exist.

Claire had just dropped down onto the bed when someone knocked on her door. Well hammered would probably be a better word, and it wasn't *someone*, she knew it would be Logan. It was sweet that he'd come after her, especially considering she was pretty sure dealing with an emotional woman was the last thing he would be comfortable doing, but talking about it was the last thing *she* was comfortable doing.

Nobody knew about her past.

Nobody.

Her friend Dahlia knew that she'd been hurt, but it was one thing to talk to her about it, Dahlia too had been hurt, it was another to tell the man she liked about her twisted family.

"Open up, Claire, I'm not going anywhere, and I will break down this door if you don't open it in the next ten seconds. One, two, three, four, five ..."

"Okay, okay," she muttered, standing only because she was sure that was a threat he would carry through with. When she opened the door, he did the last thing she was expecting. He didn't ask what was wrong, didn't demand answers, all he did was sweep her up into his arms, close and lock the door behind them, then walked to the bed and sat down, settling her on his lap.

This was just what she needed, and she had no idea how he knew it. Never in the twenty-four years since her father had died had anyone just held her. She'd never realized before just how much she needed it. So many years being deprived of comfort and support, first by her own family and then by herself, she'd thought she could survive on her own, and she could, but it was so wonderful to have Logan's support.

He didn't speak, didn't move, just sat there, his arms locked around her, and held her.

And that was exactly why she started talking.

"My mom had been tired of being married to a Ranger, my dad was away so much, she felt like a single mother. A single woman. She wanted a man who would be around more, a man who would take care of her and give her whatever she wanted. After my dad died she was free to find it. And she did. My dad had only been gone six months when she met Burke Taylor. He was rich, older, my mom was still in her twenties, he was almost forty. She married him just shy of the one-year anniversary of my father's death. Once they were married, we moved into his mansion. It was a nice house, and he paid for me to go to private school, bought me anything I wanted. At first I liked it there, but I missed my dad, I missed my friends, I missed our house that held so many memories of him, of happier times."

She stopped talking as tears flowed down her cheeks. Claire had often wondered if her father knew what would happen to her after his death if he would have rethought his options, realized he had something really important to live for.

"Your stepfather is the one who hurt you," Logan said.

"It started when I was ten, went on until I was thirteen

and started developing too much. He liked kids, preteens, once I started puberty he lost interest in me. He used to like to take me from behind, he'd put an arm around my throat, and ..."

She felt Logan go all tense beneath her, and she knew he was feeling bad for inadvertently setting off a flashback, but it was her fault, she should have asked to try something else for self-defense training.

"Claire ..."

"It's okay," she said, cutting him off. "You don't have to say anything. It's awful, it's horrible, horrific, I know that it is, but it's not the worst thing that happened to me. I told my mom the first time Burke hurt me, I thought she would pack us up and we'd leave, but she didn't. She said it must have been my fault, that I must have done something to make him do it. I was ten, I barely even knew what sex was, I didn't do anything to lead Burke on."

"Of course you didn't." Logan said it so vehemently she lifted her head from his shoulder to look at him.

"Thank you, I needed to hear that. I mean, I *did* know, but I still needed to hear it. Burke told my mom if she wanted to stay married to him, if she wanted the perks of being married to him, then that was the price she had to pay. She stayed. She wanted that more than she cared about what he was doing to me. Burke would give me gifts, say they were my payment for my services." Claire shuddered as she remembered the way he would bring wrapped gifts with him when he came to her room at night. "I became an emancipated minor when I was fifteen. I studied hard, graduated early, got a scholarship to college, and took two jobs to pay my bills so I could get out of that house. My mom and Burke are still married, and I haven't seen or spoken to either of them since the day I left. All I took with me was the teddy bear from my dad, a few photos of my dad and me, and the clothes on my back. First thing I did was buy my own with my own money and returned the clothes, I didn't want anything from them."

Logan's arms were so tight around her that it was just shy of painful, and yet she wouldn't ask him to loosen his hold for anything in the world. She could feel his rage bubbling just beneath the surface, and she knew that he had made a choice, be there for her and hold her, or break something to try to relieve some of his anger.

She was so glad he chose her.

Nobody ever chose her. Her own mother hadn't, she'd picked money and security over her own child. How could she ever trust anyone after that?

And she hadn't.

She'd never trusted anyone until this man holding her so tightly in his arms.

"Claire, I don't know what to say. I … I know ways to make bodies disappear so no one will ever find them."

That was not at all what she expected him to say, and it surprised a laugh out of her. She sat up so she could see him properly. "Did you just offer to commit murder for me?"

Logan offered a lopsided smile, and more of the wall around her heart crumbled.

"You made a joke for me." She lifted a hand and ran her fingers through his hair. "I didn't know you could make jokes," she teased.

"I don't. Not for anyone else anyway."

"I'm honored." Actually, she was so much more than honored. Logan was special, he was amazing, he was strong, solid, dependable, he wasn't the kind of man that would shove her aside because he got a better offer, and he would never allow anyone to hurt her.

Claire moved so she was straddling Logan and took his mouth in a passionate kiss, telling him about her past had freed her from it. It was still there, always would be, but now it wasn't controlling her. She needed more, wanted more. After what her stepfather had done to her the thought of sex had always made her feel ill, but not now, not today, not sitting on Logan's lap, evidence of his desire for her straining against his pants. Claire reached for the fly of his jeans.

"Claire," he warned, his hands on her hips as he tried to move her off him. "You haven't ... I don't want you to do something you'll regret."

"I won't ever regret you." She meant it too, there was nothing about Logan she would regret.

"We don't have to do this now, we have time."

"You said you were all in," she reminded him.

"And I am, but all in didn't have anything to do with sex. I can be all in and still hold off on a physical relationship until you're ready."

"I *am* ready," she told him, and meant it.

"Claire ..."

"Logan, I wasn't ready before because I didn't know you. It's you, only you, sex for me ... I'm not normal when it comes to it ... it has to be with someone special, not casual, and you told me you're all in. I am too. I want this, I want it with you."

Her words must have convinced him because he groaned once and then lifted her up and laid her down on the bed. "I wish we could do this somewhere special, you deserve a fancy dinner, flowers, chocolates, not a military base in the middle of Afghanistan."

She smiled and reached up to touch his face. "It's not the where that matters to me, it's the who. It's you, Logan. I didn't expect to ever feel this way about a man, and then you crashed into my life and everything changed."

"You know exactly what to say to convince me."

"That makes us a perfect team. I do the words, you do the actions."

"I won't argue with that. All right, sweetheart, lie back and enjoy."

Logan's lips met hers, and while he kissed her one of his hands began to play with her breasts. He touched one first and then the other, and she felt her nipples tighten under his ministrations.

"Sit up for a moment," he ordered, and when she did, he pulled her shirt over her head and then unclipped her simple white bra, baring her breasts to him.

Before she had a chance to be embarrassed he was pushing lightly at her shoulders to lie her back down, and then his hot mouth closed over one of her nipples and he sucked.

"Oh," she murmured, thrusting her chest forward, silently begging for more.

"You like that?"

"Yes," she said, moaning as he took her other nipple into his mouth, suckling at it as one of his hands brushed down her stomach, hovering just above her waistband. "I need more," she said, grabbing his hand and sliding it lower until he cupped her center through her pants. He brushed his thumb lightly across her, and she shifted restlessly.

"You ready for more?"

"Yes," she said. Her voice was breathy, nothing like she'd ever heard herself sound.

"Mouth or fingers?" he asked.

Her cheeks pinked, but she was too full of needy desire to let embarrassment break the moment. "I ... maybe ... both?"

"Both it is." Logan shot her a sexy smile, and then he was moving down her body, lifting her hips with one hand so he could pull her pants and her panties down her legs. He pulled off her shoes then tossed all her clothes onto the floor beside the bed, and then he settled himself between her legs. Embarrassment at seeing his face so close to her most intimate area was just starting to rise before his tongue stroked along her center.

Then he was licking her. First he took her hard little bundle of nerves into his mouth and sucked on it, flicking at it with the tip of his tongue, and then he stroked the length of her center in a slow, firm movement, and she wasn't sure what she liked better, they both felt so amazingly good.

"You're so tight," he whispered as he inserted one finger inside her.

Her body tensed involuntarily at the intrusion, but only for a second, and then the feel of his finger inside her, stroking deep, coupled with his lips sealed around her bud had a sensation building low in her belly. It was almost overwhelming, her body tried to pull away from it, not sure it was ready to experience something of that magnitude, but Logan never let up. He curled his fingers around, hitting a spot inside her that had her vision fading to white. And then he sucked hard, and her body exploded.

She...

She...

She wasn't even sure what she was feeling, but it was like someone had cast a magical spell on her and transported her into a body that was nothing more than pulses of pleasure zinging from her head to her toes.

When she could see again, think and speak again, she looked up to see Logan smiling down at her.

"That's what everyone talks about, huh?" she asked, tracing lazy circles with her fingertips on his stomach, between the two bandages.

"Yep."

"I can see what all the fuss is about," she said, sighing dreamily.

"Not yet you can't," he said, but then paused before moving, "do you want to stop there for tonight."

"And leave you with that problem," she said, nodding at his erection straining against his jeans.

"I can deal, if you want to stop, we stop."

"Lucky for you I don't want to stop."

Logan shot her another smile and then stripped out of his clothes and sheathed his hard length with a condom. "We'll go slow, give you time to adjust," he said as he positioned himself at her entrance.

He eased inside her slowly, melding his mouth to hers and kissing away the small groans of pain that fell from her lips as his huge length filled her. The tearing feeling pulled her out of the moment, reminding her of her first experience with sex, but Logan seemed to know how to play her body to perfection. As he kissed her, he slipped one hand between them, touching her where their bodies joined, and his attention to her and desire to show her pleasure rather than take pleasure for himself banished the bad thoughts.

Although she was sure it couldn't possibly be better than last time, or that she couldn't possibly experience it again already, as Logan began to move, thrusting in and out, his fingers stimulating her bud, she found that feeling quickly building again.

This time, her body didn't try to fight it, instead she embraced it, kissing Logan back. Her fingers trailed up and down his back, drawing him closer with each stroke. When she came, it was with a scream that would have been loud enough to be heard around the base if Logan's lips hadn't swallowed the sound, claimed it, owned it, made it his own.

She could tell he reached his own peak mere seconds after hers, felt it shudder through his body, and somehow his pleasure became her own as they shared this mind-blowing experience.

"Thank you," she whispered against his lips.

"Pleasure was all mine," he whispered back.

She wanted to keep him inside her, close like this, away from the rest of the world, but too soon he pulled out of her and disappeared into the bathroom. He returned with a warm cloth and wiped her down so tenderly that it almost made her cry. Since she'd managed to hold back the tears while she laid bare her soul, she thought she better manage to hold them back after sex as well.

"You know the best part about sex?" Logan asked as he stretched on his side on the bed and pulled her back up flush against his front.

"What we just did?"

"No," he said, and she could hear the smile in his voice. "It's this, falling asleep in each other's arms."

"Is that what you do after sex?"

"Not usually, but then again, I'm not usually with a woman I care deeply about."

His breath was warm against her cheek, his arm strong around her stomach, and his chest solid against her back. Claire felt cocooned in a little bubble of safety, and for the first time in twenty-four years, she didn't feel alone.

Because she wasn't alone.

She had her very own warrior with a big heart he kept hidden, and she wasn't letting him go.

CHAPTER 6

September 11th

2:02 A.M.

Her warm, soft body was snuggled against him, and Shark couldn't remember a time when he'd felt this happy.

His lips kept wanting to quirk up, and it had taken him much longer than it should for him to realize that he was smiling. Of course he'd smiled before, just because he was gruff and aloof didn't mean that he was unhappy, he loved being a SEAL, he loved his team and their families. His relationship with his brother, Shawn, was strained because he didn't understand how Shark could blame their mother for not leaving their father. He didn't get that it wasn't about blame, it was simply that he didn't get how she couldn't put her kids before her abusive husband, but he still loved Shawn, his sister-in-law, and their three kids.

But what he felt for Claire was something else entirely.

It was all-consuming, she was like a drug, and he was happily addicted to her. They lived in the same city, so when they both went back home they'd be able to date properly, without people trying to kill Claire, and things between them could get serious. Although he supposed there wasn't a lot more serious they could get. They'd slept together, Claire had shared her deepest, darkest secrets, and he'd been more open with her than he had been with anyone else. Ever.

They might have only known each other for five days, but it wasn't a normal five days. They'd survived a helicopter crash together and had to rely on each other to make it through dangerous terrain. She'd saved his life, he'd saved her life, she'd killed to protect him, and he'd killed to protect her. You didn't go through what they had together and not get close real quick. She'd captivated him with not just her beauty, but her strength and determination, her big heart, and her bravery. She could have left him that first day, he was trapped, unconscious, and she suspected he could be a traitor, she could have run and saved herself, but she'd stayed and killed the men who came after them. It was in that moment that she had earned his respect, and that respect had only grown with each day that passed.

Beside him Claire began to whimper, nightmares coming for her while she was vulnerable in sleep. Shark rolled Claire over so instead of being spooned against his chest she was draped across it as he moved to lie on his back. He cocooned her in his arms, gently stroking the smooth skin on her back as he touched his lips to the top of her head.

A moment later, she jerked awake on a strangled gasp.

"You're okay, Claire," he said calmly, confidently, hoping she didn't notice his racing heart. The idea of Claire hurting, even in her dreams, made him feel ill.

"Logan," she said softly, relaxing against him.

"Do you want to talk about it?" While hearing Claire tell him about what her mother and stepfather had done to her, each of them damaging her in their own way but both wounds equally as painful, it had been all he could do to hold it together and remain seated with Claire curled in his lap. He doubted hearing about whatever she had dreamed would be any better, but part of being all in was actually being all in, and that meant listening if she needed to talk.

Her hair tickled his nose as she shook her head.

That was fair enough. He knew from experience that there was nothing worse than not wanting to talk about something and being hounded to do so anyway. His mother used to do that, pull on her psychologist hat after another violent burst of anger from their father. What had she expected him to say? That he was okay with her keeping them in that house? That he understood her reasons for staying? She'd been worse after his father had been killed in prison, always wanting to know how he and Shawn were coping with the loss, like it was an actual loss. Shark couldn't speak for his brother, but he'd been relieved when his dad died, it had felt like being freed from a prison he'd been locked inside.

Instead of talking, Shark just held Claire close, made sure she knew—that she felt—everything he was feeling for her. It was way too soon to use the love word, but that didn't mean that he wasn't on his way to getting there. He'd never given much thought to falling in love, hadn't thought it would happen for him, hadn't thought he'd want it to, the example his parents had set hadn't been one he'd wanted to replicate.

Claire changed everything though.

She'd changed him.

Her hands, which had been idly tracing up and down his sides, suddenly slid between them and curled around his semi-hard length.

Shark didn't ask her if she was sure, Claire was smart and knew her own mind. If she needed this as a distraction, needed to feel connected to him, needed to feel alive, or just wanted sex because she liked it, then he would give it to her. There wasn't anything he wouldn't give to her or do for her.

"Can I be on top this time?" she asked as she propped her chin up on his chest.

"Sweetheart, we can do this in any position you want," he replied.

She gifted him with one of her sweet, sunny smiles and sat up taking the blankets with her, moving further down his body. One of her hands curled somewhat tentatively around him, and he knew that even with what they had shared last night she still wasn't completely comfortable with a man's naked body.

That was okay, they had time, the rest of their lives, for her to realize that she was never in danger with him. She could look, she could touch, she could do with him whatever she wanted.

Hooking his fingers behind his head he relaxed and left Claire to find her confidence.

As she took him in her hands, she watched his expression and his body language carefully, adjusting her grip, the pressure, and the speed, to see what he liked. She was a quick learner and soon knew exactly how to drive him wild.

Shark remained passive as long as he could, not an easy feat for a man like him who was used to being in control, in the bedroom and the rest of his life, but when he felt Claire's wet heat against his thighs, his control snapped. Reaching down, he yanked a condom from his pocket, slid it on, then gripped Claire's thighs and lifted her so she was on her knees, the tip of him brushing against her entrance.

"I'm surprised you could hold out that long," she said with a soft laugh. Then she sank down slowly taking him deep inside her. For a woman who had only willingly had sex for the first time in her life just hours ago, she knew what she wanted and quickly found a rhythm that worked them both higher.

Head tipped back, eyes closed, dark hair falling like a cascade of silk down her back, she looked like a goddess. Shark didn't hold back, taking her breasts in his hands, rolling her nipples between his fingers, kneading and palming them until she was a quivering mess, begging for release.

While Claire was in control here, he also wanted her to come, so Shark reached between them and swirled the pad of his thumb around her bud not more than twice before she came apart.

His name fell from her lips as she hit the peak of ecstasy, and Shark felt a deep sense of satisfaction as he found his release. He had given her that pleasure, he had helped her take something awful, something that scared her, and turned it around into a thing that brought her intense pleasure.

"I think I liked that even better today," Claire murmured as she sank down to press her lips to his.

"I'm glad." He was about to pick her up and carry her into the bathroom to clean her up, maybe take a shower together, when he smelled smoke.

Scooping an arm around Claire's shoulders, so she didn't tumble sideways, he sat up and saw smoke billowing beneath the door.

A second later the screech of a fire alarm pierced the quiet night.

"Get dressed," he ordered Claire as he set her on her feet then stood and began to throw his clothes back on.

"Is that smoke?" she asked, eyes wide with fear as she glanced at the door.

"Yes," he said shortly, already dressed while she had only

managed to put her underwear back on. "Hurry up, we have to get out of here, meet up with my team."

"You think this could be about me?" she asked, pausing with one leg in her pants.

"It would be a good way to create confusion, maybe get you separated and alone," he said, picking up her shirt and helping her put it on once she pulled up her pants. She winced as her injured arm went through the sleeve, and he took over buttoning the shirt so she didn't have to do it then helped her situate her arm in her sling.

With both of them dressed, he kept his weapon in his hand and then grabbed Claire's and squeezed. The idea that this could be a ploy to try to get to Claire filled him with fury and fear, and determined that he would help her end this. He'd find the man that had threatened her, scared her, and hurt her, and he'd make sure that he suffered.

"Listen to me," he said fiercely as he led her to the door. "You don't let go of my hand for anything. If I give you an order you follow it without argument, anything I tell you to do is to keep you alive. Understand?"

"Understood." Claire nodded solemnly.

Shark pulled her close, dropped a quick kiss to her lips, and then led her into a possible ambush.

* * *

2:53 A.M.

Claire's heart was hammering in her chest so fast that she pressed her free hand above it in a vain attempt to slow it down.

She had a fear of fire.

Appropriate of course, most people would be terrified at

the idea of burning alive, but she's never even liked birthday candles. Her dad used to laugh about it, put party poppers on her cake instead and have her make her wish while he pulled the string, sending confetti raining down around her. Her stepfather had told her she was being stupid and forced her to have candles on her cake, made her lean in real close to blow them out, as she got older even made her strike the match and light the candles herself—psychopath.

Now it was only Logan's hand in hers that had her leaving the relative safety of her room. There were no flames in there, and while logically she knew the smoke would eventually kill her, her fear of fire would have kept her in there until her entire room was alight.

"Why can't we go out the window?" she asked when Logan cautiously opened the door.

"Because if they're trying to flush you out, they might have someone with a gun out there waiting to take you down. This way we can blend in with everyone else," Logan replied, pulling her out into the corridor where everyone else sleeping in this building was also streaming out of their rooms. "Harder to shoot at you or get you alone if we're a part of the crowd."

What Logan said made sense, she really did know that, but as soon as they were in the corridor and she caught sight of the flames, any common sense she had flew out the window.

Claire whimpered, her body instinctively trying to pull back into the room, but Logan was bigger and stronger and pulled her along with him as he joined the throng of people heading toward the exits. As well as setting the fire the lights had also been cut, making the only light coming from the flames. The effect of the reddish-orange glow made it feel like they were walking straight into Hell, and given the likely cause of the fire, Claire felt that wasn't far from the truth.

Whoever was after her wasn't going to stop trying. If this fire idea didn't work, he would just try again and again until he got his hands on her. While Claire trusted Logan and his team implicitly, that didn't mean they were superhuman, in the end there might not be anything they could do to save her.

They were almost to the door, and she was itching to get away from the flames, out into the night where she might feel like she could breathe again when suddenly all Hell broke loose.

Gunshots started flying, a man beside her dropped. As the only non-trained person in the building while everyone else sprang into action, all Claire could do was cling to Logan and pray they got out of this alive.

One second Logan's steady presence was beside her, the next someone was slamming into her, sending her sprawling painfully onto the ground. Her bad shoulder took the brunt of the fall, and she cried out.

The sound was swallowed up by the raging fire, the gunshots which didn't let up, and the pounding of footsteps as people tried to decide whether the bullets or the flames were the bigger threat.

Someone knocked into her, and she was shoved further away from Logan. Claire had no idea if she was being deliberately separated from Logan so that snatching her would be easier, or if it was innocent men and women searching for a way to live, but in the end, it didn't matter. She was alone, she couldn't see Logan, and as people continued to move about above her, all she could do was try to find the wall so she didn't get trampled.

Claire shuffled onto her bottom and used her good arm to help her move back until she was pressed up against a wall. She tried to scan the crowd and find Logan, but it was hard to distinguish faces in the eerie red glow, especially down here on the floor.

Where was he?

She knew he wouldn't just leave her here and get himself out of the building. Had he been shot?

If something had happened to Logan then it was up to her to get herself out of here. She could do that, she just had to pretend that the fire wasn't there. Focus on the door at the end of the corridor, block out everything else. If she did that then she could get there.

Just as she was starting to stand, the wall behind her suddenly moved, causing her to fall backward. No, it wasn't the wall she'd been leaning against it was a door, and someone had opened it and was dragging her into a room.

Logan?

No. That notion was quickly dispelled when she was yanked roughly onto her feet.

"You're a hard woman to get a hold of, Ms. Barrett," a voice growled in her ear.

She knew that voice.

It wasn't the same one from when she was attacked the other day, but she'd spent enough time around him to recognize that voice anywhere.

Claire didn't bother begging for her life. What would be the point? He had to eliminate her, for him it was a matter of survival, and she had already proven that she wasn't going to back down or walk away, which meant that there was nothing she could say or do that was going to convince him to let her go.

If she was facing the end of her life, her only regret was that she hadn't met Logan sooner, that she'd only had a few days to share with him, but those days had made up for a life-time of loss, loneliness, and pain. She couldn't help but wonder what her life would have been like if she'd met him years ago.

Still, she could look death in the face, knowing that she had done the right thing in doing what she could to find the traitor. And if she was lucky and she was going to be abducted first then at least she knew Logan would do whatever it took to find her.

A gun pressed against her ribs. "We're going to walk out of here, go out the back, I have a car standing by, you're going to tell me everything you know, and then I'm going to have some fun with you."

His free hand lifted to grip her breast and Claire acted on instinct, shoving at him and ramming her knee up and into his groin.

He staggered back and then a gunshot had her screaming.

Was she hit?

Had he fired at her?

If she'd been shot, why didn't she feel any pain?

"Are you hurt?" Hands on her shoulders accompanied the frantic question, and Claire immediately relaxed.

"Logan," she said, wrapping her good arm around him and pressing her face against his chest. "I didn't know where you went."

"He has men working with him, at least two shooters, maybe three, and at least another two men who separated us."

"There's another in a car outside," she added.

His hold on her tightened as he realized what that meant. "Are you hurt?"

"No. Is he dead?"

"Yeah, he had a weapon on you, he was about to fire, we have to get you out of here." This time Logan didn't risk them getting separated again. He scooped her up, wrapped her legs around his waist, then anchored her with one arm while his other gripped his weapon.

The chaos in the corridor had calmed down, most of the people were already outside now, and no more bullets were fired. A minute later, they burst out into the night, and Claire sighed in relief.

Immediately Logan's team surrounded them and she finally felt safe for the first time since Logan had announced there was smoke coming under the door.

"She hurt?" Chaos asked.

"No," Logan replied. "There's a car somewhere around here, he was planning on taking her."

As soon as they heard that, Night and Spider took off, and she moved to put her feet down, but Logan tightened his hold, obviously not ready to let go of her yet. She was perfectly okay with that, she was right where she wanted to be anyway, and she knew how close she had come to being kidnapped tonight.

But Logan had shot him.

It was over.

There was some mess to clean up, the men who had been working for him to find, but she was safe now, and the relief was staggering. It also meant that she would be leaving soon, which meant being away from Logan, they could video call each other, and maybe it would be good to slow things down a little since they'd jumped right in at full speed. She would miss him like crazy, but they could get to know each other better, and there would be an amazing homecoming to look forward to.

"Who was it?" Fox asked.

Claire turned her head to look at him. "It was Sims."

* * *

6:05 A.M.

Shark took a seat beside Claire at the table. It had been a crazy last few hours, while he and Chaos had stayed with Claire, checked her out to make sure she hadn't been suffering from smoke inhalation or received any injuries, the rest of his team had managed to apprehend the man in the getaway car. Another four men and one woman had also been arrested and were currently waiting to be interrogated.

It was too bad Michael Sims was dead, he would have loved the opportunity to interrogate the man, find out why he'd betrayed his country, and make sure he suffered for what he'd put Claire through.

At least the threat against Claire was eliminated. She would always bear scars, physical and psychological, from this ordeal, but at least she was alive and in one piece, that was all that mattered.

Although now she'd be leaving.

She'd done what she came here to do. The traitor working with Raymond had been identified, he was dead, the people he had working for him would be dealt with, and Claire would be sent back home. He still had another eight weeks left of this two-month deployment. As much as he wanted to be there for her as she dealt with everything that had happened, he was going to have to do it from a distance, via email and video calls, rather than by her side.

"You're okay, Ms. Barrett?" Gaulding asked as he took the final seat at the table.

"Yes," Claire replied, but her hand found his, holding it tightly, and he knew that she was shaken by the night's events.

"So it was the CIA Agent?" Gaulding asked, looking

confused. "I thought we were looking at military personnel who had served with Raymond."

"We did believe that," Claire said, "but I did a little digging while everyone else was dealing with tonight's events and I found a connection between Raymond and Sims." When Gaulding nodded at her to continue, she did. "Both Sims and Raymond attended West Point, they graduated the same year. Sims was in a car accident shortly after graduation, nothing to do with the military, he was on his way back from grocery shopping and was t-boned. He suffered a spinal injury that ended his military career before it began, he decided to go into the CIA instead. I haven't had a chance yet, but I'm sure if we look into it we'll be able to find evidence that they kept in contact over the last two decades."

"But why would Sims turn traitor?" Fox asked.

"Right," King agreed. "The man only flew out here when Raymond died, and you reported what he told you, that makes it around two weeks. He hasn't been in Afghanistan before that. How did he make contact with Anvar Mir? And how did he manage to get at least six people to agree to turn on their country? Those men were prepared to launch an attack on a civilian in the middle of a military base. You don't take those kinds of risks if you don't believe in the cause."

"No way Sims could have turned them in two weeks," Spider agreed.

"Exactly," King nodded. "That takes time, it's not something that you can just do spur of the moment. We know that Sims is involved, I'm not disputing that. He admitted his involvement, and said that he intended to abduct her tonight, but there has to be more going on here than that. Raymond had been back in the US for two months before his admission to Claire and suicide, Sims only turned up here two weeks ago, and yet everyone seemed to know what they were doing and seamlessly put together a plan."

Shark didn't like where this was heading.

It sounded like King was implying that Sims wasn't the head of the snake, that he was merely another player working for someone bigger and badder, someone still out there. Still able to hurt Claire.

"Maybe Sims had been involved all this time, he doesn't have to be here in order to deal with them," Shark reminded them.

Everyone nodded in agreement, but he felt like they were just attempting to placate him. That wasn't what he wanted or needed. If they were right and someone else was involved, then he wanted to know, he couldn't keep Claire safe without all the information. He just prayed they weren't right.

"Why would a decorated CIA Agent turn traitor?" Gaulding asked. "For Raymond it was about money, but what was Sims' motive?"

"Once I knew it was Sims I looked into his background," Claire explained. "I found something that I think might have been what triggered his hatred of his country. Sims was married briefly about fifteen years ago, his wife was pregnant with twins when she was killed. It was a bombing in San Diego, Islamic extremists blew up several buildings over a period of about a month, protesting American interference in their country. You'd think that he'd blame the extremists for the loss of his family, but he's said a few things that now, looking back in hindsight, make me think that he blames America. I think he believes that if we hadn't been involved over here, there would never have been extremists setting bombs on American soil. I wish I'd seen it sooner, but we were more focused on people over here rather than a man who's never even set foot in Afghanistan before."

"No way you could have known to be looking closely into Sims," Shark reminded her.

Claire nodded but still looked frustrated with herself.

"We have to try to get one of the men working with Sims to talk. If we don't, we're never going to know if there was anyone else involved or not."

"If anyone is involved we'll get them," he said, with enough conviction that Claire turned to look at him and offered a tired smile. She was exhausted, she needed to get back to her room, get some rest. His team had a meeting to go over intel for an upcoming mission. While there may or may not still be a threat hanging over Claire's head, he thought if there was someone else still on base involved in the mess they were unlikely to try anything tonight with everyone hyperaware and on edge.

"I'll keep going through information, continue to work through the list of people we had marked as people of interest. If there's someone else involved I'll find out who they are," Claire vowed, and he admired her determination.

"First, you need some rest," he said firmly.

She frowned, and he was sure she was going to argue. She knew it was important to find out if anyone else was involved, but if she didn't get some sleep, she would miss something, and it could be something important. Instead, she nodded, looking defeated. "Yeah, you're right, I want to keep going until I find what I need, but I'm exhausted, and I'll miss something important."

"I'll walk you back to your room," he said, standing and pulling back her chair, then cupping her elbow and helping Claire to her feet.

"We'll meet again this afternoon. I'm glad you're all right, Ms. Barrett," Gaulding said.

"Thank you, sir," Claire replied. She swayed a little as she stood, and Shark slipped an arm around her waist to steady her.

"I'll walk Claire to her room and be back for our meeting," he told his team.

Once they got outside, Claire let out a deep breath and rested her head on his shoulder. They crossed to the building where Claire had been moved to. The fire hadn't completely destroyed the last building, but there was enough damage that it would take a few days, probably closer to weeks to get it operational again.

"I wish you could come lay down with me for a while," Claire said, moving so she could rest against his chest.

Shark's arms came around her automatically, holding her as natural as breathing. "I do too." Even if he was sure that she was safe for now, the idea of leaving her alone didn't sit well with him. Unfortunately, he was starting to believe that Sims was just one part of the picture, and that another, perhaps more vicious piece was still left unaccounted for.

"Do you think you're going to be called out soon?"

"I don't know. Hopefully not before we know for sure if anyone else is involved."

"How did I ever get along without you? Has it really only been five days since we met? It feels like I've known you forever like I know you deep down in my soul."

While he wouldn't have said it so eloquently, Shark felt the same way. What they'd lived through had bonded them hard and fast, and the intimacy they'd shared had only sealed the deal. He would have sworn he'd known her for years if he didn't know he'd only met her a few days ago.

"I'll be back as quickly as I can." He closed his hands over her biceps and leaned down to kiss her forehead. "Try to sleep."

"I'll try."

"Lock the door."

"I will." She gave him an amused smile.

"Don't open it for anyone."

This time she chuckled. "I'll be safe, Logan, I promise. If you get called out before you get back here then don't be distracted by worrying about me. I kind of like you and need you in one piece."

"Yes, ma'am," he said, offering her one of his rare smiles.

"You're not going to leave without a proper kiss, are you?"

"No, ma'am." Gently cradling her chin in his hand, Shark tilted her face up and touched his lips to hers. Since anyone could see them out here, he had to keep the kiss soft and brief, but there would be plenty of time to kiss her the way he wanted. If he played his cards right, they'd have the rest of their lives together.

* * *

6:39 P.M.

Her head was spinning.

So much had happened in the last twenty-four hours, and Claire had barely had a chance to process it all yet. Exhausted as she'd been, she hadn't been able to get much sleep earlier, the new room was too ... new.

There was no smell of Logan on the sheets, no memories of the two of them in there together. There was nothing but an emptiness that filled her with a sense of dread that she couldn't explain.

As a teenager, she'd lived on the streets for a brief time. It was after her stepfather had stopped molesting her, but even though that torture was over, there was still the torture of having to live in the same house as him and seeing her mother every day, knowing that she'd chosen her husband over her own daughter. Deciding she'd had enough, Claire had fled, she'd had no idea where to go, no idea what to do, no clue how to survive. She'd met some other street kids, who had told her that she had to trust her gut, but she hadn't known how to do that.

At fourteen, she'd been woefully unprepared and had almost wound up being kidnapped by a pimp, hooked on drugs, and forced to turn tricks. If it hadn't been for a police officer stumbling upon her by chance that would have been her life. Instead, she'd been returned to her home, the cops had asked her if there was a reason she'd run, and while she had debated telling them about the abuse, she figured if her own mother didn't care why would two strangers.

That experience was what had made her decide to become emancipated. She'd buckled down, worked really hard in school, started doing babysitting and house cleaning for people in her neighborhood, and got out of that house as soon as she could. She'd never learned how to trust her gut though.

Claire was a thinker, she could help other people with their emotions but struggled to deal with hers, so she locked them away and kept a mandatory distance between herself and other people. It had worked up until now.

Now she had Logan, and in allowing herself to feel the full range of emotions he brought out in her it seemed her gut had also been awakened.

And her gut was telling her something was wrong.

But she wasn't sure if it was telling her that because it was right or because she was just on emotional overload right now.

After napping for barely an hour this morning, she'd cleaned up, studied the files, and managed to narrow things down to a few suspects. Instead of focusing on a link between Raymond and personnel he'd worked with, she'd stopped trying to find associations and just started looking into anyone who may have a reason to turn on their country. Specifically, she'd been focusing on anyone with a trauma in their past that could in any way be related to Afghanistan. She'd found a couple of people of interest, but she was praying that no one else was involved.

As much as leaving here made her sad because it meant leaving Logan, she was ready for this whole ordeal to be over. It was draining having to constantly look over her shoulder, afraid that someone would come after her.

With a weary sigh, she unlocked the door to the room she'd be staying in, then stepped inside, closing and locking it behind her before leaning against it and closing her eyes. She hadn't seen Logan since he'd walked her back here this morning. She knew that he had his own things to do, his own missions to prepare for, and he couldn't be her twenty-four-seven bodyguard ... and yet she wished he could be.

She felt safe with him.

It was going to be hard walking into her apartment back in San Diego. There were going to be long lonely nights ahead, peppered by nightmares of fires, and helicopter crashes, and gunfire, and there would be no one to hold her, soothe her, comfort her. She was used to that, she wasn't a stranger to nightmares, and there had never before been anyone there to offer her the comfort she needed, but now she'd had a taste of what it was like not to be alone, and she wanted more.

She and Logan could hardly just move in together when he returned to the country. They barely knew each other, and all in didn't mean moving in together when they were all but strangers. They would go on some dates, get to know one another in a normal environment where they weren't constantly fighting for their lives, she'd meet his brother, and he'd meet her few friends. Then maybe down the road, they'd be ready to take that step.

With another weary sigh, Claire pushed away from the door and opened her eyes, glad that the new room also had its own bathroom. She'd take a nice hot shower, put on her PJs, and then climb into bed and hope Logan would come soon.

She hadn't made it to her suitcase sitting on the floor beside her bed when the bathroom door opened and a man with a gun stepped through.

Shock and fear ran through her system, and she opened her mouth to scream, praying someone else was nearby to hear her, but the man moved quickly. He ran at her, grabbing her even as she spun around to make a dash for the door, and shoved her up against the wall. One large hand covered her mouth while the other held the gun to her ribs, just as Michael Sims had done early this morning.

"Make a sound, and I shoot you. I don't need you in one piece for this I just need you alive," he hissed in her ear. "Nod if you understand."

Oh, she understood all right.

Same story, different man.

Getting herself shot wasn't going to help her situation, it was better to play along, try to figure out a way to get away from him once they left her room.

Claire nodded.

"We're going to walk out of here like nothing is wrong, men are waiting to take you away, we can do this the easy way or the hard way, it's totally up to you."

Of course she was going to choose the easy way if she had to. The whole base was on alert, seeing her alone with one man should be enough to arouse suspicion.

His hand curled around her bicep hard enough that she knew it would leave bruises, but before he could walk her to the door, someone knocked on it.

They both froze.

Logan.

It had to be him, relief made her knees weak, and she

probably would have sunk to the floor if he hadn't been holding her up.

"Get rid of him," the man whispered in her ear. "If you don't, I'll kill him, plain and simple."

What?

No!

She couldn't let that happen.

"Go." He shoved her toward the door. "Get rid of him, and say anything I even think is you trying to hint at what's happening, and I'll shoot him. I don't care anymore, I've had enough, I just want to get you out of here." The man moved his tongue around his mouth weirdly, but she didn't have time to figure out what he was doing because he moved to the door and stood with his weapon aimed and ready to fire at Logan if she messed this up.

Fighting back tears, she pasted on a smile and opened the door, careful to open it just enough to peer around. Logan stood there, all big, and strong, and capable, and she longed to throw herself into his arms, but he wasn't expecting a surprise attack, and she wouldn't risk him being killed.

"Hey," he said, smiling at her.

"Hey," she returned, gripping the door handle so tightly her knuckles were white, it was the only way she could stop herself grabbing onto Logan. "Do you mind if we call a raincheck? I hardly slept earlier, and I've been going through files all day, I just want to shower and go to bed." Claire tried to sound confident and bubbly, but her heart sank when she saw Logan blank his expression. She knew what that meant. He was back to doubting her and their fledgling relationship.

"I can stay with you if you want," he said. He was obviously confused by her about-turn because this morning she hadn't wanted to let him go, and now she was refusing his presence.

"Thank you, but I think I just need some time alone."

Claire hated saying the words because she knew that she was squashing this beautiful thing between them. All she could hope was that when he learned she went missing, he would realize that she had only been saying this under duress to save his life. "Maybe we can catch up tomorrow, have lunch or something."

Logan didn't say a word, but his expression morphed back into the empty one she remembered from the helicopter, the one that had scared her. It scared her now too, only for an entirely different reason. She'd hurt him, he thought she was brushing him off, probably thought she'd been using him, stringing him along to garner his protection. He had opened himself up to her, something he never did, and she'd broken the precious trust he'd handed her.

When he turned and started to walk away, she almost called out to him, he had to be out of range, she just had to tell him that she wasn't alone in here and he would save her again.

Before she could do it something slammed into the back of her head, and the world turned black.

CHAPTER 7

September 12th

5:40 A.M.

Shark watched the sunrise with about as much enthusiasm as one might muster for watching paint dry.

The sunrise was, of course, beautiful. The way the sky changed from dark to light, the way the growing sunlight caught on the few clouds dotting the sky, turning them pink, then red, then gold, the way the whole world seemed to come alive as the sun woke up.

What ruined the beauty of the sunrise was knowing that sunset was already coming. The sun would continue its climb across the sky, the world would be bright and beautiful, but then before you knew it the darkness was back.

It always came back.

There was no way to stop it.

Kind of like life.

There may be moments with rays of sunshine, but sooner or later, they disappeared, and you were left alone in the dark once again.

Claire had been his sunshine, she'd exploded into his life, taken it over, possessed him with her sweet innocence and strong determination, and then as quickly as she'd come, she was gone. She'd brushed him off last night like seeing him was the last thing she'd wanted. It had almost been like the idea of spending the night with him again had repulsed her.

It hadn't been him reading more into what she'd said than her actual words, she'd been blatantly clear. She'd told him she didn't want him to stay with her, point-blank said that she wanted to be alone. He'd thought what they had meant more than that. She was exhausted and strung out, he knew that and didn't blame her for it, but one minute she'd been soaking up his comfort, then the next she was pushing him away.

Why?

There had to be a reason.

He'd tortured himself all night trying to figure out what that reason was. Had she just been using him all this time? She was attracted to him, he knew that, and she hadn't been lying when she'd told him about her stepfather and what he'd done to her, no one could fake the emotion he'd felt emanating from her, but had he just been a convenient target to lose her virginity to? Maybe going through a life and death situation had made her realize she could die at any moment, and she'd wanted to make sure if she did, she'd experience what sex was supposed to be.

None of that felt right though.

He hadn't felt any guilt from her, any regret, any distance, despite her dismissive words, what he'd felt was the same pull he always felt when they were in the same room. Hell, who was he kidding? They didn't even need to be in the same room for him to feel it.

So why had she sent him away?

Since he didn't have an answer to that question, and it seemed unlikely that he would be getting one any time soon, he banished thoughts of Claire and just focused on the rising sun.

Although he was aware of his team coming to join him, dropping down into the mismatched group of chairs surrounding the old barrel that was used as a makeshift firepit, he didn't acknowledge their presence. He just wanted to be alone right now, to lick his wounds, repair the damage to the hard wall he kept around himself and his emotions, and work on getting over Claire.

Because it was over between them.

He wasn't interested in whatever game she was playing. He'd told her as much, he didn't do games, they were immature and a waste of time, time that could be better spent on other things. Whatever was going on with her, she would have to sort out herself. At least he could comfort himself with the knowledge that she'd soon be leaving here, and once she did he would never have to see her again.

Small comfort that was when his entire being ached to see her. To touch her. Hold her, kiss her, make love to her.

But life didn't always give you what you wanted. He knew that firsthand. How many nights had he laid awake in bed, praying that his mother would find the strength to pack them up and leave his worthless excuse for a father? And how many mornings had he woken up in that house, forced to live through the same cycle of anger and abuse all over again? Way more than he could count.

His mother hadn't had the strength to leave, and Claire didn't have the strength to stay. Neither woman had he been able to control, but he could control himself, and he knew what he had to do for his own sanity. He had to forget about Claire, make a clean break and cut off all contact.

"Want to talk about it?" Chaos finally asked, breaking the oppressive silence.

What kind of question was that?

Did his friend suddenly forget who he was talking to?

Shark didn't talk, he acted. And right now, his action was removing himself from the entire Claire situation.

"We're assuming this has something to do with Claire since you went to see her last night then returned like ten minutes later in a foul mood," Fox added.

They could try all they wanted, but this time he wasn't getting sucked into a discussion on Claire Barrett.

"Did she say something? Do something?" Spider asked.

Shark maintained his stony silence.

"If something happened, the best thing you can do is go to her and talk it through. Take it from the guy who almost lost his chance with the woman he loved because he didn't sit her down and talk to her," Night added.

He knew they were trying to help, but really, talking about it was the last thing he wanted to do.

"What you need to do is figure out what's going on inside your head," King said. "You have to be open and upfront with what you want from women. I'm always very clear I'm only interested in something casual and short-term, I tell them that, that way no one gets hurt. But to do that, you have to know what it is you want."

"Amen," Night said, nodding vigorously. "That's how I almost lost Lavender, I wasn't sure what I wanted, and that made me push her away."

"It isn't about me," Shark exploded, annoyed that they'd been able to draw a response out of him when he had been determined to remain silent.

"So it's about her?" Fox asked.

"She sent me away, told me she wanted to be on her own."

"Women do that sometimes," Spider said. "Sometimes it's like a test. I don't think they do it consciously, at least I know Abby doesn't, but sometimes when she's upset and hurting, she needs reassurance from me that I'm there, that I'm not going anywhere, that she has my support one hundred percent."

Was that what this was?

Was it Claire trying to see if he was going to be there for her one hundred percent?

Was it a test, and had he failed it?

Did it matter?

He'd told her he wasn't into games, and consciously or not, she'd pushed him away, and to do it to see if he would stay when she told him to go, seemed immature and beneath her. He understood where Abby might need that reassurance given that Spider had left her twice, but he'd never given Claire any indication that he would bail on her.

Whatever her motives, he'd been open and upfront with her about his commitment to their relationship and his dislike of drama and games. Whatever Claire was playing at now, she could play on her own. He was done.

"It doesn't matter, I'm not interested in whatever game she's playing. It's over."

"She seemed to really like you, dude," Chaos said. "You sure you want to walk away without even talking to her? Could be a misunderstanding like last time."

Was he sure? No.

Did he know that he was making the right decision in staying away from Claire? Absolutely.

"I'm done," he said firmly. He wasn't going to cave just because his friends had suddenly decided to be team Claire.

"I think that's a shame, I liked her," Chaos said.

"Then you go ask her out," he growled at his teammate,

then turned and stalked away. It wasn't fair to take his anger and hurt at Claire out on his team, but they were goading him, not letting it go when all he wanted to do was forget he'd ever even met Claire Barrett.

That would be easier said than done.

How did you forget about someone who was imprinted on your heart?

All he had to do was think her name, and he could remember the sweet taste of her lips, the joyful sound of her laugh, and the feel of her naked body against his.

Yep, forgetting Claire wasn't going to be easy, but she'd made her choices, and now they both had to live with them.

* * *

11:52 A.M.

Claire moaned in pain as the world came spinning back into focus.

Instantly she regretted waking up. At least in unconsciousness, she was protected from the nightmare she had been tossed into.

She was starting to wonder if Raymond hadn't deliberately chosen to confess to her before ending his own life with the intent purpose of putting her in danger. At first, she'd thought his only motivation had been guilt as evidenced by the suicide in the parking lot right after the session where he had confessed his sin, but maybe there was more to it. He'd definitely ended his life because of guilt, but the telling her part hadn't been necessary. He could have left a taped confession or a written one, he could have told his commanding officer or any one of his friends.

Instead, he'd told her.

Knowing that since he wouldn't give her the name of who he'd been working with, she would have to investigate to find out, he also had to know that in doing so he was putting her in danger.

Maybe it was payback. Raymond had asked her out several times, and each time she had rebuffed him, telling him that she couldn't date a patient, but in truth, there had been more to it than that. Yes, she would never exploit her patients' trust by dating them, but something about Raymond also that put her on edge. A glint in his eyes that he wasn't the meek and mild man he portrayed himself to be.

Well, it turned out she was right about that.

And now, thanks to him, she'd been kidnapped.

Although she wanted desperately to remain in her head, where she could perhaps pretend that her situation wasn't so dire, Claire knew she couldn't do that. Danger was all around her. She could feel it, smell it, hear it, now she had to open her eyes and see it.

After all, it couldn't be any worse than she was imagining.

With a whimper, she cracked her eyelids and peeked through them to see where she had been brought. The room was dark, dank, and cold, definitely underground. She couldn't really see much, there were no windows, and she couldn't make out where the door was because she couldn't see any hint of light anywhere. Since she couldn't see, she had no idea how big the space was, but it felt small, not tiny, but not particularly big either. If she had to guess, maybe the room was about ten feet by ten feet.

Her wrists were bound together with rope, and they'd been attached to something above her head. A pipe maybe? Whatever it was was cool and smooth, it felt like metal against her hands. The angle aggravated her injured shoulder which hadn't had a chance to heal because she kept getting attacked. The pain was bad, but not worse than the pounding inside her head. She was nauseous and dizzy, but Claire wasn't sure how much of that was due to the head injury and how much was because of her panic.

She was dressed, still wearing the same cargo pants and shirt she'd been wearing when she was taken, but they'd removed her shoes and her socks. Why would they do that? Was it so that it would make it harder for her to escape since she'd have to run on bare feet?

Because that wasn't going to be much of a deterrent.

She would gladly tear up her feet if it meant getting away from here and the men who had taken her.

At least for now she was alone. The longer she stayed alone, the better her chances at getting out of this alive. Sooner or later—and she prayed it was sooner—someone would realize that she wasn't on the base any longer. She was supposed to attend meetings with Colonel Gaulding, and she had appointments with various soldiers as part of her cover on base. Although after the fire and the shooting, that cover was probably blown.

Still, someone would realize she was gone.

They had to.

If they didn't, then nobody would be looking for her. And if nobody was looking for her, then she was completely at the mercy of these men. Her only hope was that her absence had been noticed quickly, and that already there were teams out there searching for her.

Something touched her bare foot.

Something hairy.

And then she heard the sound of something scratching across the concrete floor.

A rat.

There was a rat in here with her.

And if there was one, then there were likely dozens or even hundreds.

Claire's composure shattered, and she screamed at the top of her lungs, flinging herself violently about as she lost touch with reality and tried to break free of her bonds.

Pain from her head and her shoulder flooded her system, but she couldn't stop.

It was like she was possessed.

She had to get out of here.

She had to.

She *had* to.

"Logan," she sobbed, wishing desperately that he was here. He would know what to do, he'd get her out of here, and yet right now he hated her.

The thought was so devastating that Claire began to sob in earnest. Huge, wracking sobs that seemed to be ripped from a primal place deep down inside her. The knowledge that Logan no doubt hated her guts hurt worse than anything else. She'd gladly take her beatings, the torture, maybe the rape that was probably coming, if only it meant she could get back to him and apologize and explain that she hadn't wanted to push him away, it was that or watch him die.

A cold, detached calm settled over her and her tears dried up. Claire had no idea how long she had been gone, but she knew that if she was going to survive what was coming, she had to develop a spine of steel. She had to be strong, stronger than she'd ever been called on to be in her life. She was alone here, she didn't have anyone but herself to count on, and so that had to be enough.

She would have to learn how to take her pain and her fear and lock it away. Focus only on one thing—survival.

That was all that mattered.

Claire had something to live for. She had to get back to Logan, had to explain to him what had happened, had to beg for his forgiveness. There was no way she could die without letting that happen.

It was everything to her.

She loved him. She didn't even care that it was way too soon to be thinking that, she knew how she felt. Logan was brave, he'd survived a horrible childhood and used his own personal tragedies to save others. Underneath the stone exterior was a warm, caring man who had held her in his arms and comforted her while she cried. He'd taught her so much in the short time she'd known him she owed him an explanation.

That was going to be her focus.

It was going to be all that mattered to her.

She would repeat it like a mantra in her head when they came for her. She wouldn't let anything dislodge that one thought because if she let go of it, even for a second, then all she would be was a terrified woman held captive by dangerous extremists.

That woman couldn't survive what was coming. That woman would fall apart, she'd scream and cry and beg for her life, the pain and horror would consume her until there was nothing left.

If that happened, then Logan would never know. He'd go to his grave believing that she didn't love him, and that thought broke her battered heart.

Focus on Logan.

Find a place inside her mind to hide when the pain threatened to overwhelm her.

Use her fear as a weapon, a way to keep her strong, keep her alive.

Survive.

That was what she had to do.

Pulling her legs up to her chest, Claire curled in on herself. She was hurt, she had to conserve her strength because things were going to get a whole lot worse before they got any better.

Resting her tired, aching head on her knees, Claire huddled in the corner of her cell and latched her mind onto memories of Logan. The way it felt when his hand swept across her bare skin, the way he tasted when his mouth covered hers in a kiss that scorched her very soul, the way she'd felt full—complete—when he had been buried inside her. His black eyes that at first glance seemed empty, but when you looked closer were actually brimming with emotion, his lopsided smile, his calm, steady demeanor. He was guarded, she got that, but he had allowed her to see the real him, that was a gift he didn't give many people, and she was honored to have been given it.

She loved him, and she prayed he loved her enough to forgive her for hurting him.

* * *

4:33 P.M.

So far his plan wasn't working.

Shark had thought if he could keep busy enough then he wouldn't think about Claire. He'd thought that if he kept his body pushed to the edge, then he wouldn't think about Claire. Yet all he had done was think about Claire.

During their intel meetings it had at least been easier. He'd had to pay attention to what was being discussed because there was no way he would endanger his team by not being completely informed. They didn't have enough intel on their mission yet, so they weren't being sent out, so when their meetings were done he'd decided to run.

Running wasn't his favorite which was exactly why he'd chosen it. For some reason, he felt a need to punish himself. He should be able to turn off his feelings for Claire, he'd done it for his father, for his mother, taken their betrayals and used them as tools to fortify his heart, protect himself from further pain. If he'd done it before, why couldn't he do it now?

He'd been running for almost two hours now, a simple path around the base. His team was with him, keeping a distance, respecting his need and desire for space, but also not wanting to leave him alone.

Jeffrey Tanaka had been watching him for the last fifteen minutes, and it was starting to get on his nerves. If the man had something to say, he should just say it, only Shark didn't think he'd heard the man say a single word. All Tanaka did was stand back with a scowl on his face and watch.

Always watching.

Maybe the NSA guy was the other person involved in the plot to set bombs across the US.

After another circuit, when he saw Tanaka still leaning against the side of a building watching him, he snapped.

Veering sideways, he headed straight for the man. His team obviously got where he was running and why and picked up their pace, reaching his side the same time he reached Tanaka. Fox put a hand on his shoulder, they both knew that Shark was the biggest and strongest on their team, he could throw his team leader out of the way if he wanted, he could take Tanaka too, the man was big, but he was bigger, but Fox's touch reminded him that anger over Claire wasn't worth ruining his career.

"What do you want?" he growled at Tanaka.

The man shrugged indifferently.

"You've been watching me. Why?" Shark wanted answers, if he was a suspect again, if Claire thought he was a suspect again, then he wanted to know. Maybe that would finally do the trick and finally get him to break out of his Claire-induced haze where all he could do was think about her.

"Need to know if I can trust you," Tanaka said.

Shark felt that familiar rage wash through him. So they were back to that. Claire must have found something—although he had no idea what—while looking through files yesterday that put him back on her list.

Well, if she still thought after everything they had shared that he was a traitor, he was glad she'd pushed him away. He was better off without someone like that in his life.

"Claire is missing."

Tanaka dropped that bombshell like it didn't just shatter his entire universe.

Just like that he knew.

The reason why Claire had pushed him away.

It wasn't because she thought he was a traitor or because she thought she no longer needed him, she'd told him to leave because whoever had abducted her was in the room with her. He knew Claire, and he knew that if her kidnapper had threatened to hurt him that she would go along with whatever demands he made.

He shoved Fox out of the way, grabbing Tanaka and slamming him up against the wall. "You knew Claire was missing and you just stood there and watched me for over twenty minutes?"

Tanaka just shrugged like this entire thing bored him. "Had to make sure you weren't in on it. You've been cozying up to her, for all I knew it was to make sure she didn't see you as a threat so you could make your move on her."

"I'm not the traitor," he ground out, "and I would never hurt Claire."

"I believe you. You've been in a bad mood all day, trouble in paradise?" Tanaka asked with a smirk.

"You really going to stand there and goad him?" Fox demanded. "Claire is missing."

"I'm not the one assaulting an NSA agent," Tanaka said, gesturing at Shark's hands curled into his shirt.

"When was she taken?" Spider asked as Shark forced himself to let go of the man.

"We're not sure. She retired to her room last night. She was going to work in her office this morning, go through files unless anyone came to speak to her, and was supposed to turn up for a meeting at thirteen hundred but never did. We've searched the base, but she's not here, her room is locked, but there's no answer when we knocked," Tanaka explained.

"Last night," he said, his voice strained. "She was taken last night. I went to see her around nineteen hundred, she wouldn't open the door all the way, brushed me off, told me she wanted to be alone. He was in the room with her."

Fury at himself and a crushing sense of regret stole his breath for a moment.

This was his fault.

Instead of standing and fighting for Claire when she tried to push him away, he allowed his past to cloud his judgment. He'd believed the worst of her. All day he'd been furious at her, and she'd been snatched. Snatched because she was trying to protect him.

His fist slammed into the side of the building without conscious thought.

Pain.

He needed to feel physical pain to numb the smothering emotional pain.

Claire was in danger, had been missing for eighteen hours before anyone even noticed.

He had kept trying to figure out an excuse as to why Claire had brushed him off like what they'd shared meant nothing, but none of those excuses has felt right. Now he knew why. Because they weren't true.

"You check out her room yet?" he asked Tanaka.

"Was waiting for you. Figured you were closest to her so you'd know better than anyone else if anything in the room wasn't hers," Tanaka explained.

"You think he'd leave something behind? That seems amateurish," Night said.

Tanaka shrugged. "The guy was getting desperate, his attempts at getting Claire kept failing, all he was thinking about was taking care of her, I wouldn't be surprised if he was sloppy." Tanaka said that last part like the thought of anyone being sloppy pained him.

He prayed that her abductor had been sloppy, their ability to find Claire depended on it. He'd let her down. She'd risked her own life to protect him, and he'd repaid her by thinking the worst and spending the day trying to get himself to hate her.

In this moment, Shark despised himself.

Ruthlessly, he shoved away his own emotions. They didn't matter right now. Even if Claire never forgave him for the betrayal, he would get her back alive.

Taking off for Claire's room, he heard the others following but didn't slow down, he didn't care what they were doing, this was his fault, and he would make it right. There wasn't anything he wouldn't sacrifice to find her, if he had to spend the rest of his life, he would bring her home.

When he reached Claire's room he didn't bother waiting for a key to unlock the door, they'd wasted too much time already, time Claire didn't have. Images of what might have happened to her over the last twenty hours tortured him by running in a loop through his head.

Slamming his foot into the door did little to soothe his panic, just like the pain pulsing through his hand didn't calm him. Claire's suffering was on him, no one else.

With the door opened he stepped inside, his team and

Tanaka following him. The first thing Shark saw was the blood.

Claire's blood.

A small puddle near the door.

Not enough to indicate the wound was life-threatening but that was cold comfort. Claire had been hurt, probably knocked unconscious to make it easier to transport her.

Her clothes had been dumped out on the bed, and her suitcase was missing. Claire was probably just small enough that she could have been shoved inside it, meaning whoever took her could just walk out of her room with her body and nobody would be the wiser.

Willing down the tidal wave of emotions that threatened to knock him down, he forced himself to see through the fear, the guilt, and the terror welling inside him to look for anything that would help them find her.

There.

Something metallic.

He moved closer, scooped it up into his hand.

It was a key with some sort of insignia on the top.

It wasn't much, but right now, this was the only thing he had to help him find the woman who owned his heart.

* * *

8:47 P.M.

Finally.

Finally, he was back in control again.

Not being in complete control of the situation with Claire Barrett had left him with an unsettled feeling he hadn't been able to shake. He'd played this so carefully, been smart the whole way along, if it wasn't for Raymond and his sudden attack of conscience, no one would ever have even known what he was doing. Nothing would link him to the attacks when they started coming, nothing that anyone would find anyway.

But Claire had the power to ruin all of his hard work.

Well, she *had*.

She didn't anymore though.

Now he had her in his possession, she would be interrogated, he'd find out exactly what she knew, what she had told everyone else, and then he would know what damage control he had to perform.

He'd been waiting all day to get here to check on her, confirm with his own eyes that she was here, that he wasn't going to have to worry about her wreaking havoc any longer. He couldn't just disappear at the same time Claire had, that would have been like waving a beacon above his head asking everyone to look at him and brand him the traitor.

Not that he saw himself as a traitor.

No, what he saw himself as was someone who was righting a wrong. Loss changed a person, changed them in a way that nothing else ever could, and that's what had happened to him.

It had taken most of the day for anyone to even realize that Claire was no longer on the base. He'd thought that the SEAL would go looking for her this morning, he'd been running around after her like a lost puppy, but apparently, the man had instead spent the day sulking about Claire's brush off last night, and in the end, it had been the NSA guy who'd figured out that Claire was long gone.

Still, now they knew, and the entire base was buzzing with the abduction news, which meant that finding time to slink away had been difficult. He couldn't leave too early, but also couldn't wait until it was too late because he knew that they would be expecting that the man responsible for Claire's abduction to wait till midnight or the early hours of the morning to slip away.

While he wouldn't say that he was out of the woods yet, he certainly felt like he was on the home straight. If he made it through the next couple of days, then everything would be fine. They would quickly realize that Claire would never be found, she was his now, and once he got the answers he needed from her, he would decide what to do with her. He wasn't interested in keeping her, he wasn't interested in a sex slave, but he could probably make a bundle selling her. She was a beautiful woman, and while he himself wasn't interested in abusing her, he wasn't above selling her to get rid of her regardless of what he knew would happen to her when he did.

"Have you given her anything to drink?" he asked as he stalked through the house to the living room where Anvar and five of his men were lounging around a table, drinking, smoking, and playing cards.

"You said you didn't want us going down there, so we didn't," Anvar replied, somewhat sullenly.

Not wanting to waste time arguing with his partner, he merely nodded, pleased that they'd followed directions this time instead of going off on their own and making things worse. The last thing he needed now that everything was coming together was for Anvar to decide on his own that he knew what was best and go ahead and do it.

That wasn't flying.

Anvar might have started this and supplied most of the manpower and the money, but he had supplied vital intel and support, orchestrated weapon thefts, and had them delivered to Anvar. He'd helped plan everything, and without him, Anvar wouldn't be able to achieve what he wanted. The man should start displaying some gratitude.

"Good, she's been here for twenty-four hours now, you can take her some water and something to eat," he ordered.

Anvar's men looked to him first, not moving until Anvar nodded, then they stood and grabbed food and water for Claire. It irked him that Anvar's men didn't obey him, didn't respect him as an equal. He had his own men and women, but most of them had been taken into custody following the fire.

That was Michael Sims' fault.

Sims had acted too hastily and too elaborately. In theory, the fire and shooting were a good way to get Claire isolated, but they also created too much chaos and involved too many people, making actually abducting her harder. If the man had just talked to him first, he would have said that keeping things quiet, targeting Claire when she was alone, was the much smarter move.

It was like if you didn't do something yourself then it didn't get done right.

He'd wanted Claire kept without food or water for the first twenty-four hours because he needed her to know that there was nothing about her situation that she controlled. Control was a part of her past, her future would be whatever he decided, and once she was sold her owner would do with her whatever he pleased. Claire may as well start making the transition now, no one was coming for her. She may have found the traitor, but she wouldn't be celebrating that discovery, nor would she be telling anyone about it.

But he needed her to have some strength for tomorrow's interrogation, so she would eat and drink tonight, and then once he found out what she knew he would decide what to do with her. Maybe instead of selling her, he'd give her to Anvar and his men. As much as it annoyed him to have to work with them he had to admit that they had given him the opportunity to get the revenge he'd dreamed about in a way he would never have been able to achieve on his own. Although he hated to admit it, he did owe Anvar for all of this, even if they had worked together, so maybe he'd give them Claire as a show of his own gratitude.

Anvar's men moved the table and pushed aside a rug, revealing a trapdoor. They opened it quickly, clearly unconcerned that Claire might present any sort of threat.

At the light that spilled into the cellar, Claire moaned in pain, and knowing that she wouldn't be able to see at the moment, the light would have temporarily blinded her since her eyes would have become accustomed to the dark, he moved closer so he could see her. She was still wearing her clothes. He didn't want anyone touching her until he had a chance to interrogate her, so he'd left strict instructions to keep her isolated and clothed, but missing her shoes. He'd thought that would add a vulnerability to her that would keep her compliant. Her arms were restrained above her head, tied to a metal pipe, and she was huddled in on herself. It was cold down there, he could feel the chill from up here. While he briefly debated having a blanket tossed down there he decided against it. Again, he needed her weak tomorrow so she would be less resistant to his questions.

One of Anvar's men climbed down a ladder and untied the rope binding her to the pipe but left her wrists tied together. He threw the water and the food at her without a word, then climbed back up the ladder.

The trapdoor fell closed with a *thunk* that seemed to reverberate through him. He'd expected Claire to beg and scream, plead for her freedom, for mercy, but apparently, she was smarter than he had anticipated. For a brief moment, that caused an emotion almost like regret to filter through him, but it passed quickly.

This was what he wanted to do.

He wanted to bring pain and suffering to the country that

had robbed him of so much. His country believed that they were number one, that they had the right to meddle in cultures they didn't understand, to tell others what they had to believe and how they had to live their lives.

Because of that arrogance, his life had been destroyed.

It seemed only fair that he should pay back the people who had ruined his life by inflicting the same damage. A series of bombs at strategic locations across the US was the perfect way to do that.

An eye for an eye and all that.

Very pleased with himself and everything he had accomplished, destroying the country he despised from the inside out, he stretched his back, cracked his knuckles, and made arrangements to return the following day to interrogate his prisoner.

CHAPTER 8

September 13th

9:16 A.M.

The cold had seeped inside her to the point where Claire could think of little else.

She supposed that was a blessing of sorts, it was hard to be terrified out of your mind when your entire focus was trying to curl in on yourself enough to still the tremors that constantly rippled through your body. She had her knees pressed to her chest and her face pressed against them, her feet were achingly cold, but her pants weren't long enough to cover them, and her hands had long since gone numb from a combination of the cold and being trapped above her head.

Her entire body ached. With her hands bound as they were, she was forced to sit in basically the same position for hours. Sometimes she'd struggle to her feet to give her arms and her injured shoulder a break, but she had to stand bent over which just made her back spasm after a short while. That, plus the agonizing pain of blood flow returning to her arms and hands, pins and needles on steroids, meant she tried to get up just once an hour, or at least what she thought was about once an hour.

All she'd been given was one meal and a bottle of water, which she'd drunk far too quickly and had been merely a patch for her crushing thirst. She'd taken advantage of having her arms free by walking briskly around the room as soon as she'd wolfed down her food. The man had pulled the ladder back up with him when he left, and she hadn't found any other ways out, but at least she'd been able to pee in the corner so she didn't have to go in her pants. Besides the fact that peeing her pants would have been humiliating, there was the practical problem of the wet clothes quickly getting chilled in the cold cellar, making her colder in the process.

Now, though, she needed to go again, but she was desperately holding it in.

Why had they brought her here just to keep her locked in a cellar?

Was it to break her down?

Make her weak and vulnerable so she would be easier to deal with?

If that was the reason, then it was working.

Her earlier strength and determination to be strong, to focus on getting back to Logan so she could apologize for pushing him away had long since faded. Now her determination came in waves. One moment she would be sure she could do this, that she could survive until someone found her, but then the next, she would come crashing down as the reality that the chances of her being found were one step above zero.

Then would come the tears and the panic, she would feel like she was suffocating.

The sudden light made her moan, and Claire squeezed her eyes closed against the stabbing in her head. The severity of the headache had receded, but it was still there, and the light seemed to shoot straight through it.

Although her eyes were still closed, she could hear the thump of the ladder and then the sound of someone walking toward her.

Part of her wanted to be childish, keep her eyes closed so she couldn't see the monster stalking her way, but she wasn't a little girl anymore, and she knew that this monster was real, not a figment of her imagination. The only way to deal with such a monster was to stand your ground. Claire wasn't sure how she was going to do that, but she would have to figure it out.

Opening her eyes, she saw a man kneeling before her. He had a knife in his hand, and even though she knew he was going to use it to cut her free, she couldn't help but flinch when the blade moved toward her.

The man noticed and smiled smugly at her as he cut through the rope binding her wrists to the pipe. For a moment, the pain in her arms overtook her fear as the deadened limbs dropped down to rest on her lap. Her shoulder screamed in agony, from all the repeated abuse it kept getting, Claire wouldn't be surprised if the joint never returned to one hundred percent.

Not that that would matter if she died in here.

She hoped that he was just here to bring her more food and water, but the man roughly grabbed her arm and dragged her to her feet. She swayed unsteadily, her body falling against the only stable thing nearby; the man. He pulled her close, and her stomach revolted at the feel of his hot breath against her cheek.

He said something to her that she couldn't understand, but the meaning was clear when he reached out and grabbed her breast, squeezing it roughly, and Claire had to bite her lip to prevent her from voicing her distress. Things were going to get a whole lot worse than this, and she had to get through it, she had to stay strong. She had to.

Someone shouted from above, and the man quickly released her breast but kept his hold on her.

Leaning in close, he said in heavily accented English, "He say we have you after."

The words made her shiver, and she couldn't quite hold back her whimper. She knew that the possibility of her being raped by her captors was high and yet hearing him voice it suddenly made it very real.

How was she going to do this?

Was anyone even looking for her yet?

She had no idea how long she'd been here, but she knew each hour that passed her chances of being found dropped dramatically.

Could she really accept she was going to die here?

Claire wanted to cling to hope, but sitting here cold and hurting for hours in the dark had drained away that hope.

She was draped over the man's shoulder, and he awkwardly climbed up the ladder and deposited her in a chair in the middle of a large kitchen. The room wasn't modern by American standards, but neither was it primitive. The walls and the floor were stone, and there was a wooden table and chairs which had been shoved to the side. Wooden counters bordered two walls, and there was a large range against a third. Sunlight streamed through two windows, one above the sink and another on the adjacent wall.

The rope binding her wrists was cut and then each of her arms were tied to the chair's arms, her legs were likewise bound to the chair's legs, and although Claire knew what was coming, she couldn't help but be temporarily distracted by the warmth of the room. It was the first time since she'd woken up in the cellar that she'd been even close to warm and her body eagerly absorbed the sensation even knowing that this was but a brief reprieve in her suffering.

There were six other people in the room with her. Four of them lounged around the table, watching her with interest. It was clear in each of their expressions that they were looking forward to getting their hands on her.

The fifth man, one she recognized as the leader of The Atash, Anvar Mir, stood just to the left of her chair, his eyes were dead, empty, devoid of emotion, and she knew that he would enjoy inflicting pain. The final man was the one she had been sent here to find, and she knew exactly what he wanted from her.

Answers.

He wanted to know if she had told anyone about him.

"Ms. Barrett," he said, nodding at her in greeting, "it didn't have to end up this way. I told you to leave, you chose to stay, I'm sure you understand why I had to bring you here."

Claire knew that anything she said to this man was only going to be the wrong thing, so the safest bet was probably to keep her mouth shut. Besides, he needed to know what she knew and who she'd told. Self-preservation was a strong thing. The only way he knew for sure that he was in the clear was to get answers from her. If she didn't give him those answers, then he had to keep her alive.

"Was I on the list of people you were looking into, Ms. Barrett?" he asked.

She pressed her lips into a line and remained silent.

He nodded at Anvar, and even though she was prepared for the blow to the side of her head, it still rattled through her, drawing a cry of pain from her lips.

"We can do this the hard way or the easy way, Ms.

Barrett," the man told her, but she knew that wasn't really true. This was only stage one of her descent into Hell, and she knew once his interrogation was over she'd be handed over to the Afghani men, whether she answered his questions or not.

Her only chance was to gamble with the fact that he was driven to know what she knew so he knew what damage control he had to perform if he wanted to remain a free man. It was a big gamble and one that was going to bring her pain, but she believed it was her best bet at remaining alive.

"Have you told anyone that you suspect me?"

This time she braced herself for the pain of the coming blow. A fist rammed into her stomach, shoving the air from her lungs, and she gagged and choked as the world spun around her.

"Do they know? Do they know it's me?" he demanded, his voice rising as his desperation bled through.

She might be afraid for her life, but he was equally as afraid for his. Claire took some grim satisfaction in that even as a fist caught her in the cheek, and then her nose. She could feel hot sticky blood on her face, knew her nose was broken, possibly her cheekbone as well.

Blows kept coming, to her head, her stomach, her chest, and she could hear the questions repeated over and over again. What did she tell anyone about him? Would they be coming for him? Did they know it was him? Did they believe Sims was the mastermind and that no one else was involved?

It got easier and easier to keep her mouth shut as the pain took over, her entire body shook violently, she knew she was crying, thought she could hear her voice echoing in her head begging them to stop. Images of Logan flashed through her mind, he told her to be strong, promised that he was coming, but he was just a hallucination. He couldn't save her.

No one could save her.

Her fate had been sealed the moment Raymond walked into her office.

Pain, suffering, torture, and death.

That was all her future held.

* * *

7:22 P.M.

An abundance of energy burned through him, a mixture of guilt and fury, with a heavy addition of exhaustion. Shark had barely slept last night. Every time he closed his eyes, images of what Claire was enduring at that same second tortured him. The guilt was a relentless thing inside him, reminding him that if he had trusted Claire—who had given him no reason not to—then she would be safe now instead of in the hands of a traitor who intended to help an extremist cell set bombs across his country.

He had vowed to get Claire safely out of the desert, and he'd done it. He'd made that same vow to get her back alive now, and he prayed that he would be able to fulfill it.

His team along with another SEAL team approached the farmhouse, but Shark already had a sinking feeling in his gut. There were no lights on in the house, and everything was too quiet. It didn't look like anyone was there.

Still, it was the only lead they had, and they had to follow through on it.

If they were lucky, Claire would be tied up here somewhere, left behind while the man who had abducted her had fled.

That wasn't likely, and yet Shark clung to that hope as they spread out and entered the building. The farmhouse was three floors, a large kitchen, a living area, and a bathroom downstairs. Three bedrooms on the second floor, and the third floor with two additional bedrooms that looked like they had belonged to children at some point, as there were toys scattered about.

There was no one there.

With the building cleared, they all returned to the kitchen and Fox flipped the lights on. As soon as the room was illuminated they all noticed the trapdoor. There was a chair in the middle of the kitchen, blood on the floor around it, and Shark's stomach dropped when he saw it.

If they were right and this was where Claire had been taken, then chances were that was her blood.

He fought the urge to be sick and instead whipped his weapon up to aim it at the trapdoor. A rug had been hastily thrown over it, but in their hurry to leave—no doubt tipped off by the traitor on the base—they hadn't put it down properly, which meant the trapdoor was still visible.

Was Claire in there?

Had they got what they wanted from her then discarded her body like garbage?

Could she still be alive?

Covering Spider and Sam "Mozart" Reed from the other team, as they approached the trapdoor, Mozart flicked the rug out of the way then Spider grabbed the handle and swung the trapdoor open. It was dark down there, and no bullets came flying out at them, still they cautiously checked out the space to be safe.

There was a ladder leaning against one wall, but Shark didn't bother waiting for it, he jumped down into the cellar, desperate to see if Claire had been left down there. Kason "Benny" Sawyer and Night dropped down with him, but it only took a second to determine that the cellar was empty.

Frustration speared through him, he'd been so hopeful that Claire would be here and that they had got to her in time, but she wasn't here, maybe never had been, and they were back to square one. They still didn't know who the traitor was, but the key that had been found in Claire's room had led them to this farmhouse.

It had to be related, but either they were too late or they'd been wrong, and Claire had never been brought here.

"Ropes," Benny said, crouching by a pipe in the corner.

"And someone peed over here," Night said from the opposite side of the room.

"So someone was kept down there," Matthew "Wolf" Steel, the leader of the other SEAL team said from the kitchen above them.

"And recently," Night added.

"Looks like they were kept tied to the pipe," Benny said.

Had it been Claire?

There was no way to know for sure, but it made sense. The key had led them here, and there were obvious signs a prisoner had been in here recently, plus what was in the kitchen indicated the prisoner had been interrogated and they knew that the traitor would want to know what Claire knew.

The thought of Claire tied up down here made his blood turn to ice. It was cold in here, and the stone floor would have been uncomfortable to sit on. If her wrists had been bound to the pipe based on her height, it would have meant she was forced to sit on the ground, arms above her head. Not only would that be extremely painful as blood flow was restricted, but her injured shoulder would have caused her excruciating pain.

Shark swore viciously and would have punched the stone wall of the cellar if his hand wasn't still throbbing from his last tantrum. At least he'd pulled the last punch enough that he hadn't broken his hand, the last thing he needed was to be benched.

"We don't know for sure it was her," Benny said softly.

Only of course they did know.

It was her.

He knew it.

He could feel her fear, her pain, her overwhelming terror etched into every molecule of the room.

"We'll take a sample of the blood, we can't get a DNA test done, but we can at least see if the blood type matches Claire's," Christopher "Abe" Powers said.

Shark nodded, feeling numb now. He couldn't deal with anything else, couldn't deal with the horror of knowing that Claire was suffering because of him. How was he supposed to live with himself?

The ladder was lowered down, and he climbed up on autopilot. Even if they could get Claire back alive, she would never forgive him for allowing this to happen to her.

Back in the kitchen, his gaze fixated on the blood on the floor. Like the blood in her room back at the base, there wasn't enough to indicate that someone had bled out in here, but there was enough to know that someone had suffered.

Panic clawed inside him, trying to rip him apart from the inside out. It had been a long time since he'd felt panic, not since he was a very small boy, too small to fight back against his father. He'd used that panic to grow strong but now it threatened to overwhelm him.

"It's a good thing they took her with them when they left," King reminded him.

Shark just nodded dully.

A good thing the woman he was falling in love with was still in the hands of violent extremists. While he knew what King meant, it certainly didn't feel like there was a single good thing about this entire situation.

"We'll get her back, man," Chaos said, slapping him on the back. "I know it doesn't feel like it right now, and looking at that ..." He waved a hand at the chair in the center of the room, the shorn ropes discarded on the floor around it, and the spatters of blood. "But none of us are giving up on you or on Claire."

"Never," Faulkner "Dude" Cooper agreed.

While Shark appreciated that, it didn't ease the knot of panic sitting heavily on his chest. They might never find Claire, and even if they did it could take weeks, months, or even years. Abby had been gone for fourteen months before they'd found her quite by accident.

"Guys, someone's coming," Hunter "Cookie" Knox said from where he'd been standing by the door.

Immediately they all snapped to attention. They flicked the lights out and positioned themselves so they could apprehend their suspect as soon as he entered the building.

"Anvar?" a tentative voice called out. A woman's voice. That was the last thing he had been expecting.

Neither he nor his team moved.

A moment later, the lights were turned on.

A woman stood, dressed in traditional Afghani clothes, clutching a small infant in her arms. Who was she?

She froze when she saw them, hesitated for a moment, then spun around as though deciding fleeing was her best option.

Abe had circled her so he was between her and the door. The woman looked from Abe to the rest of them, circling her with their weapons aimed at her and her child, and she backed up against the nearest wall.

"You will not stop us," she cried out in Dari. "It is coming, and we will prevail, Insha'Allah."

"Ma'am, place the baby on the floor and kneel down, hands on your head," Wolf instructed the woman in Dari.

Instead of complying, the woman laughed hysterically, smiling at them manically as she shook her head. "We will come in flames, you cannot destroy us, and you cannot stop us. Insha'Allah, Insha'Allah, Insha'Allah."

Since she was holding an infant, it would be harder to restrain her, but Shark nodded at Abe, and the two of them sprung toward the woman. Shark wrapped an arm around her neck, pulling her back and off-balance, while Abe snatched the baby.

The woman thrashed in his hold like a wildcat, but she was much smaller than him, and Shark shoved her up against the wall, yanked her arms behind her back, and secured her wrist with zip ties.

Her wild gaze met his when he spun her around. "The American whore will be the first, but she won't be the last."

He froze.

Claire.

She had to be talking about Claire.

These people were into blowing things up which meant wherever they'd taken Claire, they intended her to be the first death in their crusade to seek revenge on the US and presumably attempt to take over the world.

CHAPTER 9

September 14th

11:32 A.M.

She still couldn't get warm.

Different location, same problems.

No, strike that, she'd much rather be back in that cellar, cold, and hurting, and alone. Being left alone was so much better than this.

Claire shivered and pressed her back closer into the corner, anything to get as far away from the bed as she could. Her entire body was on fire from the pain of her beating. Her ribs had already been bruised in the crash, and now she was pretty sure that at least one was broken. She couldn't take a breath without it feeling like someone was sticking a knife into her chest. Her face hurt too, and her stomach, her wrists and ankles were torn up from fighting against the ropes, and then there were the bruises from being held down.

She shivered again, wanting to weep for everything she'd been through and everything she knew she still had to endure before they killed her.

No longer was she thinking about surviving this, she wasn't, she knew that. There would be no getting back to Logan, no explaining to him why she'd sent him away, no apologizing, no seeing if he could forgive her so they could have a future. Claire wasn't leaving this place alive, she had accepted that, just like she had accepted that she was going to die with Logan hating her.

All she prayed for now was a quick death.

She couldn't survive much longer like this.

She didn't want to.

Claire had been unconscious by the time they'd untied her from the chair in the kitchen and brought her here. This room had a window with a tattered curtain. She'd looked out of it at one point, but her sense of hopelessness had grown when she'd seen no other houses or any signs of life nearby. Wherever they were it was remote, no one was going to stumble upon her, no one was going to find her here. She was on her own in a way she'd never experienced before.

She thought she knew what it was like to be alone, she'd lost her father, and when her mother remarried, in a way, Claire had lost her too. Then had come the abuse and her mother's reaction to it, and Claire had felt like she had no one, but that wasn't quite true. She'd gone to school, had teachers she liked and respected, a few friends, not close ones but people to talk to, and she'd had jobs, walking dogs, and babysitting, and anything else an underage kid could do. There had been people in her life, so she hadn't been truly alone, not like this.

Here, she was locked in a room. There was a metal cuff

around her left ankle, secured to a chain embedded in the concrete floor. The only other people here were the men who had abducted her, who had beaten her, who had ...

Her gaze darted to the bed and then skittered quickly away. She didn't want to touch it again, although she knew at some point that choice would be taken out of her hands. Last night she'd slept on the floor. The cold, hard concrete had aggravated her injuries, but despite the fact the bed had a thin mattress, a dirty pillow, and even a blanket that would have offered her a little warmth, she'd chosen the floor and would continue to do so.

The longer she spent here, the number she became.

Yes, she hurt, yes she was hungry, thirsty, cold, and terrified.

She felt all of those things, and yet they were fading away as a haze settled over her. It was like being in a fog, you knew that there were other things out there, but it was hard to see them because all you could see was the fog. That was how she felt right now, she knew that there was more pain coming, culminating in her death, but right now, there was a silent cloud surrounding her.

She liked it this way.

The fog was peaceful, quiet, soothing almost. It smoothed away the edges of the horror she was living because right now, she couldn't quite see it.

Maybe it was shock, maybe it was the injuries she had sustained, maybe it was simply acceptance of her fate, but whatever it was, she wasn't fighting it. If she had to suffer a horrific death, no rule said she had to experience every second of it. If she could allow her mind to float away, then why shouldn't she do that?

It was definitely the best option she had.

That should be her focus.

Retreating into the dark recesses of her mind where nothing and no one could touch her.

If she found a place deep enough and dark enough then she could stay there, she could deaden her emotions, she could pretend she was somewhere else.

With Logan.

He was still her happy place even if he wouldn't think it. If she tried really hard, she could imagine his large hands skimming her body, smoothing away the pain of her bruises and broken bones. She could imagine him touching his lips to each injury in the softest of kisses, then cradling her gently in his arms, promising her that he would take care of her.

Claire could feel herself slipping away, but one tiny part of her brain was screaming at her. Warning her that if she did this, if she checked out, drifted too far away, then she wouldn't be able to come back. It would be breaking a rope that couldn't be repaired. Once it was done it would be done, she'd be gone for good, and if by some miracle she was found and survived against all the odds, then she'd never be able to rebuild her life.

Sometimes once you did something, there was no going back.

"No one is coming," she reminded herself aloud. "Do it."

But the more she tried to let go, the more her brain rebelled against the notion, insisting that it wasn't the way.

Giving up wasn't who she was.

It wasn't what she did.

There hadn't seemed like a way to have a future the first night her stepfather had come into her bedroom. She'd felt lost, broken, like her life was over before it had even really begun. But she hadn't accepted that, she'd fought to get out of that house, get the job she wanted, make a home for herself, and then over these last few days she'd even found a way to let a man into her life and her heart.

She hadn't given up.

She'd fought even though it had seemed pointless at first.

Claire hadn't given up when she'd woken up after the helicopter crash, hadn't even considered it as an option. She hadn't given up when those two men had accosted her in the mountains, hadn't given up when Logan had been shot, hadn't given up after someone had left the note under her door, or attacked her as she walked to her room, or set a fire to ambush her.

She hadn't given up any of those times. So why was she allowing herself to give up now?

"Come on, Claire, you're better than this," she roused herself.

And she was.

She was stronger than she gave herself credit for. In the end, no one else might ever know that she had fought as hard as she could to escape, she might—probably would—still die anyway, but *she* would know that she fought, and that would be enough. The only person she had to rely on right now was herself, which meant that the only person she could let down was herself, and she wasn't going to do that.

Somehow, she found strength she hadn't known she had and pushed to her feet. The chain binding her to the floor was long and allowed her to roam the entire room. Besides the bed, there was a table and two chairs, and two buckets, one for her to use as a toilet and one with water for her to clean herself.

Maybe she could use the chair to knock someone out when they brought her food?

But that would still leave her chained up.

It was the chain that was the real problem. If it had been rope, she might have been able to untie it or find something to saw through it, but she couldn't do that with metal. She knew she was outnumbered here, and that they were somewhere remote, but Claire thought her best chance at escape was to wait until they unchained her and then have a weapon she could use against them.

She didn't necessarily need to take them all down, she just needed to get away from whoever unchained her. She could incapacitate them, then go out the window and run, find a place to hide. She had one thing working in her favor, so far she hadn't really fought back. They thought she was weak, an easy prisoner, they wouldn't be expecting her to try anything.

Well, she was going to prove them wrong.

She was either going to escape or die trying.

Invigorated, Claire began a systematic search of her room, she could do this, she knew she could.

* * *

2:40 P.M.

Shark paced outside the interrogation room where Hanifah Mir had been sitting ever since they'd brought her back here yesterday. He'd wanted to start the interrogation immediately. The woman knew what was going on, knew about Claire, had admitted that she was involved in the terrorist cell. The longer they let her sit there, the higher the chance they wouldn't get Claire back alive.

Standing there doing nothing while answers sat just on the other side of the door was killing him.

Tanaka had refused to start the interview until he was ready, Shark hadn't bothered to listen to the NSA guy's reasons, he didn't care what they were. There was only one thing he cared about, and that was finding Claire.

His team and Wolf's were all here with him, lounging against the walls. He'd told them already they didn't have to stay with him, he wasn't going to fall apart. He didn't fall apart. It was why everyone called him Shark. He was nothing but an emotionless killing machine, he did his job, rid the world of evil, and that was it. Beyond his team and their families, he didn't have friends, didn't have much of a relationship with his brother, hadn't had much of one with his mother before she had passed away.

He had nothing.

Then all of a sudden he had Claire.

He didn't know how it happened. He certainly hadn't been looking for a woman when he got onto that helicopter, and there was no way he could have foreseen the crash and everything that had happened since, just like he couldn't have foreseen falling for Claire. But he had.

Fallen right off the deep end.

She'd given him things he hadn't even realized he needed or wanted. She filled a dark hole inside him, she settled the anger he'd harbored since the first time he watched his father slam a fist into his mother's stomach. He still remembered that day, he'd been four. He was supposed to keep an eye on his brother, who'd been two, while their mom took a shower before taking them to daycare and going to work. Instead, he'd gotten distracted by a spider scuttling across the ceiling, he'd watched it instead of Shawn, who had gotten into the kitchen cabinets and proceeded to open every packet of every food he could find.

When his father had staggered out of bed and found the mess he'd lost it, his mother had come running in from the bathroom, she'd apologized, promised to get it all cleaned up and replace everything, but of course his dad couldn't resist lashing out. He'd punched his wife in the stomach, shoving the air from her lungs and her breakfast from her stomach. She'd thrown up all over the floor, then collapsed into her vomit, writhing on the floor, trying to breathe through the pain.

That day something inside him had broken.

It had gotten worse over the years, watching the abuse, begging his mother to leave and take him and Shawn with her, knowing she never would. In the dark recesses of his brain maybe he'd thought if he could save enough people, prevent enough people from being hurt, maybe he could undo what his father had done. Closing himself off had been the only way he could survive. There had been too many emotions inside him, in a way he absorbed the pain of each person he had protected. The more he internalized their suffering when he stepped in to help them the more his emotions grew, and the more they grew the more he shut down.

Then along came Claire, and suddenly, he felt something good, light.

How was he supposed to go on after getting a taste of that? Especially knowing he was to blame for everything that happened to her.

"If I let you come in there with me, are you going to be able to keep your mouth shut?" Tanaka demanded as he strolled down the hall.

Shark immediately straightened. "You letting me go in while you interrogate her?" That was better than he'd been hoping, he'd thought Tanaka would make him stay outside, expected him not to even let him listen in.

"If you can stand in the corner of the room and look like that, all angry and quietly intimidating, then you can come in," Tanaka replied.

"Man, he has your number," Chaos joked in an attempt to lighten the mood.

Only Shark wasn't interested in improving his mood, his entire focus was on finding Claire. "You want me in there to scare her."

"You're the perfect man for the job," Tanaka said with a half-smile.

"Let's go," he said, already heading for the door.

"We'll be right out here," Fox told him, and everyone nodded their support.

Inside the room, Hanifah Mir sat cuffed to a table in the middle of the room. She'd been given nothing to eat since arriving here and nothing to drink other than a couple of bottles of water. Despite being in this room for going on twenty-four hours, the woman sat straight in her chair, her eyes spitting fire at them as they entered.

Shark delivered a glare of his own to the woman before stalking to one of the corners and leaning back against the wall, his arms crossed over his chest. He knew he was an intimidating presence with his height and size, and he let every ounce of the darkness inside him show on his face.

"Your brother is Anvar Mir, correct?" Tanaka asked Hanifah in Dari.

"Anvar is going to bring about a new world," Hanifah said, her voice strong and fierce despite the fact that she had to be starving and exhausted.

"We know about his plans to plant bombs across the US," Tanaka said. The man had slid into a chair on the opposite side of the table. He lounged in his seat, looking relaxed and completely at ease.

"That is merely the beginning," Hanifah shot back, sounding proud of her brother and his plans to destroy another country.

Tanaka nodded agreeably. "I have no doubt about that.

Anvar has big plans. What about you, though, what are your plans?"

The question seemed to throw the woman, and she cocked her head quizzically. "I am to serve Anvar and my husband."

"Ah, yes, of course, that's your place as a woman," Tanaka agreed.

"Right." Hanifah nodded, although she still looked at the NSA guy like he was trying to trick her. Shark certainly hoped Tanaka was trying to trick the woman because he wasn't here to listen to them discuss the role of women in Muslim culture.

"You're also in charge of raising the children, right? Have you given any thought to what will happen to your baby if you go down along with your brother and your husband?" Tanaka asked. "Because that's what's going to happen, Hanifah. You're involved in the abduction and torture of an American citizen. You've admitted to being part of a plot to set bombs on American soil. I know this is all Anvar, it's his plan, this is all him, you don't have to go down with him. If you give us information that leads us to the location of the kidnapped psychologist, then we can make a deal. You'll still be around to raise your child."

Hanifah looked at him as though he were an idiot. "It's a girl. My husband and my brother wanted a son, a son who would follow in their footsteps, who would make the world a better place. Who would help to lead his people to victory. You can keep the girl, she is a disappointment."

So much for using her baby as leverage to get her to talk.

Shark took a step forward, and Hanifah's gaze danced in his direction, it was almost imperceptible, but he noticed the way she shifted slightly away from him. She was afraid of him. Good. He could use that to his advantage.

Taking another step toward her, he planted his hands on

the table, leaned in until his face was mere inches from his. "Who is your husband? It's not one of your brother's men, is it? Your husband is American, military, he's the traitor that the psychologist was brought here to find."

Hanifah looked fearfully at him, not offering an answer, but he knew he was right. He'd seen the baby, and it was too pale-skinned to be the child of two Afghanis. It made sense, Anvar was working with the traitor, a man who needed a reason to turn on his country. What better reason than because he had converted to Islam, that he was married to an Afghani woman who'd had his child?

"Who is he, Hanifah? Who is your husband?" Tanaka asked. From the man's tone, he knew that the NSA guy believed the same thing he did. They had sat before them the wife of the traitor. Even if the woman wouldn't give up her husband's name, when word got to him that they had his wife in custody, he was sure they could use that to bring him in.

"I will never tell you, infidels," she spat the word out. "He is one of us now. He is going to help to bring you down, he wants to be part of bringing in the new world order. He has chosen the side of Allah. He is a hero to me, and to my people, I will never turn on him."

"You won't have to," Shark said smugly. "Once he knows we have you and his daughter here, he won't be able to stay away. If you're not smart enough to make a deal for information to help us find Claire, I know he will be. Self-preservation is stronger than any religious affiliation. You're going to rot in a prison cell for the rest of your miserable life, and when I find your brother, I'm going to kill him for what he did to the woman I love."

CHAPTER 10

September 15th

8:45 A.M.

Despite her weakness and the exhaustion that was ever-present, tugging at her mind and sometimes pulling her under for brief bouts of restless sleep, Claire was actually feeling much better today.

Better mentally.

Her bruised and battered body still ached, especially her broken face and ribs, but determination continued to flow through her blood. She was not going to give up, it was as simple as that. As soon as she had decided that she would not allow these men to break her spirit, a weird sort of strength seeped into her.

Last night she'd fought the men when they'd dragged her to the bed, she'd earned herself several more blows and new aches and pains, but it was worth it. She'd screamed at them that she was never going to break, that it didn't matter what they did to her, she wasn't going to give them the satisfaction of killing her spirit. She was their prisoner in body only, but her mind and soul were her own, and she was going to do whatever was necessary to protect them with everything she had.

She was going to do Logan proud.

When he eventually found her—and she had no doubt that whether he hated her or not, when he learned she was missing obligation would have him and his team doing whatever necessary to find her—even if she was already dead, her broken body would tell the story of how hard she had fought.

That comfort was what had kept her going yesterday. There had been nothing useful she had been able to find for a weapon, but she had spent a lot of time hammering away at the concrete around where the chain was embedded in the floor. Since she didn't have anything to use as a hammer, she was using the chain itself to batter away at the floor.

It was working too.

Slowly but surely the concrete was starting to crumble.

Depending on how long they kept her here, she might actually be able to get herself free. That thought was what kept her going when her hands cramped so badly that tears leaked out of her eyes, but she didn't give up.

She was *never* going to give up.

The door to her room opened, and Claire quickly dropped her chain and shuffled slightly so she was sitting close enough to the damage she was doing to the floor that no one would be able to notice.

The man, she thought his name was Anvar, carried a bowl of stew and some bread toward her. He looked angry today, usually when he came into her room he was cocky, arrogant, taunting her with her upcoming death, laughing that someone from her country had betrayed her.

Today though, he was furious.

He threw the food at her, the bowl shattering and food sloshing all over her and the floor around her.

For a moment, he ranted at her in Dari, and while she couldn't understand the words, she could feel the venom spitting from them and pressed herself back against the wall, shrinking in on herself to make her as small a target as possible. While she wasn't letting these men win and destroy her, she also didn't want to do anything to draw attention to herself. She wanted a chance to get herself out of here alive.

When Anvar switched to English, she looked up at him.

"American whore, your people will pay for taking my sister," Anvar sneered.

His sister?

She didn't even know he had a sister.

Her people had found his sister?

That had hope flooding through her, invigorating her more than the food could have done.

If they'd found Anvar's sister, then that meant not only were they looking for her, but they had made progress in finding her. They must have located the first building she was at. She hadn't seen any women at this house. If they knew where Anvar had kept her, and they had his sister, then they would be able to find her here, all she had to do was stay alive until that happened.

Struggling not to let her excitement show, Claire merely adjusted her gaze so it was focused back on the floor.

"They will not find you," Anvar said, stepping closer and grabbing her chin, roughly yanking her head back so she was looking at him again. "You will be dead soon, but you can take to your grave the knowledge that they will suffer too."

Turning and stomping from the room, Anvar slammed

the door shut behind him, still muttering about how he was going to make the infidels pay. When he was gone, Claire bypassed the food, despite her ravishing hunger, and picked up the pieces of the shattered bowl. There were nine of them in total and a few tiny shards too small to be of any use to her. Most of the pieces were large, big enough that if someone came to clean up the mess, they might notice something missing. There was one shard that was the perfect size, it was small enough that she could conceal it in her palm, but big enough that it could be used as a weapon.

Claire held it in her hand, this could be the answer to her prayers.

When one of Anvar's men came for her, and sooner or later they would because she knew Anvar was going to kill her, using her to kickstart his reign of terror, she could use the shard of china to incapacitate them and then make a run for it.

No.

Not incapacitate.

She was playing this to live not just prolong the inevitable.

She had to plan to kill not just injure the person to give herself time to flee.

Kill.

Could she really do that to another person?

Claire knew that she'd shot people to protect herself and Logan after the crash, but firing a gun and being close enough that her victim's blood would wind up on her skin were too different things.

No, she reminded herself again.

Not her victim.

These men were her captors, they'd beaten her, held her down and raped her, and they were planning on killing her.

She was the victim here.

Not them.

If she had the opportunity, killing them was what she had to do to save her life.

With her weapon sitting on her lap, Claire grabbed the bread and began to gobble it up hungrily. She was starving enough that she scooped up whatever of the stew she could from the floor despite the fact that it made her feel like an animal. She needed her strength and had to be prepared for her opportunity, which meant eating whatever she could and getting some sleep.

When she'd finished the bread and whatever stew she could salvage, Claire rested her head back against the wall and closed her eyes. She hadn't really expected to fall asleep, but the next thing she knew, someone was crouched beside her and was unlocking the metal cuff from around her ankle.

Instantly, she snapped awake.

This was it.

The man noticed she was awake and gave her a smile that made her shudder. "You going to make video," he said as he grabbed her elbow and hauled her to her feet.

Claire didn't wait.

Didn't hesitate.

She just flung her hand out, aiming right for the man's jugular.

She sank her weapon in deep, and the man's eyes widened in surprise before going dark with horror as blood flowed from the wound.

Not just flowed, blood was gushing, and Claire knew she had hit her target and severed the man's carotid artery.

Keeping her weapon in her hand, she hurried across the room to the window. It opened easily, and she was thankful they hadn't found a need to lock it since she was chained up. She wasted several precious seconds hauling her injured and weak body up and out the window, but then her bare feet touched the ground, and this tiny taste of freedom pushed her pain to the back of her mind.

She ran.

She had no idea where she was going, and right now she didn't really care, she just had to get as far away from that house as she could.

When she heard voices shouting she knew they had discovered the man she had killed. She wasn't far enough away yet. As soon as they looked out the window they would see her. She had to find a place to hide.

Frantically, she scanned the landscape, but there was nothing she could see that would hide her. They were in a valley, there were no rocks or caves in sight, neither were there any other buildings.

Tears streamed down her cheeks, she couldn't be this close to freedom only to be caught again.

Somehow she managed to push her battered body harder, running on when her legs shook and threatened to collapse beneath her.

The shouting voices were closer now.

They'd seen her, were chasing her, would catch her.

She knew it, but still, she couldn't give in to the inevitable.

There.

Up ahead was a car.

If she could get to it, maybe she could escape that way.

Claire pushed harder, keeping her body moving by sheer force of will. Her lungs heaved as she struggled to draw in enough air, the food she'd eaten earlier swirled in her stomach, threatening to come out the same way it had gone in.

The car was closer now, just a dozen or so yards away.

For a moment, she thought she might actually make it.

She could hear the pounding of footsteps behind her,

anyone else—gave him no choice, he would do whatever was required to get the information he needed to rescue Claire, then once she was safe he would gladly deal with the consequences of his actions.

"We can't just go storming in there and accuse the Colonel himself of being a traitor," Fox reminded him.

"Why?" As far as Shark was concerned, that was the perfect way to do it. "If we go in and pussyfoot around, he's going to have a chance to come up with a lie. We need to catch him unawares."

"Actually, that might work," Wolf said thoughtfully. "So far he thinks he's safe, that we're not onto him. If we go in there and confront him, we might actually be able to catch him in a lie, or he'll realize it's over and cut a deal to save his own life."

"And if we're wrong?" Fox asked.

"Then it's one more person to cross off our list," Shark said, shrugging out of Fox's hold. "I'm going, you guys can stay here if you want."

"As if," Chaos muttered as they all trailed him from the room.

Their support meant a lot to him, his team and Wolf's, but while he was quite prepared to go on a suicide mission, whether it cost him his life or his career, he couldn't ask his friends to do the same. They had families, lives, people who counted on him, he had no one but Claire, and he wasn't going to let her down.

Outside the Colonel's office, he stopped. "This could go bad, I can't ask you all to risk your careers for Claire."

Eleven sets of narrowed eyes looked back at him.

No one said a word, but Spider brushed past him and opened the door to Gaulding's office. Shark beat down a smile at his friends' show of support and surged forward into the office. He didn't hesitate, just went straight to the

Colonel who had started to rise from his chair, wrapped one of his huge hands around the man's neck, and shoved him back into his seat.

"Where is Claire?" he asked through gritted teeth.

Fear flared in the man's eyes before he hid it. "You want to get yourself arrested?" Gaulding asked.

"Someone saw you driving a Humvee around base the night Claire was abducted," he said, fighting the urge to start beating the man until he gave up Claire's location.

Gaulding licked his bottom lip, his eyes darting around, taking in the twelve special forces operatives who surrounded him. He had to know that it was over, that he'd slipped up, that there was no way he was going to be able to get out of this. His only chance was to bargain for a better deal by saving Claire.

Defeated, Gaulding sank back against his seat, the fight draining out of him. "It isn't me, but I know who it is."

"Name?" Shark demanded.

"He ... I ... it's ..." Gaulding hesitated.

"Why are you protecting him?" Cookie asked.

"He's my son," Gaulding replied.

"Son?" Abe asked.

"There's no record of you having a son," Night added.

"I didn't know about him until last year. His mother is a woman I knew in college. It was casual between us, she never told me she was pregnant. Then last year she died, and my son went looking for his biological father. I didn't know he was the traitor." Gaulding's pleading eyes traveled to each one of them, begging them to believe him. "It wasn't until the night they took Ms. Barrett that I found out. He called me, asked me to shut down security cameras temporarily. That was when I knew. He said I owed him for never being a part of his life, for abandoning him and his mom, but I didn't abandon them, I never knew he existed."

Shark didn't care about the man's personal life, all he cared about was the name of the traitor and the location of where Claire was currently being held.

"Who is he?" Wolf asked.

"Captain Cameron Hank," came Gaulding's soft reply.

The name rang a bell, Shark was sure he'd heard it somewhere before, but he couldn't place it until Fox sucked in a shocked breath.

"Captain Hank and nine other soldiers were taken prisoner by a terrorist cell two years ago. Hank was the only one to return alive after being held captive and brutally tortured for almost two months," Fox said.

Gaulding nodded.

"Anvar Mir was the leader of that cell, wasn't he?" Abe asked.

Gaulding nodded again.

"He bought his freedom by converting to Islam, he married Anvar's sister, and agreed to betray his country," King said.

"From what I heard, Cameron came back a different man. He recovered, declined a medical discharge, and passed his psych evaluations to return to active duty," Gaulding explained.

Before they could ask about the location of both Hank and Claire, the Colonel's laptop pinged with an incoming email.

"It's from Hank," Dude told them as he checked out the computer. "And it has a video attachment."

Shark's blood turned to ice. He released the Colonel and turned to face the laptop. The sense of foreboding he felt telling him this wasn't good news. "Open it."

Both SEAL teams exchanged glances. "Shark, I think you should wait outside," Fox said gently.

"No," he said simply. If that was a video of Claire, then he owed it to her to watch it.

Dude didn't move until Fox nodded at him, then he opened the email and clicked on the video.

Immediately, an image of Claire popped up. She was in a room, her wrists tied together and secured to a chain that hung from the ceiling, she could barely reach the floor, balancing precariously on her toes.

She was naked.

Her face was a mess of bruises, swelling, and dried blood, one eye completely swollen closed. Bruises covered the rest of her body too, her chest and stomach were a mottled mass of blues, blacks, and purples. There were smaller bruises on her arms and thighs.

Finger-sized bruises.

They'd held her down while they'd raped her.

Shark saw red.

His blood pounded deafeningly in his ears, and he lunged at the computer as though he could somehow reach through it to the men who had hurt Claire. He wanted to kill every single one of them, slowly and painfully, and then he wanted to gather his woman in his arms and find a way to make all her pain go away.

Hands grabbed at him, dragged him away. He fought as hard as he could, swinging his fists and trying to wrench free of their hold.

He had to get to Claire.

She needed him.

"Shark, man, you need to calm down," Fox said.

"Calm down?" he roared. How exactly was he supposed to do that? Didn't anyone understand that Claire was his, and he was the reason she'd been beaten to within an inch of her life and gang-raped by sadistic terrorists?

"You have to, she needs you," Fox said simply.

He dragged in several ragged breaths, willing his heart to slow down before it beat its way out of his chest. They were right. Claire needed him, and he was no help to her if he fell apart, blinded by rage and guilt.

Everyone watched him carefully, but there was no pity in their gazes, only understanding. He wasn't the only one who had been forced to watch as his woman was in danger. Spider, Night, and Fox had all gone through this same hell. Wolf and his team had too. They had all gotten their other halves back alive, and Shark prayed the same would be true for him.

"Play the video," he ordered as he shrugged off the hands of his teammates.

"Shark, I don't ..." Dude began.

"Play it," he barked. He would watch it, he had to. They had to find any clues as to where Claire was being held.

Dude hit play, and the video resumed. Anvar walked into the frame, he held a whip in his hand. Shark sucked in a pained breath, tried to prepare himself for what was about to happen, tried not to look at Claire's one good eye as it widened in understanding.

But nothing could prepare him for the sound of the whip slicing through the air then making contact with Claire's exposed skin.

Nor for the small whimper of pain that fell from her lips.

She was so tough, she held in her cries as best as she could, but the hits kept coming, one after the other with no time for her to catch herself between blows. Her body swayed as she kept losing her balance, but it wasn't until the tenth strike that she began to cry. She lasted until almost twenty before she began to beg for mercy.

Shark curled his hands into fists, welcoming the pain in his injured hand. What he wouldn't give to take the pain Claire was currently suffering and make it his own. She didn't deserve this, she was sweet, strong, compassionate. She'd turned her personal tragedy into a way to help other families from suffering the same loss she had when her father committed suicide. She'd come here, knowing she was putting herself in danger, to do the right thing.

Just when he thought he couldn't bear watching another second of her torture, hear another one of her sobbed pleas, Anvar stopped.

He walked around so he was in front of her and ran his fingertips along the leather straps of the whip, coating his fingers in Claire's blood. "Tomorrow is the beginning of a new world. It starts with her, but millions will die. There is nothing you can do to stop it from happening."

The video ended, the screen went black, but those images were burned into his mind's eye along with Anvar's words. They had only hours left to find Claire before it was too late, and Shark had no idea how they were going to do it.

* * *

10:03 P.M.

Cameron Hank was still feeling a little queasy from filming the video they'd sent to his father earlier today.

It wasn't watching Claire Barrett be tortured, he'd known exactly what the woman's fate was from the second he had broken into her room on base, knocked her unconscious, and spirited her away, leaving her in the hands of a ruthless group of men. No, it wasn't Claire's pain, suffering, and humiliation that had him sick to his stomach, it was the memories that it brought back up.

Memories of his own imprisonment and torture.

He had been like Claire once upon a time. An innocent

American working to make the world a better place, to protect the country where he was born, the country he thought had his allegiance.

But where was that same country when he needed them?

He had spent fifty-eight days in captivity. Kept in a dark cellar like the one Claire had been put in at the farmhouse. Only, unlike Claire, he had been kept there, in the dark, chained to the floor, barely fed, dying for a single sip of water, lying in his own filth for almost two months. The only reprieve he got was merely jumping from the frying pan and into the fire.

They would come for him every day. Dragging him down to the room at the end of the long corridor, a room with death and suffering etched into each stone.

It seemed that every day they found some new way to torture him. Knives cutting into his skin, whips flaying him open, pliers ripping out his teeth or fingernails, broken bones, beatings. They would immerse him in tubs filled with ice and laugh as he shook so badly he felt like he was going to shake himself to pieces. They would tie his wrists together, attach the rope to a metal hook in the ceiling, then they would light a fire beneath him and laugh as they watched him try to keep his mangled body up and away from the flames.

It had taken him an entire year to recover physically from his injuries, but he worked hard every day at physical therapy, determined to get put back on active duty. He had to, it was the only way to get the vengeance he needed to heal from his ordeal.

There was no going back now.

He had made his choice, picked which side he was on. It hadn't been a hard choice. While he spent fifty-eight days in Hell, his country hadn't been there for him. They hadn't come for him. He had sat in his cell, dreading his turn in the torture chamber, forced to listen to his men's screams, their hoarse pleas for mercy, then watch as, one by one, they succumbed to their injuries.

No one had come for him.

No one had rescued him.

No one had cared that his mother, the only person who had ever loved him, was suffering right along with him. The trauma of his ordeal had affected her deeply, and she had suffered a massive heart attack upon learning of his suffering, eventually passing away several months later.

He had lost everything because of the country he had dedicated his life to. He had served, but when he needed them, they hadn't been there for him.

When Anvar had come to him, asked him if he wanted to join in the fight against the almighty United States of America, it had been an easy choice. In the end, he hadn't even hesitated. When he'd been offered a way out of the hellhole he'd been trapped in, he had grabbed it enthusiastically with both hands. If it had the added bonus of making his father suffer all the better. He hoped the man had enjoyed the video he'd sent, hoped it made him sick to watch the psychologist's pain, hope it made him feel impotent to know there was nothing he could do to stop what was coming.

He had joined The Atash, the fire, an extremist group that was determined to take over the world, starting with the destruction of America. He had married Anvar's sister when he arrived back in Afghanistan, joining himself to the family by blood when his wife became pregnant. He converted to Islam and accepted his role in bringing about a world in which Allah and Allah alone reigned supreme.

Those decisions had led him to this point. His wife and child were now American prisoners. The men and women he had secretly begun converting to Islam, who saw the light and agreed to help The Atash's cause rather than suffer the consequences of being branded an infidel were all American prisoners. His father, sooner or later, would turn on him, informing everyone that he was a traitor to his country.

Even if he wanted to, going back wasn't an option.

If he did he would be arrested, charged with treason, and sent to Leavenworth. No way was he ever going to be anyone's prisoner ever again. Hence his safeguard. Cameron touched his tongue to one of his remaining teeth where the cyanide capsule sat, ready to be put to use if it came down to it.

Death was preferable over capture.

Any previous prisoner would tell you that. He was sure if it came down to it, Claire Barrett would choose death if given a choice between continued torture or an end to her suffering.

He was no different. He had no intention of being a captive again, either by the country of his birth or the men he had pledged his allegiance to. He knew that Anvar was a psychopath, one who wouldn't hesitate to turn on him if it was in his best interests. No one knew about the suicide capsule, and no one was going to know about it until it was too late, it was his personal insurance policy.

Cameron parked the car outside the building that would be the beginning of the end for the rest of the world. This was it, he wasn't going back to the base. From now on, his role was as a full-fledged member of The Atash. There was no more inside information he could offer them, no more access to weapons and explosives, now he would rise to the top as the greatest soldier for Allah the world had ever seen.

He unbuckled his seatbelt, opened his door, and climbed from the car, then opened the back door and pulled out the unconscious body of Claire Barrett. In a way, he envied her the role she was playing in this crusade. She would be the very first death, the starting point for a crusade that would take over the entire world.

Her body hung limply in his arms as he carried her into the large empty building, there was a single cage in the middle of it, and he took the woman to it and laid her gently on the floor inside. With her multitude of injuries there would be no comfortable and pain-free position to put her in, so he merely set her down and left her there, knowing that she would not be suffering for much longer.

He closed the cage door and locked it, sealing Claire's fate. The bombs would be set, and her death would be live-streamed across the world. Everyone would see what had happened to her and know that all infidels would meet the same fate.

Out of the fire would come rebirth.

A new world.

With but one God, there would be no more countries, no more cultures, everyone would worship Allah. Everyone would be united as one. No one would ever get left behind again. Loyalty would be the new motto.

Cameron felt a sense of peace settle over him as he looked at the unconscious woman. She didn't understand her role, but that didn't matter, she was serving a higher purpose, making the world a better place, righting the wrongs that had been done to him, and for that, he owed her a debt that given all eternity he could never repay.

"Peace be with you," he whispered as he reached out and touched the woman's hair which pooled around her head like dark silk.

With Claire in place, all that was left was to set the bombs, and then tomorrow night, they would be detonated, and the battle would begin. There was no stopping it, every-thing was just a formality now, once this first bomb went off the fire would be started. The bombs would be taken to the

US, loyal members of The Atash would start setting them, and every day the kingdom of Allah would be closer to taking over the world.

With perhaps the first genuine smile he had given since that day two years ago where his team was ambushed and tossed into a Hell he wasn't supposed to survive, Cameron turned around, intending to help Anvar and the others set up the bombs and the cameras that would film it.

Only he never got a chance.

His fears of imprisonment and his suicide capsule turned out to be irrelevant. Anvar stood there, weapon pointed at his head, that evil smile, the same one which had taunted Cameron as he was helplessly tortured, on his face.

"You are no longer any use to me," Anvar said, then fired his weapon.

Captain Cameron Hank, a one-time military hero, sole survivor of his team, and traitor to his country, was dead before hitting the ground.

CHAPTER 11

September 16th

8:52 A.M.

Claire woke slowly.

Painfully.

Her entire back from her ankles to her shoulders burned like it was on fire.

She remembered every second of the vicious whipping she'd been given. She remembered the sound of the leather whooshing through the air and the sharp sting as it made contact with her skin. She remembered the wet, sticky feeling of her blood flowing down her skin and the pain, the agonizing pain as the blows rained down on her, flaying her open.

At some point, she must have passed out because she had been moved again.

As bad as the pain was, it was the regret that hurt the most right now. When she'd seen that Anvar was going to film her, her plan had been to shout her apology to Logan and tell him that she loved him. She wasn't exactly sure who Anvar was going to show the video to, but she had been confident that at some point Logan would see it, and then he'd know the truth about that night.

Faced with her impending death, that was what was most important to her. If she knew that Logan didn't hate her, then dying didn't seem quite so scary.

But Anvar had started whipping her before she'd had a chance to look at the camera and say what she'd planned to say. She'd tried to hold in her cries of pain, she knew that seeing her being hurt would upset Logan whether he knew why she'd pushed him away that night or not, but in the end, she couldn't keep silent. The pain had been too bad, and by the end, she'd been begging through her tears for them to stop.

Claire didn't have time for regrets though, she was awake now, and she had a whole new set of obstacles to attempt to find a way to overcome.

Moving slowly because her entire body was one pulsing ball of agony, Claire slowly pushed herself up into a sitting position. Since her entire back was a mess, there was no comfortable way to lie down or sit, so she curled her fingers around the metal bars in front of her and used them to help her leverage herself up so she was standing.

Biting down on her bottom lip so she didn't start weeping, she just didn't have time for tears right now, Claire took in her surroundings. She was in a large room, it kind of looked like a hangar at an airport, only there were no planes inside. Gritting her teeth, she turned in a circle, checking out every inch of the room. One wall had a huge roller door, further confirming her suspicions that she was at an airfield. Besides that, there was only one other door on the far side of the building. There was also a small staircase leading to what looked like a small room, maybe an office or observation room.

She was in a metal cage in the middle of the room. It was about eight feet high and about six by six. There was a metal floor and a metal ceiling, and the bars were spaced about eight inches apart.

Helplessness rushed through her and Claire had to fight back tears. She was doing her best not to give up, to find a way to escape, to keep fighting, but no matter what she tried it never worked out, and she just kept finding herself in a worse position than she'd been in before.

She sank to the floor of her cage, wincing as her shredded bottom touched the cool metal of her cage. She was so tired, exhaustion buffeted her in angry waves, and it was a struggle just to keep conscious.

Maybe she should stop fighting.

It would be so nice to just fade away into the empty quietness of unconsciousness. It had a peacefulness that she so desperately craved.

Claire carefully lay down on her side, resting her head on her folded arm. She let her eyes drift closed and tried to focus on nothing. Not her situation, not Logan, not regrets, and all the things she would do differently if given the chance.

As she emptied her mind she started to relax, her pain melted away, a sense of acceptance settled over her.

She was going to die.

She couldn't stop it.

Maybe it was time she stopped trying.

Claire.

Logan's voice echoed through her mind so clearly that

she startled and shoved up, crying out as her ripped back protested the sudden movement.

She scanned the hangar, but it was still empty. There was no one here, but …

Her brow furrowed as she noticed something she hadn't before. She wasn't alone in here, there was a body lying next to her cage.

"Hello?" she called out. If he was alive maybe he could help her get out of here, he wasn't restrained as far as she could see.

As quickly as hope flared to life inside her, it died.

Blood.

There was a huge pool of blood around the body.

The man was dead.

Claire drooped down again, resting against the bars, trying to sit on the sides of her thighs and not her backside to alleviate the pain. She recognized the man even though he was lying face down. It was Captain Cameron Hank. The traitor. The man she had been sent here to find. She knew he had been captured and horribly tortured. When offered a way to live he'd taken it, converted to Islam, married Anvar's sister, and joined The Atash and agreed to sell out his country.

In a way she understood, he'd done what he had to do to survive. She supposed she couldn't blame him for that. But she couldn't really forgive him either, because of him she was sitting here facing certain death.

Claire frowned as she noticed something lying half in and half out of Cameron's pocket.

A key.

Hope came rushing back like a tidal wave. If that key was to her cage then she could get herself free.

Never in her life had Claire been so pleased that she was on the skinny side and that the ordeal of the last ten days had caused her to lose more weight. Her stomach growled almost in appreciation that its suffering hadn't been for naught, and she couldn't help but smile.

All she had to do was get that key, get out of here, then find somewhere to hide where she'd be safe. Someone would come looking for her, she knew it, especially after that video Anvar had made.

Lying down on her stomach, she ignored her pain, it was only going to slow her down, and stretched her arm between the bars.

The key was tantalizingly just out of reach, mere millimeters from her fingertips.

No way was she giving up.

Gritting her teeth, she pushed up as close as she could against the bars, her shoulder screamed in pain, but she still couldn't get close enough.

All she needed was another millimeter or two.

Pulling her arm back, Claire switched to the arm with the shoulder she'd dislocated in the helicopter crash. After all the trauma it had been through she knew it hadn't had time to heal, maybe it could pop back out so she could get those extra millimeters.

It was worth a try.

Claire slid that arm between the bars, shoved against them, and felt the joint move. Since she was alone, she didn't bother to hold back her scream of pain, but it worked. Her fingertips brushed the key and she curled them, pulling back so the key moved within easy reach. Removing her arm, she held it tucked against her chest, then used her good arm to scoop up the key.

Shuffling on her knees she moved to the door of her cage. Needing both hands to do this, she grit her teeth and put one hand on either side of the lock.

Tears of relief flowed down her cheeks when the key slid

into the padlock, and she opened it. She shoved the door open and stumbled out of the cage, landing heavily on her knees.

She was out.

Free.

Well almost.

Somehow she got to her feet, her back ripped and tore open all her wounds, her broken ribs stabbed at her lungs with each ragged breath she took, but no way was she giving up now.

No way.

When she reached the door, a scream of denial tore through her.

There were multiple bombs wired to it.

Why did this keep happening?

Even though she knew what she would find there, Claire stumbled toward the roller door and found exactly what she thought she would.

More bombs.

She was trapped in here.

"No, no, no. It's not fair," she wailed as sobs tore through her aching body.

Through her tears, she noticed a camera set up facing her cage.

Anvar intended to live-stream her death. She hurried over to the camera, but there was no red light, nothing to indicate that it was turned on. He must be waiting till he was ready to set off the bombs before activating it. When he did turn it on, he'd see that she was no longer in her cage. He couldn't use her death to start his revolution if she wasn't in the frame.

Satisfaction mingled with her despair. She might be going to die, but Anvar was going to have to come all the way back here and throw her back in that cage if he wanted to film her death. At least she was going to make him work for it.

* * *

8:59 P.M.

Finally.

It had been a long day, they'd tracked Anvar's movements and eventually ended up here at a small airfield that the terrorist had used to traffic weapons. Shark was praying this was where Claire was being held, but they'd already cleared two other properties in the last twenty-four hours and come up empty. The first there had no signs that Claire had ever been there, but the second was the one where the video had been filmed.

Seeing her blood puddled on the floor had almost sent him off the deep end—that and the fact that he kept showing up too late.

What if he was too late this time?

What if Claire was already dead?

"Focus, man," Fox said softly, keeping his voice quiet so the words were for his ears only. "She's not dead, he wants to film it. We have people watching for the video, so far there hasn't been anything. Claire is alive."

He gave a sharp nod, mostly in agreement, but just because she was still alive now didn't mean she would be when they found her. If she wasn't here, then they were running out of places to check.

The two SEAL teams approached the large hangar. There was no one around, no one shot at them, the place appeared to be deserted.

Another dead end?

Something felt off, and Shark scanned the building, trying to put his finger on what it was. They had theorized that Anvar intended to blow Claire up. The Atash had been setting off bombs across the Middle East and intended to plant bombs across the US. If they'd brought Claire here to kill her, then why weren't they here?

Unless ...

"Wait," he called out. Everyone looked at him, and he continued. "Anvar is smart enough to keep his links to this place hidden, yet he practically left a trail of bread crumbs leading us here. The only reason I can think of to do that is because he wants to take out as many Americans as he can."

"He brings Claire here, leads us to her, and we blow her up when we go running in to save her, getting ourselves killed in the process." Wolf nodded his agreement.

"We need to disable the bombs before we go in," Dude said. He was the explosives expert on Wolf's team.

"You think he wired the doors?" Shark asked. He might not be as good with bombs as Dude was, but he knew a thing or two about setting them.

Dude nodded. "He was hoping we would just go rushing in without thinking."

Shark rolled his eyes at Anvar's stupidity. SEALs weren't reckless like that, even if he hadn't figured out that Anvar would wire the building before they tried to enter they would have noticed the explosives.

"I'll get us in there," Dude promised as he knelt before the door.

While he and Dude worked on dismantling the bombs so they could get inside, the rest of both teams spread out to search the area, see if there were any hints of where Anvar and his men had gone. As much as his focus was on finding Claire alive, he also knew that they had to find Anvar. The man was a threat to national security. Even though his mole was now exposed, he no doubt already had people in the US who were ready and waiting to receive their orders to start setting bombs.

Inactivity, waiting, knowing that Claire could be just on the other side of the wall waiting for him, praying that someone came for her, that *he* came for her, was another layer of Hell he had to experience.

"Got it," Dude announced almost fifteen minutes later, looking up at him with a satisfied smile.

"We're going in," Shark said into his comms. Weapon in hand, he finally stepped inside the hangar.

First thing he saw was a metal cage in the middle of the room and a body lying beside it.

The body was too large to be Claire, but still he and Dude crossed toward it slowly. The rest of the room was empty, no threats that he could see, but he didn't lower his guard.

Dude knelt beside the dead man. "Cameron Hank."

"He outlived his usefulness," Shark said, heading for the stairs. Claire had to be up there. Somehow, she'd gotten out of the cage, but she must have seen the bombs and known she couldn't get out of here without setting them off.

"We have incoming tangos," Spider announced through their comms.

"At least a dozen, maybe more," Mozart added.

"Do you have Claire?" Fox asked.

"Not yet," Shark said, taking the stairs three at a time. He had complete faith in both his own team and Wolf's to deal with the approaching tangoes, so he kept his focus on Claire. The office was dark when he threw open the door. There were two desks, a small kitchenette, and a filing cabinet with the draws sitting open and empty.

Weapon still raised in case one of Anvar's men was here, he moved carefully around the room, praying with each step he took that he would find Claire.

He did under the second desk.

She was lying on her side, her knees drawn to her chest, she was naked, and he could see tremors wracking her body.

Claire lifted her head, screaming when she saw him.

Immediately, he let go of his weapon and dropped to his knees in front of her. He reached for her, one part of his brain telling him he would scare her further, make her believe he was there to hurt her, but he had to touch her.

Shark hauled her into his arms, as careful as he could not to cause her further pain. She stiffened for a moment, but then she sank into his embrace.

"It's okay, Claire, it's me."

"I know," she said, pressing her face against his neck. "You're really here."

"I'm here," he agreed, cradling her against his chest. As much as he'd love to sit here forever, just holding her, letting her slight weight convince him that she was alive, that he'd found her in time, they had to get moving. "This is going to hurt, sweetheart, but we have tangoes on the way so I don't have time to check out your injuries."

When he went to shift her so that he could carry her, she curled her fingers into his BDUs, and looked pleadingly up at him. "I'm sorry, Logan, the night I told you I needed time alone he was in my room, he said he'd shoot you if I didn't get rid of you."

Her words were slurred together and weak, but he could feel her determination in every word. While she'd been fighting for her life, being beaten and tortured, she'd been worrying about explaining herself to him. If he didn't love her already her concern over not hurting him would have made him fall.

"I know, Claire Bear," he said, leaning down to touch his lips to her forehead.

"You got her?" Dude asked from behind him.

"Yeah, I got her."

"Good, then we have to get out of here."

"Bombs," Claire said softly, "the place is wired ... how did you ...?"

"We found the bombs," he told her. "Dude here is an explosives expert. He was able to disarm them, but it looks like Anvar changed his plan, he's moving in with some of his men, my team and Dude's will hold them off, but we have to get you out of here."

"I wasn't in the cage," Claire said. "I got out, he wanted to film my death, mine and whoever came to rescue me, he had to come back, his plan doesn't work if he doesn't get the films."

He had seen the camera downstairs, and he had no doubt that Claire's assessment was correct. Anvar wanted to invoke fear and what better way to do that than to have a face to the beginning of his crusade. Filming Claire's death showed everyone how serious he was, how dangerous he was.

"Here, wrap her in this," Dude said as he handed him the emergency blanket from his first aid kit.

Shark wrapped it around her then very carefully scooped her up. Claire cried out as his arms pressed against her wounds, but there was no way to carry her without touching them, and he knew by looking at her she wasn't strong enough to walk out of here on her own.

Her muffled cries made him want to break things, preferably the monster who had taken great pleasure in torturing her.

"I'm sorry," he murmured.

"It's ... okay ..." she said, panting through her pain.

Since what Claire needed she couldn't get here, Shark did his best to ignore her shaking and the little whimpers she was making. Instead, he stood with her in his arms and followed Dude down the stairs.

They had no sooner stepped out into the night than gunfire erupted around them.

* * *

9:36 P.M.

Claire cried out, her back felt like it was on fire as her open wounds hit the ground when Logan threw her down, covering her body with his own.

"Sorry," Logan muttered, and she could hear the recrimination in the whispered word.

"I'm okay," she assured him. She was pretty sure that wasn't true, her back burned with agony, and she thought she had a fever—some of her open wounds had no doubt become infected. The broken bones in her face and her broken ribs added to her overall pain level, and her head pounded with a headache that wouldn't let up.

Still, she was alive, and Logan was here, and she just wanted to go home.

Someone was shooting at them, and while Claire knew they weren't out of the woods yet, she was so tired that it was hard to care.

Besides, she wasn't on her own anymore, she had Logan and his team, and apparently another SEAL team here as well. She trusted all of these men, even the ones she hadn't met, and it was so nice just to not be alone that she couldn't stop tears rolling down her temples.

She could hear Logan's whispered voice talking to someone, but she had pretty much reached the end of her rope and was content for now to just rest and let Logan take care of things. He was better at it than she was anyway, he actually knew what he was doing, and she hadn't done such a great job so far.

"We're going to move, Claire. I don't want you to do anything, I'm getting you out of here," Logan said, his mouth right above her ear.

That she could do.

She wasn't sure she had enough strength left to do anything but lie here like a ragdoll anyway.

Logan didn't seem to care, he just picked her back up and started running with her. She didn't know where they were going, nor did she care, as long as they were moving away from the guns and the terrorists, that was all she wanted.

Claire just focused on clinging to consciousness and biting on her bottom lip to keep the screams of pain from escaping. She had no idea how many men were here trying to kill her and the SEALs, and she didn't want to do anything to draw undue attention to herself, or Logan who was risking his life to save her.

He dropped to his knees behind a Humvee and handed her off to another man, one she'd never met before, it had to be one of the men on the other team. She knew he was a SEAL too, and she had no doubt he was perfectly capable of protecting her, but she reached out instinctively for Logan, she needed him.

"Don't go," she begged. She hated that she sounded so weak and whiny, but she couldn't make herself let go of him.

His fingers trailed through her tangled hair before his large palm cradled her head. "He hurt you, he has to die."

The way he said it, so quiet and deadly, made it clear that in his mind he had to do this for her. Like the idea that she could survive what she'd just lived through hinged entirely on him being the one to eliminate the man responsible.

She had to force her fingers to uncurl from Logan's BDUs, but she did it.

"Don't get hurt," she whispered.

"Nothing is going to keep me from you," he vowed. Then he touched his lips to hers in the softest of kisses and disappeared.

"Your man will come back to you," said a large man with dark hair, dark eyes, and scars on his face. "I'm Mozart, by the way."

"Hi, M-Mozart," she said. Her teeth were chattering, she hurt so badly, but she didn't want to complain, so she did her best to grit her teeth through it.

Apparently, she did a pretty awful job of hiding it because Mozart reached down and lifted her up and laid her in the back of the car, on her side, facing the back of the seat.

"Just rest, Claire, I'm going to get you something for the pain," Mozart told her, resting a gentle hand on her shoulder.

Morphine sounded perfect right about now, she'd basically do anything someone told her to if they said it would take even the edge off her pain.

Gunfire still peppered the night, and Claire just wished this was all over.

"Once I give you the shot, I'll see if I can find you some clothes," Mozart said, his hand on her hip eased the blanket back.

Before he could administer the drugs, the world exploded around them.

The Humvee was tossed sideways, and the jolt of pain as her body slid out and hit the ground was enough to knock her unconscious.

She had no idea how long she was out, but she was being dragged across the ground when she came to. When she looked up she saw the face of her own personal demon.

Anvar Mir.

He'd come back just like she thought he would. He

needed to film her death, in his mind it had become a vital part of his crusade.

And now he had her.

Tears of anger, and frustration, and grief spilled down her cheeks. She'd been so close to escaping again only to wind right back in this man's clutches.

"It's over, Anvar."

Claire startled at the voice, looking up she saw that she and Anvar were surrounded by a bunch of menacing-looking Navy SEALs. Despite the fact she was in the clutches of a psychopathic terrorist, she breathed a sigh of relief.

Logan and his team would save her, her faith in him was complete and unshakeable.

"Your men are dead, Anvar," said one of the big men. She didn't recognize him so he must be on Dude and Mozart's team.

All of the SEALs were armed, but Anvar wasn't, and she wondered why he didn't just give up. He had to know that he was never going to get what he wanted.

Anvar's dark eyes were wild, and he reached down and produced a knife, which he promptly pressed against her neck. He dragged her to her feet and held her between himself and the SEALs, only they surrounded him leaving the man turning in circles that made her dizzy as she was dragged along with him.

"You can kill me, but you can't end my mission. The world will be consumed by fire. You can't stop Allah, he will reign, and all who deny him will burn," Anvar screamed.

None of the SEALs seemed concerned about his rant, and when Claire's eyes met Logan's he locked his gaze on her, she saw his determination, his confidence that he was going to save her and she felt herself relax. Logan's gaze shifted to whoever was standing behind her, and he gave a single nod, she had no idea what he had planned, but she trusted him.

Anvar was still spinning around as though he were trying to find a break in the circle of SEALs. Their backs were to Logan when something slammed into her and Anvar from behind.

The knife was gone from her neck, then Anvar's hold on her was broken. The extremist's arms were replaced by one of the SEALs who snatched her up and quickly carried her away.

"It's okay, Claire, I'm Wolf, and this is over now."

"Is Anvar …?"

"Shark is taking care of him," Wolf said. His voice was soft and soothing as he headed for a helicopter that appeared in the sky. It touched down, and Wolf climbed inside and carefully set her on a seat.

Claire saw that a couple of the men had followed them and stood protectively at the door to the helicopter, ready to protect her if another threat arose. She saw Mozart amongst them and was glad that he hadn't been hurt when the bomb went off.

She tried to relax, tried to breathe through the pain, tried to believe that it really was over and that she was going home alive. She wasn't doing a very good job of it. After trying to escape and failing, it was hard to believe that she was free now.

Then Logan was there, he scooped her up and lay down on a stretcher on the floor of the helicopter, draping her across his front. This position meant the open wounds on her back weren't pressed against anything, and she loved that Logan knew what she needed without her saying anything.

For a moment she didn't speak, neither did he—although that wasn't surprising—she just lay there and soaked up his warmth and strength. He was solid beneath her, his hands curled lightly around her hips, the beating of his heart beneath her ear went a long way toward helping her relax.

One of the guys—she was too tired to open her eyes and see which one—took her arm and hooked up an IV.

"You came for me," she said softly.

"Of course," Logan said.

"You killed Anvar."

"He deserved it. Sleep now, Claire, it's over, you're safe, you can rest."

"Are you going to leave me?" Whatever had been injected into her IV was starting to work, making her feel like she was floating away.

"Never."

His firm declaration made a small smile curve up her lips and she snuggled closer against him. Feeling safe for the first time in days she was able to let go and drift off, knowing Logan wouldn't let anything happen to her.

CHAPTER 12

September 17th

6:47 A.M.

It had been dark when he'd found her, and he'd been distracted by the incoming tangos. With people shooting at them, bombs going off, and ridding the world of the man responsible for her suffering, Shark hadn't had a good chance to see all of Claire's injuries.

Now, as she lay in a hospital bed under the harsh fluorescent lights, evidence of what she had lived through was shockingly obvious.

Eight of the cuts on her back had been deep enough to require stitches, and several were already showing signs of infection. She had two broken bones in her face, three cracked ribs, and one that was broken. The shoulder that had been dislocated in the crash eleven days ago had received so much additional trauma that it would require surgery when she was stronger. She was receiving IV antibiotics as well as painkillers and had been sedated so that her body could get the rest it so badly needed.

In addition to her injuries, she'd been badly dehydrated and had been mostly starved during her five days in captivity.

Lying in the hospital bed, propped on her side so that her shredded back didn't have to take her weight, she looked small and frail. Her skin was pale, the bruises on her face stood out in stark contrast. The skin around her wrists was torn from the ropes used to restrain her, and he knew her ankles were similarly injured.

As bad as her injuries looked, Shark knew the internal ones were going to take a lot longer to heal. There was some internal damage from Anvar and his men gang-raping her, which the doctor had assured him would heal, but it was the psychological damage that had been done that he was most worried about.

Claire hadn't woken since she'd fallen asleep in his arms on the helicopter, and he hadn't left her side. He had respectfully turned his back when the doctors had performed their internal exam, but otherwise, he'd kept his promise not to leave her.

A promise he was soon going to have to break.

She was going to be transferred to Germany later in the day. She'd stay there for a few days, and then when she was stronger, she'd fly back to the US.

He couldn't go with her.

He wanted to, more than anything. The thought of Claire going home alone, weak and in pain, to suffer through flashbacks and nightmares made him feel ill. But he and his team still had another eight weeks to go before they would be going home.

Right now, eight weeks felt like a lifetime.

It was one thing if Claire was going home to be surrounded by a loving family, but her father was dead, she had no siblings and no relationship with her mother and stepfather. She'd be going home to deal with everything on her own.

Shark scrubbed his fingers down his face. He wanted to reach out to Claire, hold her, but aside from not wanting to wake her, he wasn't sure she would welcome his touch. It was different in the helicopter. She was scared and hurting, but she'd been through Hell, and had been hurt in the most horrific way a woman could, and when she woke up, she might not be comfortable with him touching her.

Or being in her life.

She'd been worried the whole time about lying to protect him, but he was the one who'd let her down, and she had to realize that.

He shifted in his chair, clamping his fingers around his knees so he didn't reach out to her. He had no idea where they stood, what happened next, it was one thing to have said goodbye to Claire on the base and watch her fly home, but neither of them had expected things to develop into the nightmare they'd become. After her ordeal, he was sure that starting a new relationship was the last thing on Claire's mind. He wanted to do the right thing, wanted to give her space and time, but he had no idea what his place in her life was right now. Or what she wanted it to be.

A small whimper escaped Claire's lips, and she began to shift restlessly on the bed. It was the first time she had stirred, and he hated that she would have to relive her ordeal over and over again. Shark wanted a way to fix this for her, but the way he fixed things for people was to eliminate the problem, usually by using his fists. He'd already done that, Anvar Mir was dead, but that didn't erase what Claire had lived through, and he felt woefully unprepared for the job of helping her deal with what had happened. The fear of saying the wrong thing was almost paralyzing.

"Logan."

The whispered plea hit him straight in the heart, and he moved from the chair where he'd been sitting watching Claire, to stand right beside the bed. Carefully, he traced his fingertips down her cheek, avoiding the bruises that marred her perfect skin. "Wake up, Claire Bear," he said softly.

She snapped awake at his words, her wild gaze traveling the room before settling on him, and he felt her entire body relax. "You're here," she murmured and gave him a small smile.

"Promised you I would be."

"Yeah, you did." She smiled again then shifted uncomfortably.

Immediately, he itched to find a way to help her, but all he could do was stand there, his hands hanging uselessly at his sides. "Do you want some water?"

"Yes, please."

Happy to have something to do, no matter how small, he picked up a cup of water on the table beside her bed. There was a straw in it, and he slipped an arm around her shoulders and elevated her slightly so she could take a sip. When she pulled her mouth away he set the cup back down, but when he went to release her, Claire grabbed at him. There were bruises on her knuckles, but her grip on him was strong.

"Don't go, don't let me go," she begged.

"I don't want to hurt you." He brushed a lock of hair off her cheek and tucked it behind her ear. He'd resisted touching her while she was asleep for fear of her waking disoriented and afraid he was one of the men who had hurt her, but now that she was awake, he didn't want to take his hands off her.

"I don't care, I just want you to hold me, I … need you to hold me," she said, her dark eyes shimmering with unshed tears.

With her left arm immobilized in a sling, it would be more awkward than it was on the helo, and he had to be careful of the IV taped to the back of her right hand, but Shark picked her up, doing his best to black out her moan of pain as his arm pressed against her wounds, lay down on the bed, then turned her over and draped her across his chest. Her head tucked under his chin, her injured arm was between them but it didn't seem to be bothering her, and her free hand rested above his heart as her cheek pillowed on his right pectoral.

"This is nice," Claire said with a soft sigh.

Yeah, it was.

It was heaven.

He could get way too used to holding her like this way too quickly if he wasn't careful. There was a lot they needed to discuss. Their future was anything but certain, but now wasn't the time to have that talk. They'd discussed all in, but that was before Claire's world had imploded, it was presumptuous of him to assume that was still the case, and yet holding her like this felt perfect.

Perfect to him anyway.

But even though Claire didn't seem to be repulsed by his touch, she'd been gang-raped, he would guess multiple times, in addition to being beaten and almost killed, right now she was still in shock, she hadn't processed everything, when she did, being with a man—any man—might not be something she could handle. Maybe something she would never be able to handle. He would wait for her forever, but what she had endured was heavy stuff, and she might not ever recover from it.

"I knew you would come for me," Claire said softly, her

fingers tightening slightly against his chest. "Even when I thought you might hate me."

"I would never hate you. Ever," he added for emphasis.

"I didn't give up, I fought them, kept trying to get away, I even killed one of them, but it wasn't enough."

"You're wrong, sweetheart," Shark told her, sweeping his hands up and down her sides where she wasn't bruised. "What you did was enough, it kept you alive, and if you hadn't gotten out of that cage at the airfield, then Anvar would still be out there. Because of you, because of how hard you fought for your life, a dangerous man is dead."

Claire's tears dripped onto his t-shirt, and she tilted her head up to touch her lips to his jaw. "Thank you for not giving up on me."

"Thank you for not giving up on yourself."

"Sometimes I wanted to."

"Because you're human, Claire. No matter how much you wanted to, you didn't. You are the strongest person I've ever met, and I couldn't be more proud of you. Now rest, Claire Bear, close your eyes and let your body begin to heal. I'm here, I've got you, you're safe."

He felt her relax against him a few minutes later as she drifted away. It felt like holding his heart in his hands, his heart that he was going to have to hand over to strangers in just a few hours. Shark lay there for a long time holding her and praying he wasn't about to lose her.

* * *

5:11 P.M.

. . .

Fear gripped her as she jolted out of another nightmare, but she was immediately soothed by the presence of the large man she was draped over.

Claire let out a slow breath to calm her racing heart. It hadn't sunk in yet that she was safe, that Anvar was dead, that the traitor was also dead, that it was all over. She was starting to wonder if it ever would sink in. She knew she was being pessimistic, it hadn't even been twenty-four hours since Logan had found her, and most of the time she'd been asleep, but she was about to be sent to Germany and then back home, where she would have to deal with everything alone.

How was she going to do that without Logan?

He shouldn't make her feel so safe, she'd only known him for eleven days. Half of that time they'd been separated and she'd been in the hands of violent men who hadn't hesitated to take that violence out on her, but right now, he was the only thing helping her hold it together. It didn't make sense, and the psychologist side of her wanted to explain away her feelings for him with theories about how he'd saved her life, protected her, been the only thing standing between her and certain death. But her heart knew that it loved the man who was cradling her so gently against him.

It seemed like he was finally asleep, he needed the rest. She thought he probably hadn't gotten any more sleep than she had since Cameron Hank had abducted her. He'd watched over her like he'd promised her he would in the helicopter, he'd stayed with her when she'd been debriefed, he'd held her while she slept, he'd soothed her when she woke from a nightmare, but he was also soon to walk out of her life.

They hadn't discussed the future yet.

Before everything had gone to Hell, they'd been together, a couple, they'd both been all in, they'd planned on keeping in touch while he finished his deployment and then picking things back up when he returned to the US. Now though? She had no idea what the future held for them. Did Logan even still want her? Her body was a mess of injuries that would take months to recover from, and then there were the psychological injuries that would never completely heal. Logan knew that she'd been raped, he knew that she'd been beaten and whipped, he knew that she was damaged now. Maybe that had been enough to turn him off.

No.

She was being silly.

Logan already knew that her stepfather had abused her and that hadn't turned him off. In fact almost the opposite, he'd wanted to protect her from that old pain, take it away for her, and make it better. He wouldn't have stayed with her here at the hospital, held her so gently if he didn't care about her. Claire had to believe that and cling to it with everything she had because she was about to lose the one thing that comforted her.

"You're awake," Logan said, his voice rumbled through the chest she was pillowed on.

"So are you," she said with a smile.

"Sorry I fell asleep," Logan said and seemed genuinely remorseful about it.

That made her chuckle. "You need sleep, Logan. Even big, tough SEALs aren't immune from the need for sleep."

"I want to be here for you while I can," he said, "I can sleep later."

After she was gone.

Just like that, her momentary good mood faded away.

"Well, soon I'll be gone, and you won't have to worry about me anymore," she said, faking a brightness to her tone that was the opposite of how she was feeling.

Apparently Logan wasn't buying her fake cheer. "I didn't

mean it like that, Claire. I'm going to worry about you when you're gone."

Was that all it was?

He was just worried about her?

Claire hated these doubts that were making what was already a horrendous situation even worse.

One thing she knew for certain though was that any minute now she was going to be flown out of Afghanistan and she didn't want to leave without knowing exactly where she and Logan stood. If all he felt for her was pity, guilt, or general worry because the two of them had briefly been lovers, then she wanted to know. She wanted to be prepared to end things now and move forward alone.

Since she needed to be able to see his face to know if he was lying to her, she propped the elbow of her good arm on his chest and met his gaze directly. "Logan, I know a lot has happened in the short time we've known each other. We went from battling together to get to safety after the crash, to lovers, in the blink of an eye. But then I was taken, and now ..."

"Evening, Ms. Barrett," said a pretty young woman who smiled warmly at her. "We're here to pick you up."

"Now?" She needed some time to talk to Logan first. She had to know where things stood between them, she didn't want to allow herself to lean on him, to get used to his presence in her life if he wasn't going to be there long term. Claire knew she had a long battle ahead of her to reclaim her life and it wasn't going to be an easy journey, the last thing she needed was to invest in someone who had no plans to stick around.

"Yes, ma'am," the woman replied.

She looked up at Logan who was watching her with an inscrutable expression. Was he relieved to be handing her over to someone else? Did he feel like he was off the hook now and could move on with his life? Or did he feel the same sense of crushing loss that she did? Like they were about to say goodbye to a piece of their own body.

"Can we have just one moment? Please. It won't take long," she promised.

"It's okay, Claire, we don't have to figure this out right now," Logan said as he gently rolled her off him and onto the gurney the woman had brought with her. Claire winced as her back touched the mattress, and Logan's large hand smoothed her hair before he positioned her on her side.

"Logan." She caught his hand when he went to take a step back. "Don't you think we should talk before I go?"

"You've just been through a horrific ordeal, I don't think you need to be making any big decisions right now. You have to focus on you, on healing," Logan said, but there was a distance in his eyes that made her feel like this was final.

Tears burned the backs of her eyes, but she wasn't going to let him see her cry. If he wanted to end things now then she couldn't stop him. If what they'd shared hadn't meant the same to him as it had to her then she couldn't change that. She couldn't make him love her, and she didn't want to be with someone who didn't.

Since she didn't know what else to say, and she didn't want some awkward goodbye, nor could she watch him as she was taken away, Claire closed her eyes, wishing she could shut out everything that had happened to her the same way she could shut out Logan's image.

She was covered in a blanket, her IV was transferred to a pole attached to her new bed, and then she was wheeled toward the door.

Claire kept expecting Logan to call out to her, tell her he loved her, tell her he'd call her, tell her he'd email, tell her something.

But he didn't.

He didn't say anything.

Just as they turned to head down the hall, Claire peeked her eyes open, wanting so badly to see Logan walking toward her, offering her something that would tell her he cared. Instead, all she saw was him standing beside the bed, his arms crossed over his massive chest, his face impassive.

Well, she guessed that was the answer she needed.

Whatever had changed Logan's mind no doubt had something to do with her abduction. Either he now saw her as damaged and too big a problem to take on, or it was his own guilt keeping him in place. Whatever the reason, in the end the result was the same, she was leaving here alone, she had to find a way through the mess her life had become alone, just like when she'd fled her stepfather's house she had no one to count on but herself.

Because she knew that the only way to get through this was to focus on the future and not the past, Claire focused her gaze in front of her and dug deep to find any scrap of strength she had left.

CHAPTER 13

September 20th

1:27 P.M.

He'd made a mistake.

Shark knew that.

Owned it.

Problem was, he didn't know how to fix it.

He had panicked.

Him.

Panicked.

Everything had been going fine, Claire had mostly been sleeping in his arms, but then it was time for her to leave and she'd wanted to talk. He'd been positive she was going to say she couldn't be in a relationship right now so he'd shut her down. He'd given her some lame line about how they didn't need to get into anything now, how there was no pressure on her to make any decisions right now. Both of those had just been excuses, in truth, he'd been terrified that Claire was about to send him away.

"You gonna tell us anytime soon why you're in such a bad mood when we got your girl back alive?" Fox asked, startling Shark out of his thoughts.

"She's not my girl," he shot back. The last thing he wanted to do right now was talk about this. Shoving to his feet, he headed for the door, he'd go to the gym, work out for a few hours, try to figure out if there was a way to salvage the situation with Claire.

"Where are you going?" Wolf asked as he and his team strolled into the room.

Great.

Now he had two SEAL teams full of meddlesome men to deal with. Weren't SEALs supposed to be big on muscle and small on talking about feelings? It used to be that way, but he'd watched as one by one his teammates fell for their other halves, and now they seemed all in for discussing emotions and all that other mushy stuff he avoided like the plague.

No way he could deal with his team and Wolf's too.

"He messed up with Claire," King informed the other team.

"Been moping around about it since she left," Chaos added.

Shark shot a glare at his friends. Did they really think he needed six more mother hens trying to fix this and play matchmaker? He was the only one who could fix the mistakes he'd made—if they could be fixed.

"You messed up?" Cookie asked, dropping down into a chair.

"How'd you manage that?" Abe asked.

"Seemed like a slam dunk, she was way into you," Mozart added.

"I thought you guys were flying out after we found Claire," he muttered, irritated with his team and the other one for shoving him into the spotlight when he wanted to just slink away quietly and lick his wounds, but more irritated with himself for messing up what he had with Claire.

"Nope, we're hanging around. You get to enjoy the pleasure of our company a while longer yet," Dude said with an amused smile.

"So, what did you do?" Benny asked as he lounged against the wall.

Shark wasn't at all comfortable with this level of attention, he preferred to blend into the shadows, do what needed to be done then disappear again. He didn't like praise, and he certainly didn't want to be in the spotlight because he had messed something up.

Still, his friends were here, with the exception of Chaos and King they were all married, and most of them had made at least one mistake with the women they had ended up falling in love with. Did he really have anything to lose by asking for advice on how to make things right with Claire?

In the end, it boiled down to one thing. Claire had become the most important thing in his life. Was he really just going to let it end that way?

No.

He wasn't.

And if the only way to fix this was to talk to these guys and get their thoughts, he would shove aside his feelings and have this conversation.

"I haven't spoken to Claire since she left," he admitted.

"Did she ask you not to?" Dude asked.

"I thought she was going to. Right before they came to take her away she said she wanted to talk. I thought she was about to say she needed time and space so I told her that she didn't have to make any decisions right now and that we shouldn't talk," Shark explained.

"So you sent her away with everything up in the air?" Spider asked.

"And then never contacted her?" Night added.

"I don't have her contact information," he uttered somewhat belligerently.

"Lame, man," Fox said with a shake of his head.

"We have a file on Claire, we have her cell phone number and her email address," King said, looking disappointed in his lame excuse.

"She doesn't have her cell on her, and she probably doesn't have access to email, so I couldn't contact her either of those ways," he muttered.

"You're a SEAL, you telling us you couldn't find a way to contact Claire? You know where she is, you could call the hospital and ask to speak to her," Cookie said like it was the most obvious thing in the world.

Raking his fingers through his hair, Shark shoved out a breath. "I don't want to hear her end things."

"You don't know for sure that she would have ended things," Wolf reminded him. "You didn't give her a chance to talk to you about whatever was on her mind."

"She was gang-raped, beaten, and tortured. How can I even ask her to think about starting a relationship with me? It would be one thing if we'd already been together for a while, but we met five days before her life was turned upside down. How selfish of me is it to think I should be her priority right now."

"Isn't it up to her to decide what she wants and what she can deal with?" Wolf asked. "I made that mistake with Caroline when we were first together. I tried to decide what was best for her, let my own insecurities almost ruin the best thing I've ever had. Claire is a big girl, she can decide for herself what she can and can't deal with."

"And what if she can't deal with me, with us?"

"Then at least you'll know for sure, and you can move on," Wolf said.

"And what if she can deal with me? How do I make this better?" To be honest, he was almost as afraid of Claire wanting to be with him as he was of her turning him away. He fixed problems with his muscles, his strength. Did he have what it took to help Claire through the emotional rollercoaster she'd been thrown onto?

"You know about Fiona, right?" Cookie asked.

Shark nodded, he knew that Cookie had rescued her from being a sex slave in Mexico. He also knew how much Fiona had struggled after she was rescued.

"It was hard, man, I'm not going to lie to you. Fiona struggled a lot. You're not always going to say or do the right thing, sometimes you won't even know what the right thing is, but if you care about her, then all you need to do is be there. Ask her what she needs. Sometimes she'll need you to hold her, sometimes she'll need space, some days she'll need you to remind her she's strong and other days she'll need you to be strong for her. It's not going to be an easy road for her or for you, but there is light on the other side."

He appreciated Cookie's advice, but none of that meant anything if he'd already burned his bridges with Claire. "There's a chance she won't forgive me."

"You're talking to someone who messed up pretty badly with Alabama in the early stages of our relationship, I can tell you that earning someone's forgiveness isn't always easy, but if it means enough to you, you'll find a way to do it," Abe told him.

It meant enough to him.

Claire was important enough that he would find a way to

make things right, then he'd find a way to support her while they were on opposite sides of the world, and when he got home, he would make sure she knew for certain he was never going to leave her.

"So, do you need to go find a phone and call Germany, or are you going to continue to sit around and sulk and wonder what could have been?" Fox asked.

Like that was a question.

His friends whooped and hollered and cheered when he got up to find a phone.

Shark's hands shook as he picked one up and dialed the number that he'd memorized days ago for the military hospital in Germany.

When someone answered he asked to speak with Claire Barrett and was then put on hold. His hands were sweating as he waited to hear her voice, and he shifted uncomfortably from foot to foot. He'd fight for Claire, he already knew that, but he was praying for a miracle that when he explained why he hadn't wanted to talk she would understand.

"Hello?" Claire's hesitant voice came down the line.

For a moment he couldn't talk. It might have only been three days since he'd last seen her, but it felt like a lifetime. How badly he wished he could be there to drag her into his arms and kiss her. "Hello, Claire."

"Logan?" She sounded confused to hear his voice and he worried that didn't bode well for him.

"I owe you an apology. The day you left, when you said you wanted to talk I was afraid you were ending things between us, that's why I didn't want to hear what you had to say. If that's what you want, I'll respect your wishes, but it's not what I want, Claire. I want you. I'm sorry I haven't contacted you before today, I guess I needed the guys to hit me over the head with some common sense. If you can forgive me, Claire, then I'm here, I'll support you as best as I can from here until I can get back to you. I'll be there on the bad days to hold you and tell you that we'll get through it together, and I'll be there on the good days to celebrate with you. I'll love you, and support you, and protect you with everything I have and everything I am."

"Love me?" Claire asked.

Damn. Was it too soon to say that? Of course it was, they'd only met two weeks ago. Yet it was how he felt and he wasn't going to lie about it.

"Yes. I love you, Claire."

The sound of her weeping carried down the phone line, and he was positive that she was about to tell him that she didn't love him back, but then he heard her laugh through her tears. "I thought you didn't want to talk because you thought I was too damaged or because you were too guilty about what happened, but, Logan, I love you too."

"You do?"

"Of course I do. I wish so much that you were here with me but just hearing your voice helps, and knowing you love me makes me feel like I'm not in this alone."

"You're not in it alone," he said firmly. "I love you, Claire Bear."

"I love you too."

Shark wasn't sure he'd ever get used to hearing those words, they weren't ones he'd heard growing up, and he'd learned to hold people at arm's length, keep a safe emotional distance between them. But Claire had changed that, and hearing her tell him she loved him changed him.

CHAPTER 14

November 2nd

8:08 A.M.

"Stay safe," Claire said to her friend Dahlia Black.

"I will, I'll have an entire entourage of over-protective big brothers and cousins who I'm guessing aren't going to let me out of their sight," Dahlia said. Even though her friend had just flown to the other side of the country to deal with an ordeal from her past that no longer wanted to stay there, Claire could hear the grimace on Dahlia's face in her tone.

"They love you," she reminded her friend. What she wouldn't have given to have an entourage of her own to be by her side these last several weeks. Instead, she'd come home to an empty apartment, fought through the ever-present terror as best as she could, and did her best to put herself back together. Dahlia had been there for her, and she appreciated that, but it wasn't the same as having a family.

At least she had Logan.

Even though he was on the other side of the world, he'd done the best he could to support her, and Claire knew that the distance between them and his inability to be physically there for her left him feeling impotently frustrated. Because she didn't want him to feel worse, she did her best to hide her struggles from him. And she was struggling—a lot.

"They do," Dahlia agreed, somewhat reluctantly, and Claire knew that going back to her hometown was hard for her. She didn't know everything about Dahlia's past, but she knew a bit, enough to know that Dahlia had vowed never to return to River's End and it was only because she was being blackmailed that she had got on that plane early this morning.

"Keep me updated."

"I will. I'm sorry I had to leave you alone. Maybe you should call up those friends your man tried to set you up with."

"Yeah, maybe," Claire said vaguely, already knowing she had no intention of calling the wives of Logan's teammates. Abigail, Lavender, and Evie had all seemed like lovely people the one time she'd met them, and their kids were definitely adorable, but she didn't want strangers right now, she wanted Logan. Unfortunately, you didn't always get what you wanted.

"I have to go, I'm about to rent a car," Dahlia said.

"Okay, thanks for letting me know you arrived safely, I hope your brothers and the FBI can get this sorted out."

"Me too. Bye, Claire."

"Bye." As she hung up the phone and set it down on her kitchen table, Claire pushed to her feet and wandered aimlessly around her small apartment. This place used to be her little sanctuary. She'd chosen each piece of furniture so carefully, the large sectional in the living room where she spent most of her time these days, preferring to sleep there than the big bed in her bedroom. There was her little reading nook, big comfortable rocking chair, pretty wooden bookcase, fairy lights strung around a canopy she'd hung from the ceiling and draped around the chair. The kitchen table and chairs she'd found on the side of the road, they'd looked old, and didn't like the idea of them just being thrown away, so she'd brought them home, sanded and stained them, and now they looked perfect in her kitchen. This place no longer made her feel safe and cozy, now it felt like a prison of loneliness she was never going to be paroled from.

With a sigh, Claire shoved away her sadness, she could hardly be angry that Logan couldn't be here because of his job when it was only because of that job that she was here alive, and mostly in one piece. Her injuries were healing but slowly, surgery on her shoulder last month had set her back a bit, and she was still weak, partly because it had been a long road to recovery and partly because she wasn't really taking care of herself. Nightmares meant she didn't sleep much, and an undercurrent of fear meant she didn't have much of an appetite. She hadn't been back to work yet, and other than medical appointments, she rarely left her apartment.

She had just shuffled back into the kitchen to make herself a piece of toast, and was planning out in her mind what she was going to do today, when there was a knock at her door.

Claire froze.

The only people who knocked on her door were delivery people, but she didn't have anything she was expecting today.

While she knew that Anvar Mir was dead, The Atash mostly disbanded, there was always the possibility that one of the members of the extremist group who was already in the US would track her down and seek revenge on her. It was unlikely, Anvar had probably never shared her name with anyone, but there'd been that video of her and someone could identify her from it.

Cautiously, she crept across her apartment to the front door, then peeked through the peephole.

She gasped when she saw who was standing there.

Her hands shook as she unlocked the door and wrenched it open.

By the time she threw herself into his arms, tears were already streaming down her cheeks.

Logan caught her easily, lifting her feet off the floor as he clutched her to him. When she'd left Afghanistan, she'd been positive he didn't want her. Those first few days in Germany she'd cried more about losing Logan than she had about what she'd been through. But then he'd called, and he'd told her he loved her, and he'd contacted her almost every day since. There'd been times when he was on a mission and she'd had to make it through the day without hearing from him. Those video calls with Logan were the only highlight in her life right now and the only reason she was still standing. Without him, she was pretty sure she would have fallen completely apart.

"How …? Where …? You're not supposed … I thought you weren't back for another three days," Claire babbled as she clung to him.

"We finished a few days early, got back late yesterday, debriefed all night, I came straight here. I thought about calling but I wanted to surprise you, and I didn't want to waste a single second before I could hold you again."

"This is the best surprise ever." Claire buried her face against his neck, letting her tears flow without trying to hide them. She felt Logan press his lips to the top of her head and hold them there and she knew without a shadow of a doubt that the distance between them had been every bit as hard on him as it had on her.

Eventually he set her down, but his hands remained on her shoulders, and his dark eyes searched hers. "I'm sorry I wasn't here for you. You know I would have been if I could, right?"

Seeing her big, strong, tough SEAL looking so insecure made her heart tighten in her chest. Logan really did love her. She couldn't deny there had been times over the last several weeks where she had selfishly been angry at Logan for not being here even though she knew it was outside his control. Claire didn't like being selfish, but she was only human, and it was hard when she woke alone, screaming and drenched in sweat from a nightmare, not to feel abandoned.

Lifting her hands to cover his, Claire maintained direct eye contact. "I know that, Logan. I can't lie and say it was easy dealing with everything by myself, but you were there for me as best as you could be and that meant everything to me."

"I hate that you were alone, and I wish I could promise you that I can be here for you now, but you know my team is still on rotation, right? That we might get called away again. I hope we won't, other than PT I hope I can be here with you the rest of the time."

"I know you might get called away," she assured him, trying to paste on a brave smile but pretty sure she failed. Having Logan dangled in front of her, being able to soak up his strength and the security that his arms offered, only to have him yanked away and sent on another mission would be awful, but she'd deal with it if she had to. The last thing she wanted to do was make him feel guilty about his job.

"If I get called out then I'm going to make sure you're not alone this time," he said, a hint of reproach in his tone. Logan hadn't been happy when he'd heard from his friends' wives that she had thanked them for their concern but sent them away. She hadn't wanted to feel ungrateful she just couldn't deal with strangers and her emotions about her ordeal at the same time.

"I didn't mean to offend them, I just ..."

Logan cut her off with a gentle kiss. "They weren't offended, they understand better than most what you're going through. They just felt bad because they hated the idea of you being alone almost as much as I did. But I wasn't talking about my friends. Wait right here, I have a surprise for you."

Releasing her, Logan turned and walked down the steps from her second-floor apartment, Claire had no idea what surprise he had in mind, but truly nothing could be better than having the man she loved back by her side and knowing that as hard and painful as this time in her life was, it wouldn't last forever. She had the rest of her life with Logan to look forward to, bright days of shared happiness and joy, marriage and kids, there would be more hard times, but they'd face them together.

Together.

That in itself gave her enough reason to smile genuinely for the first time in months.

* * *

8:35 A.M.

Shark felt completely relaxed for the first time since Claire had gone missing. She was alive, safe, back home. She didn't resent him for not being able to be there for her when she needed him—although he could tell it had been hard for her—and nothing was standing between them. No distance, either physical or emotional, they could finally be together.

Knowing that sooner or later—although he was praying for much later—he would be called away had gotten him thinking. He didn't want Claire alone. She had shut out his friends because she wasn't comfortable with strangers, so he'd thought outside the box.

Opening his truck's back passenger side door, he reached for the pink leash. He hadn't come straight here from debriefing; he'd made one short stop along the way. The golden retriever looked up at him with warm brown eyes, and he was sure the dog smiled at him. A friend of his team and former SEAL, Eagle Oswald, owned and operated a security firm with his siblings, and they worked with several dog trainers. He'd explained Claire's situation to Eagle, and his friend had hooked him up with someone who could provide her a dog trained to help with her specific needs.

"Come on, girl," he said to the dog as she jumped down out of his truck. He closed the door and locked it, then led the dog up the stairs to where Claire was still standing in her open doorway.

Her eyes widened when she saw the dog, then flew from it to him and back again. "Is that …?"

"She's yours," he said. "Her name is Goldilocks, she's a two-year-old Golden Retriever, she is an assistance dog who is trained to help someone who suffers from PTSD. She'll help you if you have a panic attack, she'll wake you if you're having a nightmare. She's been Public Access Tested and can go anywhere with you."

"She's mine?" Claire asked, looking disbelievingly at the dog who was sitting and wagging her tail, patiently waiting for a pat. "You got me an assistance dog?"

"So you'll never have to be alone again."

Claire flung her arms around him and hugged him hard.

"Thank you, that is the nicest thing anyone has ever done for me." She kissed him quickly on the lips then dropped to her knees beside the dog. "Hello, beautiful girl," Claire gushed, holding out her hand for the dog to sniff. Once it had, Claire began to pat her, stroking the soft, golden fur lovingly, and Goldilocks immediately began to lick her hand, then moved closer so she was pressed right against Claire.

Shark smiled at the pair, it looked like they were bonding already, and he knew that he would feel so much better when he had to leave Claire, knowing she had someone watching over her. Goldilocks was as much for his benefit as she was for Claire's.

"Here, take her leash, let's get you two inside," he said. It was a particularly windy and chilly November day here in Southern California, and he wanted to get his girls in where it was warm.

"Oh," Claire said, her smile dipping as she took the leash and allowed him to usher her inside. "I don't have anything for Goldilocks, no toys or food, no bed or bowl, nothing."

"Why don't we catch up for a bit, and then later today, we'll go and buy her everything she needs." He'd deliberately not bought anything for the dog because he wasn't sure yet where she'd be living, he intended to talk to Claire today about the two of them living together.

"Do you want something to eat?" Claire asked.

"Nope, I just want to hold you." He scooped her up and carried her over to the sectional. The couch was set up facing an entertainment stand that had an electric fireplace, and he switched the fire on before sitting down and settling Claire on his lap. Goldilocks immediately jumped up to snuggle beside them.

"This is nice," Claire murmured, snuggling closer.

"It is," he agreed, holding her tighter. For several minutes they sat together in silence, just enjoying being together.

Their entire relationship had been far from conventional. They'd relied on one another to remain alive as they trekked across the Afghanistan desert, then jumped straight from zero to one hundred in the few days they'd spent together on base. Then they had spent the last eight weeks apart, it was time for them to get some normal. "How are you doing? Really, Claire," he added when she opened her mouth and he knew she was going to tell him what she thought he wanted to hear.

"I'm ... struggling," she whispered, dropping her eyes as though admitting that out loud somehow made her seem less in his eyes.

Knowing how much the admission cost her, Shark touched a kiss to her forehead, then captured her chin between his thumb and forefinger and tilted her face up so he could kiss her lips. "Thank you, for being honest with me."

"It's so hard, Logan," she said, a thread of desperation in her voice.

"I know."

"I'm so tired." Weariness seemed to bleed from every pore, and she sank deeper into his embrace.

"I know, sweetheart. But I'm here now, and I'm going to take care of you. Goldilocks and I both are."

She smiled up at him. "I'm so glad you're here."

"Me too. I don't ever want to be away from you if I don't have to be. I know it's soon, and I won't push you if you're not ready, but I want us to live together, Claire. Your place, or my place—although yours is much more homey than mine which is just a place I sleep when I'm not away—I don't care. Or we can look for a new place together, a house with a yard for Goldilocks, space for us to grow into over the years when we get married and have kids. I don't want to go home and leave you here alone, I want to be with you every second that I can."

Claire stiffened in his arms. "Logan, I'm not ready to …" she trailed off, but her heated cheeks told him what her words couldn't.

"I'm not talking about sex, Claire. You'll be ready for that whenever you're ready, I know what you went through, I know every horrible thing they did to you and I would never pressure you for more than you're ready to give. I love you, Claire, and I told you that I only do things one of two ways."

"All out or all in," she said for him.

"Right."

"Isn't it too soon for us to live together? I mean, we've never even been on a real date."

"Something I plan to rectify once we go shopping for the dog. And I don't care how long it's been since we met, I love you and I want to be with you. That is all I care about."

Claire smiled and relaxed into him again. "I love you too, and the idea of being away from you makes me all cold inside. Okay."

"Okay?"

"Let's live together. You're right, who cares if we haven't known each other for very long, what we went through together was intense, made each minute more like a day. I don't want to waste time that could be spent together apart, so let's move in together. You can stay here for now, but let's look for a new place together because I want everything you just mentioned. I want a home that belongs to both of us, a home where we'll get married and start a family. A home that gives both of us what we missed out on when we were kids. A home that's full of laughter and happiness and love. Love that stands strong even during the hard times when there is anger and sadness because that's what a home is. It's love standing strong as the entire gamut of emotions rage around it. Emotions are real, and we're both only human, sometimes I'm going to let you down, and sometimes you're going to let me down, but there isn't anything that could make me stop loving you."

This woman was perfection.

She'd just so eloquently said everything he was feeling but would never be able to put into words.

Since he couldn't top what Claire had said, nor did he want to, Logan framed her face with his hands, his thumbs brushing softly across her cheekbones as he drank in the feel of her soft skin. His eyes met hers, seeking her permission, and when she gave a small nod he swept his lips across hers. Her sweet taste permeated every ounce of his being, and he made love to her with his mouth, prepared to wait as long as it took for her to be ready to let him touch the rest of her body. He didn't care, the only thing in this world that was important to him was protecting the woman in his arms.

She was the most precious thing he had, he'd die for her, kill for her, become a better man for her. He'd love her completely, offering her everything that he had and everything he was. She had helped him learn to feel again, given him a reason to hope, she loved him unconditionally, and he would repay that love by cherishing her every day of the rest of their lives.

Find out how what happens when Grayson "Chaos" Simpson arrives home to find a woman in his bed in the next book in this action packed and emotionally charged military romance series!

WINTER WONDERLAND

DEAD OR ALIVE

LITTLE GIRL LOST

FORGOTTEN

Count to Ten Series

ONE

TWO

THREE

FOUR

FIVE

SIX

BURNING SECRETS

SEVEN

EIGHT

NINE

TEN

Christmas Romantic Suspense Series

CHRISTMAS HOSTAGE

CHRISTMAS CAPTIVE

CHRISTMAS VICTIM

YULETIDE PROTECTOR

Conquering Fear Series

(Co-written with Amanda Siegrist)

DROWNING IN YOU

OUT OF THE DARKNESS

ABOUT THE AUTHOR

Jane Blythe is a USA Today bestselling author of romantic suspense and military romance full of sweet, smart, sexy heroes and strong heroines! When she's not weaving hard to unravel mysteries she loves to read, bake, go to the beach, build snowmen, and watch Disney movies. She has two adorable Dalmatians, is obsessed with Christmas, owns 200+ teddy bears, and loves to travel!

To connect and keep up to date please visit any of the following

Email – mailto:janeblytheauthor@gmail.com
Facebook – http://www.facebook.com/janeblytheauthor
Instagram – http://www.instagram.com/jane_blythe_author
Reader Group – http://www.facebook.com/
groups/janeskillersweethearts
Twitter – http://www.twitter.com/jblytheauthor
· Website – http://www.janeblythe.com.au

There are many more books in this fan fiction world than listed here, for an up-to-date list go to www.AcesPress.com

You can also visit our Amazon page at:
http://www.amazon.com/author/operationalpha

Special Forces: Operation Alpha World
Christie Adams: Charity's Heart
Denise Agnew: Dangerous to Hold
Shauna Allen: Awakening Aubrey
Brynne Asher: Blackburn
Linzi Baxter: Unlocking Dreams
Jennifer Becker: Hiding Catherine
Alice Bello: Shadowing Milly
Heather Blair: Rescue Me
Misha Blake: Flash
Anna Blakely: Rescuing Gracelynn
Julia Bright: Saving Lorelei
Cara Carnes: Protecting Mari
Kendra Mei Chailyn: Beast
Melissa Kay Clarke: Rescuing Annabeth
Samantha A. Cole: Handling Haven
Sue Coletta: Hacked
Melissa Combs: Gallant
Lorelei Confer: Protecting Sara
Anne Conley: Redemption for Misty
KaLyn Cooper: Rescuing Melina
Janie Crouch: Storm
Liz Crowe: Marking Mariah
Sarah Curtis: Securing the Odds
Jordan Dane: Redemption for Avery
Tarina Deaton: Found in the Lost
Aspen Drake, Intense

KL Donn: Unraveling Love
Riley Edwards: Protecting Olivia
PJ Fiala: Defending Sophie
Nicole Flockton: Protecting Maria
Alexa Gregory: Backdraft
Michele Gwynn: Rescuing Emma
Casey Hagen: Shielding Nebraska
Desiree Holt: Protecting Maddie
Kathy Ivan: Saving Sarah
Kris Jacen, Be With Me
Jesse Jacobson: Protecting Honor
Silver James: Rescue Moon
Becca Jameson: Saving Sofia
Kate Kinsley: Protecting Ava
Rayne Lewis: Justice for Mary
Heather Long: Securing Arizona
Gennita Low: No Protection
Kirsten Lynn: Joining Forces for Jesse
Margaret Madigan: Bang for the Buck
Trish McCallan: Hero Under Fire
Kimberly McGath: The Predecessor
Rachel McNeely: The SEAL's Surprise Baby
KD Michaels: Saving Laura
Lynn Michaels: Rescuing Kyle
Olivia Michaels: Protecting Harper
Wren Michaels: The Fox & The Hound
Annie Miller: Securing Willow
Kat Mizera: Protecting Bobbi
Keira Montclair, Wolf and the Wild Scots
Mary B Moore: Force Protection
LeTeisha Newton: Protecting Butterfly
Angela Nicole: Protecting the Donna
MJ Nightingale: Protecting Beauty
Sarah O'Rourke: Saving Liberty

Victoria Paige: Reclaiming Izabel
Anne L. Parks: Mason
Debra Parmley: Protecting Pippa
Lainey Reese: Protecting New York
KeKe Renée: Protecting Bria
TL Reeve and Michele Ryan: Extracting Mateo
Elena M. Reyes: Keeping Ava
Deanna L. Rowley: Saving Veronica
Angela Rush: Charlotte
Rose Smith: Saving Satin
Jenika Snow: Protecting Lily
Lynne St. James: SEAL's Spitfire
Dee Stewart: Conner
Harley Stone: Rescuing Mercy
Sarah Stone: Shielding Grace
Jen Talty: Burning Desire
Reina Torres, Rescuing Hi'ilani
Savvi V: Loving Lex
Megan Vernon: Protecting Us
LJ Vickery: Circus Comes to Town
Rachel Young: Because of Marissa
R. C. Wynne: Shadows Renewed

Delta Team Three Series
Lori Ryan: Nori's Delta
Becca Jameson: Destiny's Delta
Lynne St James, Gwen's Delta
Elle James: Ivy's Delta
Riley Edwards: Hope's Delta

Police and Fire: Operation Alpha World
Freya Barker: Burning for Autumn
B.P. Beth: Scott
Jane Blythe: Salvaging Marigold

Julia Bright, Justice for Amber
Anna Brooks, Guarding Georgia
KaLyn Cooper: Justice for Gwen
Aspen Drake: Sheltering Emma
Emily Gray: Shelter for Allegra
Alexa Gregory: Backdraft
Deanndra Hall: Shelter for Sharla
Barb Han: Kace
EM Hayes: Gambling for Ashleigh
India Kells: Shadow Killer
CM Steele: Guarding Hope
Reina Torres: Justice for Sloane
Aubree Valentine, Justice for Danielle
Maddie Wade: Finding English
Stacey Wilk: Stage Fright
Laine Vess: Justice for Lauren

Tarpley VFD Series
Silver James, Fighting for Elena
Deanndra Hall, Fighting for Carly
Haven Rose, Fighting for Calliope
MJ Nightingale, Fighting for Jemma
TL Reeve, Fighting for Brittney
Nicole Flockton, Fighting for Nadia

As you know, this book included at least one character from Susan Stoker's books. To check out more, see below.

SEAL Team Hawaii Series

Finding Elodie
Finding Lexie
Finding Kenna (Oct 2021)
Finding Monica (May 2022)
Finding Carly (TBA)
Finding Ashlyn (TBA)
Finding Jodelle (TBA)

Eagle Point Search & Rescue

Searching for Lilly (Mar 2022)
Searching for Elsie (Jun 2022)
Searching for Bristol (Nov 2022)
Searching for Caryn (TBA)
Searching for Finley (TBA)
Searching for Heather (TBA)
Searching for Khloe (TBA)

The Refuge Series

Deserving Alaska (Aug 2022)
Deserving Henley (Jan 2023)
Deserving Reese (TBA)
Deserving Cora (TBA)
Deserving Lara (TBA)
Deserving Maisy (TBA)
Deserving Ryleigh (TBA)

Delta Team Two Series

Shielding Gillian
Shielding Kinley

Shielding Aspen
Shielding Jayme (novella)
Shielding Riley
Shielding Devyn
Shielding Ember
Shielding Sierra (Jan 2022)

SEAL of Protection: Legacy Series

Securing Caite (FREE!)
Securing Brenae (novella)
Securing Sidney
Securing Piper
Securing Zoey
Securing Avery
Securing Kalee
Securing Jane

Delta Force Heroes Series

Rescuing Rayne (FREE!)
Rescuing Aimee (novella)
Rescuing Emily
Rescuing Harley
Marrying Emily (novella)
Rescuing Kassie
Rescuing Bryn
Rescuing Casey
Rescuing Sadie (novella)
Rescuing Wendy
Rescuing Mary
Rescuing Macie (novella)
Rescuing Annie (Feb 2022)

Badge of Honor: Texas Heroes Series

Justice for Mackenzie (FREE!)

Justice for Mickie
Justice for Corrie
Justice for Laine (novella)
Shelter for Elizabeth
Justice for Boone
Shelter for Adeline
Shelter for Sophie
Justice for Erin
Justice for Milena
Shelter for Blythe
Justice for Hope
Shelter for Quinn
Shelter for Koren
Shelter for Penelope

SEAL of Protection Series

Protecting Caroline (FREE!)
Protecting Alabama
Protecting Fiona
Marrying Caroline (novella)
Protecting Summer
Protecting Cheyenne
Protecting Jessyka
Protecting Julie (novella)
Protecting Melody
Protecting the Future
Protecting Kiera (novella)
Protecting Alabama's Kids (novella)
Protecting Dakota

New York Times, USA Today and *Wall Street Journal* Bestselling Author Susan Stoker has a heart as big as the state of Tennessee where she lives, but this all American girl has also spent the last fourteen years living in Missouri, California,

Colorado, Indiana, and Texas. She's married to a retired Army man who now gets to follow *her* around the country.

www.stokeraces.com
www.AcesPress.com
susan@stokeraces.com

Made in the USA
Coppell, TX
08 December 2021

67546263R00154